THE GREEN POOL

An Inspector Carmichael Mystery

THE GREEN POOL

An Inspector Carmichael Mystery

Helen L. DiNapoli

with cover art by Roni Haas

iUniverse, Inc.

New York   Bloomington

The Green Pool
An Inspector Carmichael Mystery

iUniverse books may be ordered through booksellers or by contacting:

iUniverse
1663 Liberty Drive
Bloomington, IN 47403
www.iuniverse.com
1-800-Authors (1-800-288-4677)

Because of the dynamic nature of the Internet, any Web addresses or links contained in this book may have changed since publication and may no longer be valid. The views expressed in this work are solely those of the author and do not necessarily reflect the views of the publisher, and the publisher hereby disclaims any responsibility for them.

ISBN: 978-1-4401-2424-2 (pbk)
ISBN: 978-1-4401-2423-5 (cloth)
ISBN: 978-1-4401-2422-8 (ebk)

Library of Congress Control Number: 2009923036

Printed in the United States of America

iUniverse rev. date: 2/27/2009

Dedication
To my children, Sutton Porter
and Joseph DiNapoli

CONTENTS

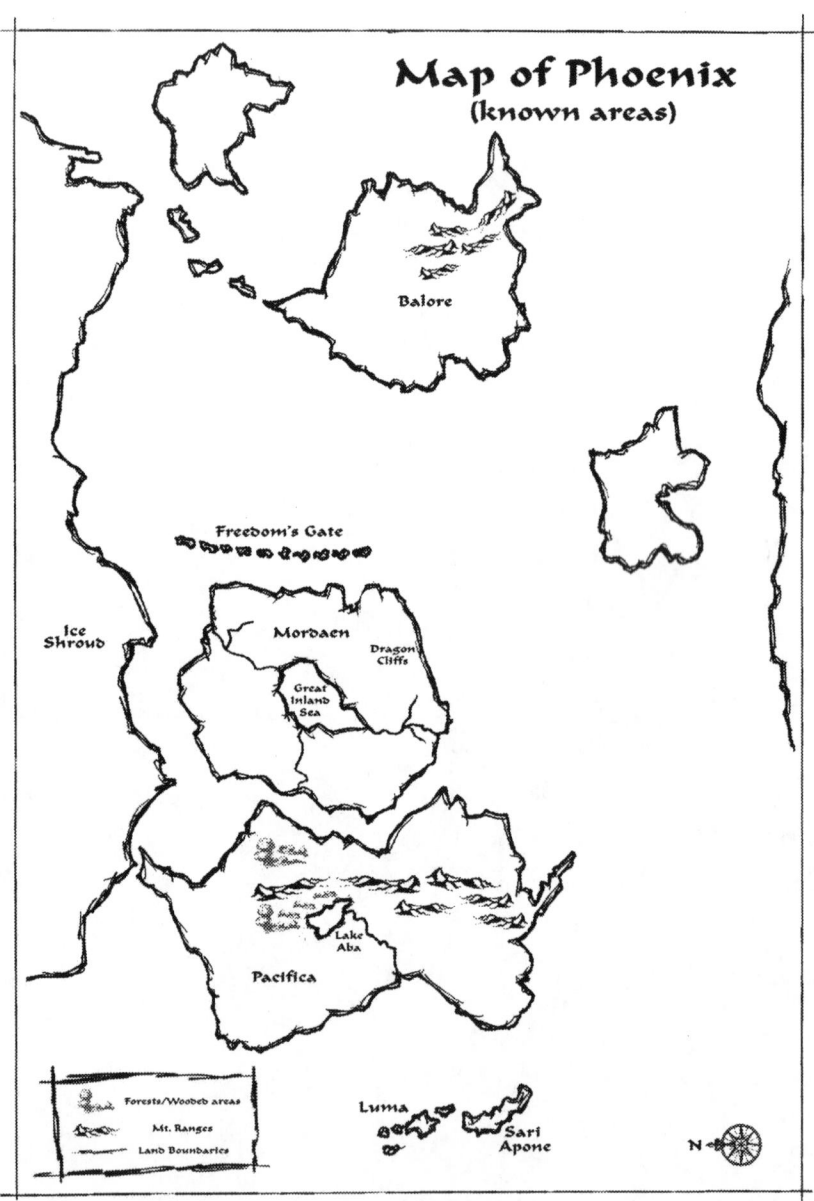

Map of Phoenix
(known areas)

INTRODUCTION

Earth survived a near miss of a massive sphere at the turn of the twenty-first century. This nearly planetary-sized body, which intruded from reaches of the outer solar system, would, in future years, take on the mythical characteristics of an angel of death—a lethal heavenly emissary in the minds and the culture of the surviving humans. Though the heavenly traveler didn't succeed in wiping out all of the major life forms during the subsequent pole shift, it did cause cataclysmic worldwide upheavals of continents. Some continents sank beneath the roiling oceans, and new land masses rose with devastating eruptions from uncountable volcanoes. The mantle of smoke and ash that blanketed the globe came to represent, in legend, the shadowy veil of the angel of death and cast a pall of enormous proportions over the chaos below. Corresponding eruptions from the passing body contributed to the vaporous shroud and caused a drastic change in the plant and animal life on the earth.

When the angel's veil cleared, the sun shone on a new object in the night sky. Smaller than the devastated planet, the captive sphere was larger than the traditional moon, though more distant, and its new orbit around the sun made it clearly visible in the night sky after the moon rose and reached its apex, particularly when it was waxing or waning. This new, ominous red orb, named Khensu, dominated the evening heavens and struck fear into the hearts of what remained of mankind. Those remnants of humanity renamed their celestial home Phoenix, in honor of the beautiful bird that rose from the ashes, and they renamed their traditional moon Horus—in closer orbit now—for its victory over the usurper body. And even that bloodthirsty, almost-destroyer of mankind acquired the element of beneficence, for it represented success over incredible odds and an increased virility and remarkable longevity in humans.

On the embattled surface of Phoenix, humanity, in scattered groups, began to draw together. They sought shelter and the comfort of some semblance of government and organization. The cities they had lived in were gone, and their technology was shattered. The geography of the planet had been rearranged, as if a mighty hand had reached down and wrenched their civilization from them, and there were those who loudly informed others that this had been caused by the wrath of God. They had become complacent and filled with the pride of their technology. Having no choice, the majority allowed themselves to be led by those whose authority they accepted. Apocalyptic speeches fell upon the eager ears of a populace that had begun to view the result of the terrible disaster that they had survived.

Whether it was the chemical mix produced by the exchange of debris and gases from the passing planetary body, or other disruptions from the chaos on the planet, in many species of life, mutations began to appear. Those mutations resulted in the return of creatures of myth and legend, as if the planet had reverted to a bygone age. Dwarves, elves, and newly frightening beasts of the animal kingdom now walked upon Phoenix, along with the human race. Strange creatures inhabited the oceans and, most terrifying of all, whispers of huge dragons swept through the skies above their huddled communities. Parents warned children not to wander too far from the camps; unobserving adults could find themselves sucked into the maw of one of the swooping beasts. The puny weapons they could devise at first proved unsuccessful against most of the larger predators. It was only in a moment of desperation that the most powerful weapon of all was discovered—one that would forever change the shape and content of their new world.

One day, on a hunting expedition accompanied by the village priest, a group of the village's most able hunters were surrounding a large horned beast, their spears raised. The kill was almost in sight when a huge shadow swept over them. Looking up, the group beheld an enormous dragon, suspended in the sky above them. The beast seemed to grin as smoke drifted from its dilated nostrils; then it tucked its huge head and dropped toward them. All cowered in terror beneath the soaring dragon as the huge creature swooped in a circular pattern, aiming directly for the small group. Only the priest stood alone in his faith and raised his staff in defiance at the beast. At once, a bright light flashed from the head of his staff and struck the dragon's great head. A flash of flame and smoke burst from the dragon as the creature plummeted to the ground; the crash knocked some of the party off their feet. They all rose and stared in shock, first at the enormous carcass of the dragon, then at the priest, who appeared as stunned as the rest of them. It was only later that they would assure themselves that it was not the staff but the man holding it that had brought down the dragon. That man, John Bondonai, was to be the first recorded wizard in the post-cataclysmic era. Among the humans, magical powers had been reborn.

Upon the discovery of the magical abilities of John Bondonai, the priesthood set about attempting to discover whether this ability was an anomaly specific to that particular person. Whether it was for the purpose of anointing him with some form of sainthood or special status in the priesthood or—more likely—of finding some way to get rid of this embarrassment to their order was never clear. As soon as word circulated about the wondrous event, gossip drifted back to the priests that it was not the first time an unexplained magical event had taken place; it was being seen more often in newborn children. Each case was investigated and the unusual auras that occurred on the third day of birth were noted. The priests were disturbed and angered that these events were attributed to commoners with nothing particularly notable about them, least of all their spiritual perfection. Naturally, they rationalized; this must not be consistent with the same power that was within one of their kind. It was determined that such occurrences were against the teachings of their holy order, and the children would have to be put to death, as they surely were possessed of devils.

It was not long before the populace revolved against such a practice and a faction, led by John Bondonai himself, gathered and eventually overthrew the priesthood. Led by John Bondonai himself, they gathered and eventually overthrew the priesthood. The success of this revolution was marred only by the assassination of John Bondonai by a zealous and distraught priest, who slipped into Bondonai's camp tent on the eve of the victory celebration and stabbed him to death.

After the Religious Wars, the word *wizard* was used in connection with these people, and because Bondonai was a noted figure of his time, his name was often used to denote someone with such power. It was a necessary transition to some form of theology that could encompass those with the power and still provide comfort and a semblance of control over the people. It was not questioned that the standard beliefs that had survived the cataclysm no longer meant anything, not in light of the changes in men after the rebirth of their world. In the place of those beliefs, a philosophy grew, one based on spiritualism and more closely in tune with nature and man's relationship to the earth and the elements.

With the passage of the years, cities, townships, and villages were formed on the large continent, and the name *Pacifica* was given to this new home of humans. Exploration of the scattered islands in the western sea produced no other sign of humans, inviting settlement from adventurous seafaring folk. The Bondonai became customary (though often feared) figures to the people. The ruling class that grew from the initial warring factions also found these powerful people useful.

The city of Sanctuary that arose at a confluence of two large rivers, within easy traveling distance to the western seacoast, hailed as their leader King Stephan in 132 p.c. (post cataclysm). His line became the first great ruling family of the new world and continues unbroken to the present day. On his right hand sat a Bondonai, Gladstone, son of John Bondonai, a wizard of the gold class, who had conducted the magnificent ceremony that consecrated Stephan's royalty. Thus was precedent set, which would be followed from that time on, of rulers and peers of the realm being blessed and served by the most powerful of wizards.

With the crowning of the first king, the cities grew and the countryside of Pacifica was eventually divided up among local landowners, calling themselves barons of their domains. It had been discovered that human magic, unlike elven magic, was divided into five classes. Each class had its own particular distinctions that appeared to also be tied to the color of the child's aura on the third day of birth.

The *gold class* represented the highest level of power. Those endowed with this power had the ability to draw upon the very force within the planet and all of nature, including the living things upon the earth. These individuals had the power of sight, which allowed them to read the auras of others of their kind. They also had the power of clairvoyance in varying degrees, and some even exhibited the gift of prophecy, though such things were often viewed with suspicion. In addition to their individual power, the gold class could enhance that power by linking up, physically as well as mentally, with others of their class to produce a force of terrific and earth-shattering magnitude.

The *blue class* signified a power, spiritual in nature, that could heal the body as well as the mind and soul. Though female children were most often endowed with this gift, occasionally a boy child would be born with it.

The *green class* signified a power attuned to the flora and fauna. Those with this gift could communicate mentally with birds, fish, animals, and even the smallest plant and command them as well as draw upon their power, if necessary.

Those of the *red class* were attuned to the power of the elements. These Bondonai were able to command the weather and use the power generated by that connection. They were also able to call upon the elements within the rock and the earth beneath their feet and bring to life a dormant volcano.

The *white class* appeared to have a symbiotic power that allowed them to draw upon the particular gifts of the other classes of Bondonai with which they could be linked. Alone, their power was limited to manipulating small objects within a minimum range and for a limited period of time. Generally of varied degrees of ability, their position was enhanced by their station. When placed in service, they could be linked to the master Bondonai and thereby gain a portion of the power represented by that class.

The first 150 years after the rebirth saw major changes and was often a time of terror and uncertainty for humanity. It was learned—almost fatally, from the abuse of incredible power—that children born of two wizard parents could be disastrous, giving them unpredictable and often terrifying power.

Realizing that only by setting up laws could they be assured that such a disaster would never happen, King Stephan made use of Gladstone Bondonai's stature in the wizard community to support the creation of the wizard guilds. A High Council of the Bondonai was elected at their first conclave in 150 p.c., each guild having a representative on the council. By their direction, each of these guilds of the Bondonai was integrated into human society, depending upon the areas that would best utilize their powers. (Only the gold class wizards were set apart to bind themselves to service in the royal house and within the peerage of the realm—though truth be told, any gold-class wizard could break his vows of service with a unanimous agreement of the High Council).

The Revealing was established for each child on the third day after birth, to determine whether the child had the power. In a solemn service, the parents presented their children to the local Bondonai wizard or wizardess, amid chanting and pageantry. The child was placed in a large cistern filled with water. The Bondonai would lower the child into the water and wait expectantly. If the child sank immediately, it was snatched up, dried off, and given back to its parents. If the child floated and evidenced a colorful aura, it was pronounced to have the gift and taken from its parents, to be raised within the guild, based on the color of its aura.

The Gold Guild, containing the most powerful wizards, used their power best with the ruling class as a political tool. Elaborate ceremonies were developed for everything from crowning a new king, when that event became necessary, to carrying out diplomatic missions. If regional conflicts or a full-blown war among baronies broke out, each side had its head Bondonai. Luckily, few disputes had been allowed to develop to such a degree since the Mud God War, due to the balance of power. Therefore, the Gold Guild became councilors to the ruling class.

The Blue Guild became the healers, and though each family of the ruling class sought to secure one of these as their own, the edicts laid down by the Bondonai Charter forbade individual service of any wizard class, the exception being the Gold Guild. The peasantry was more than content to have a Blue Guild wizard in their township or village. This class was also closest in nature to the ancient priests, in that the spiritual functions were often overseen by a Blue Guild Bondonai.

The Green Guild became the agriculturalists and naturalists of the new world. They were consulted on everything from the growing of one's flower garden (only the ruling class was given this honor) to the care and treatment of the earth. They were the main functionaries at festivals that signaled the spring and fall equinoxes to celebrate the sowing and reaping of crops. They were also the veterinarians and took care of the animals that were needed for work and play.

The Red Guild wizards worked alone and in cooperation with the Green Guild, often controlling the weather to assure the ultimate production of food for the populace. They also were useful in choosing the quarries for excavation of the granite and other materials needed for building the cities and baronial castles that began to appear in Pacifica.

The White Guild was probably the most important in the everyday workings of the new world, as they were the administrators that made the functioning of government run smoothly. In cooperation with all of the other guilds, they maintained the systems that made the citizens and those in authority comfortable, compatible, and safe. They were also the least favored of the wizard guilds, being the new-world bureaucrats. The members of this guild formed the service directly responsible to the king that would become the Royal Bureau of Investigation. Out of its ranks would emerge an investigator with unsurpassed skills of detection and the guile to succeed within the political maze of competing factions of human authority, dwarf clans, and the elven communities that made up their world—one Inspector Sandoval Carmichael.

PROLOGUE

In a misty glade deep in the forest called the Grimwood, a young female faerie darted between the shafts of shadow and sunlight that played over a round-topped knoll in the center of the clearing. Her delicate wings thrummed in agitation, glowing iridescent in brief shots of sunlight as she circled the knoll, her small pointed ears directed toward its center deep within the ground. Silence answered her. Hovering over the center of the grass-covered knoll, a frown drew her peaked brows together, and her little mouth twisted in consternation. Sighing, she darted off, only a little dot of light to eyes not accustomed to spotting faeries.

Reaching the edge of the glade, the faerie hovered for a moment. Still suspended, the tiny figure shimmered and coalesced into the full-sized form of a young female clad in a flowing, rose-colored dress, tied beneath her small breasts with a cord of gold. The young faerie glanced behind her back and nodded at the absence of her wings. She closed her eyes in concentration and clapped her hands together. On the ground next to her feet, a silver tray laden with food appeared. She expelled a satisfied breath, gathered up the tray, and walked to the base of the knoll. She didn't have to look for the small round entrance beneath the mound—human eyes would never have found it, as it was concealed by tall grass. She knew it was there. With one fluid movement, she turned and backed into the opening, drawing the tray behind her.

Immediately enveloped in darkness, her eyes adjusted with little pause. The tunnel she faced inclined gradually in a gentle descent. Her feet took it with tiny, mincing steps, apprehension visible in the fixed downturn of her mouth. Shortly after the tunnel bottomed out to a level walk, she saw the door ahead.

She stepped up to the door and studied it intently. It was a heavy wooden door, made of rough oak slabs banded together with wide brass strips. Only the trained eye of the faerie (or maybe that of a wizard) could discern the faint quiver in the air around the door that told her the spell placed on it was still holding strong. Cocking her head, she leaned a pointed ear close to the wooden surface. All was quiet within. She whispered one word, grasped the curved brass handle while still balancing the tray in her other hand, and pulled the handle down. The door released and swung easily outward, as if commanded by another silent hand, leaving just enough space for her slim body to slide into the room. As soon as she stepped over the threshold, the door slid silently shut behind her. She didn't have to turn to look behind to know that no sign of a door would show in the mortar; no crack would give away its presence or hint at the section of the wall in that room from which it would appear the next time she entered or exited.

The room was oddly in contrast to its outward appearance, as if she'd stepped through a barrier of time and space. Created to give the illusion of a room in a fine castle, its walls had the texture of smoothed mortar that rose to an eight-foot ceiling, braced by heavy wooden crossbeams. From the far wall, a fire glowed in a large stone hearth, before which a table and a comfortable, stuffed high-back chair were placed. The table held a glowing oil lamp. Against another wall was a bed with clean linens, a woolen coverlet, and a pillow. To her right sat a polished oak table and two chairs. Stepping to the table, she set down the tray and turned to the chair before the fire. She could see the man's bronzed arm draped along the chair arm, though the rest of his body was hidden from sight. His hand held the stem of a delicate glass, shaped like an open flower, which he twisted slowly with his strong fingers. The golden liquid in the glass caught the light from the fire in the hearth. The young faerie stepped forward, her bare feet making no sound on the soft grass-green carpet that covered the center of the room.

"And what sweet things do you bring for my midmeal this day, Tillie?" The man's rich baritone voice broke the silence.

"Sweet fruits and nut bread, with butter and honey," Tillie answered softly, moving around the table and looking down at him. A tentative smile touched her mouth.

Rolf Andelar cocked his head slightly sideways and looked up at her, his strong fingers still slowly turning the glass. His long dark hair drifted over his shoulders. Wisps of curls framed a face still bronzed from the sun, though he'd surely been in this place for months, maybe years, if faeries counted them. Tillie stared into his eyes, green, like the waters of the pool beneath the Glaistig's falls. His muscular frame and the coloring of his hair and eyes looked more human than elf and would fool anyone, as long as they didn't spot the pointed ears beneath that wavy hair. This elf was unlike the delicately statuesque Florian elves that inhabited the Grimwood. Had Tillie not seen others of the Ileana clan on occasion, still haunting the Grimwood in search of their leader, she would have thought him a mutant. But she knew better now. She also knew that the heavier, muscular bodies of the Ileana concealed their ability to move with a lithe grace, just as the Florians could exhibit strength incredible for their slim, delicate-looking bodies.

He doesn't look as old as Nortenaine, Tillie thought, but she knew he was actually older. His beautiful face (she thought the word beautiful, rather than masculine, even though the angles of his face were sharper than most elven men) was unlined, as if worry hadn't touched him. Yet she knew that the news she carried would change that look forever.

As if reading her mind, Rolf's brows drew together, and he placed the glass carefully on the table. "You look pensive, my young friend." Rolf reached out and took Tillie's hand. "I expected someone other than you this day. Have you news for me? I have not seen Lilliana in months. But she had promised she would come back to me with the first breath of spring. Though I can't feel it, my senses tell me the season is upon us."

Tillie felt his hand grow cold in hers and knew he had sensed what was in her mind. His fingers tightened as he drew her down next to him. Tillie turned her face away from the darkness that drew across his face.

"No time for games, little faerie. Why didn't Lilliana come?"

"I have news of her, lord," Tillie mumbled, unable to control the trembling of her frail body.

Rolf released her hand and stood abruptly, gazing down at her. His voice rasped with barely held control. "They've found us out?"

"Oh, no, sir!"

"Well, what then, girl? Don't quiver and mutter; just tell me!"

"She—Miss Lilliana—told me …" Tillie burst into tears, covering her face with her hands, her small body shaking.

Rolf grabbed her shoulder with two strong hands and shook her roughly. "What is it? Tell me, damn it!"

"Oh, lord! Lilliana means to throw herself from the falls above the green pool!"

"What?" Rolf shoved Tillie back, his face glowing red. "They've discovered us and threaten to banish her? We knew this might come. But, when—how long ago did you speak with her?"

Tillie stammered, tears streaming down her pale face. She tried to speak, but only a high-pitched squeak was expelled. Rolf stared at her, bursting in frustration, his fists clenched. Then he threw his body forward and slammed a fist into the nearest wall.

"Blessed Queleastor! I must know!"

"Just a short while ago, lord. I met her on the path to the knoll. She … looked terrible. I mean, she told me she must do it."

"Why? Why would she do such a thing? I must get out of here and stop her!" Rolf threw himself at the wall, sliding around the room, his long fingers probing for any crack or imperfection to define the doorway to freedom. He slammed his hand against the blank wall. Pulling himself back, he shook his mane of dark hair from his face and began to breathe deeply.

Then, as calmness came over him, he looked steadily at Tillie. The intensity of his gaze threw her into trembling again, and she turned away, uncertain terror growing within her.

"You know, Tillie." His voice was deadly calm. "You know and will tell me, or you'll not leave here alive."

Tillie began to sob in earnest, the words interspersed with sporadic gasps of breath. "She is pregnant with your child, lord. She's known it for some time and can hide it no longer, as her time is due. She despairs, knowing her family will never accept the child." Tillie's voice trailed off.

Silence filled the room that had now grown smaller and more confined. Rolf stood, transfixed, his face drained of color. Just as Tillie was sure she couldn't stand another moment of silence, she heard his step and looked up. Rolf stood over her, his green eyes glazed and staring at some spot above her head. His hands were clenched together before him, as if in prayer. From deep within him, a sound rose, like a hum, low and vibrant, building until it burst from him like the howl of a crazed beast. Swinging around to face the wall, he aimed his clenched fists toward the heavy barrier as the pitch of his voice grew unbearable and the walls of the room began to quiver. Releasing his grip, he threw his arms wide, and a burst of power hit the wall with a thunderous boom that blew a gaping hole in that barrier, revealing the tunnel beyond, and threw Tillie off her feet to land behind him on the rug. Tillie sat up, her ears ringing, eyes unable to focus. Strong hands yanked her roughly to her feet, and her eyes cleared to see Rolf's, a wild green fire within them, glaring at her.

"Do you think they could hold me here? That their spell would suppress my power? What silly fools! The only reason I stayed was to be near her. I meant to take her from here but knew she had to be ready. If she's done ill to herself, they will pay when the might of the Ileana falls upon them!"

Tillie's mouth opened but no sound issued. Turning, Rolf charged from the room where he had been kept a prisoner, not by brass and wood but by his love for Lilliana. Tillie stared around her; then, charged by an urgency born of her terror, she ran through the tunnel and broke free into the dappled sunlight. Calming herself in order to concentrate, she closed her eyes and shimmered into the tiny form with iridescent wings. Batting her little wings as fast as she could, she drove forward toward the green pool, all the while cursing herself for her folly.

The small point of light shot through the tall trees, bobbing and weaving, and reached the green pool ahead of Rolf, who was madly thrashing his way through the brush behind her. Hovering near the edge of the pool that rippled and sparkled from the waning sunlight, she looked up and saw Lilliana emerge from behind the falls. The elf maiden hesitated and looked about wildly. The force of the water cascading over the falls blew a fine spray about her that slapped at her dress, flattening the wet cloth to her skin. Her once serenely beautiful face was framed by a matted tangle of wet blonde hair, making a ghostly web through which wide blue eyes gazed, unseeing. Her delicate mauve gown was dirty, splotched with blood; her hands were scratched and torn from the vines covering the precarious climb to the ledge of the falls. The light cloak that she had been wearing in the last few months to conceal her condition lay cast aside, draped over a bush below.

Tillie tried to concentrate for her transformation when she heard a low chuckle. Flitting to a nearby tree branch, she sheltered herself behind a leaf and looked down. Below her, as though through a haze, she saw what appeared to be an elven woman, amazingly beautiful with large almond-shaped brown eyes, red smiling lips, and silky blonde hair. Her sumptuous form was covered by a green gown shot with silver that rustled softly in the light breeze.

"I see you, faerie sprite. You have nothing to fear from me." The voice was soft and alluring, even to Tillie's ears. "I have assisted the princess as I would. She chooses her own path. There are none who can help her now."

Without another word, the woman slipped into the green water of the pool and slid beneath the surface just as Rolf stumbled into the grassy clearing that surrounded the pool. He spotted Lilliana immediately as she struggled to get her footing on the slick, rocky path.

"Lilliana!" he screamed, looking about in desperation for a way around the pool to reach her. "I'm here, my love! Whatever you've done, you had to do. Please—wait for me! I'll come to you! We'll leave this place together!"

Lilliana froze and stared down at her lover. A stronger breeze whipped at her and caught her hair, blowing it from her face. Her eyes were shadowed with dark circles, and the delicate cream skin of her face was ashen and lined, as if she'd aged magically since Tillie had last seen her. A gasp escaped her lips, and she threw open her arms, as if to embrace Rolf. At that moment, a shadow appeared to engulf her and she pitched forward, her arms still outspread, as she tumbled headlong from the path's edge.

Tillie watched in horror, clutching her leaf, as Lilliana plunged into the churning water beneath the falls. Her ears rang with the scream of agony that rose from Rolf's throat. The little faerie shut her eyes tightly, her body shaking. When she finally opened them, she looked down and saw Rolf pulling Lilliana's body from the water. Weighted with sorrow, tears streamed down Tillie's face and blurred her vision. She could only watch silently as the once tall, proud elf lord drew Lilliana's dead body into his arms and sobbed uncontrollably.

Tillie threw herself down on the branch and wrapped her little iridescent wings about herself, trying to shut out the terrible sounds.

"What is this lie?" Rolf gasped, his hands moving gently over the slim, cold body.

Tillie unwrapped herself, brushed the tears from her face, and was about to fly down to him when a sound from the forest froze her in place. A chill ran down her spine, and she folded herself even more tightly into the leaf as a shrouded figure slipped out from the cover of the trees, a sword grasped in one hand.

Sucking back a sob, Rolf turned toward Maelthor, Nortenaine's vessel and the spiritual guardian of the Florian elves. The shock on his face was immediately replaced with resignation. A bitter smile touched his lips.

"It is not for you to judge me," he said wearily and half-turned back to the elf maiden in his arms.

Rolf caught movement out of the side of his eye—the upraised arm with the sword. He turned back to Maelthor. "Do what you will," he called out, his voice already sounding like the ominous ghostly wail of the dead to Tillie's ears. "But take my curse with you. There shall be no peace in this place 'til her death is avenged. I call upon the god of the first elves, Chaska, and his issue, Queleastor, first warrior and guardian of this world, to quit this place and take their light and life from the Florian!"

Maelthor swung the huge sword, and the air whistled as its arc took the weapon in a wide sweep, the severed head of Rolf Andelar following the finishing upswing of its blow. As Rolf's head dropped and rolled to the ground beneath Tillie's perch, Maelthor reached down and plucked a ring from the elf maiden's finger.

Shouts and the thrashing of brush and limbs heralded the arrival of a group that burst from the cover of the trees. Below her, Tillie saw Nortenaine, the Florian lord and nephew of Lilliana, along with several other elf warriors. Their forward momentum was halted as they took in the scene before them. Rolf's arms continued to clutch Lilliana's limp form to a body devoid of its head. Maelthor jammed his hand quickly beneath his robe, but Tillie saw something drop to the ground with a brief glint before it disappeared in a clump of bright lady slippers.

Nortenaine grabbed Rolf's body and threw it aside, kneeling next to Lilliana. He brushed the hair back from her cheek, lifted her head, and touched her cold lips with his own. A howl escaped him. The Florian lord fell back on the grass, his eyes staring upward, not seeing the men circled around him.

"As my vision told you, Nortenaine, he has killed the flower of the Florian clan—my sister and your revered aunt. Now he has paid the price," intoned Maelthor.

Tillie bit her fingers to keep from calling out, though her faerie sight followed the spirit of Rolf Andelar as it rose from the elf's body. The glowing spirit form spread its arms, unseen by the eyes of the elves that stood over the inert body on the grass, and folded them together in a last embrace. With that action, the light in the small clearing around the green pool faded, as if dark clouds had shrouded the sun.

CHAPTER 1

ORDERS FROM HEADQUARTERS

Inspector Sandoval Carmichael lounged in a crudely crafted wooden chair, the seat and back made of banded leather strips, a floppy-brimmed leather hat almost concealing his long black hair that was liberally streaked with grey. His black eyes squinted at the book open on the table before him. Any person passing through the camp who was unacquainted with the famous inspector wouldn't have recognized a wizard of the White Guild, considering his white robe was brown with dust. Sandoval was oblivious to this fact, as well as to the heat, which was unusually intense even for a midsummer day in the northern regions, caused in part because the rocky expanse upon which they were encamped was bare of vegetation. The outcropping of granite acted like a natural mirror, reflecting the heat and shriveling any errant weed or blade of grass that attempted to take root there.

Such was the cost of Sandoval's obsessive investigations into the ancient history of his world that it took him to any part of Pacifica when the smallest hint or whisper of a find drifted to his ears. Always eager to get rid of his most irritating employee, Director Tantilus of the Royal Bureau of Investigation would generally authorize any excuse Sandoval could invent to visit various parts of the kingdom. Those excuses *never* mentioned artifacts, for Tantilus would refuse to allow one of his investigators to just pop off any time he pleased on what Tantilus considered silly treasure hunts. Crafting a convincing purpose was an art that Sandoval Carmichael had developed over uncounted years and often involved his friends. Whether it was marauding bandits hitting the stores of Bergen Ale made by the Dwarves of Thunderstorm Mountain, or a mysterious disappearance of racing stock from the herds of the Lestrami people, or some crisis in a particular part of the country that demanded his diplomacy and investigative skills, he could generally back it up with desperate pleas for help to the director or sometimes with appeals that went straight to the king.

Suspicion narrowing Tantilus' blue eyes and fueling a rage that often caused the unruly white hair to stand out on his head, he would glare at the calm, answering gaze that Sandoval returned. Knowing that it was probably a put-up excuse created by this most frustrating employee, Tantilus nevertheless had little recourse but to allow Sandoval to go, particularly when these requests always pointedly requested Inspector Sandoval Carmichael and often cited a previously solved theft, feud, or recovery of some item of great worth. Sandoval would usually bemoan the conceit of the wealthy and powerful who felt that wizards of the White Guild should be forever at their beck and call, while Tantilus would feel the heat rise in his face and was sure that if he didn't cool down, it would burst out of his ears like blasts of steam. Acquiescence was always safer than wasting his own staff's precious time in disproving the validity of the request, though he vowed that one day he would catch his smug inspector pulling a fast one.

The current excavation had been brought about by a young dwarf, one Waldo Snufflebeam, falling down a long-unused shaft on the side of a mountain overlooking the unexplored region east of the Thunderstorm Mountain range. What he was doing there wasn't as interesting as the item he carried back to the halls of his home in the bowels of that range to the north. Upon laying eyes on the item, a message had gone out by carrier pigeon to a small cottage in the Carthwait barony near Darren's

Choice, which was the home of Inspector Carmichael. The resulting urgent call to Director Tantilus requesting the services of Inspector Carmichael to discover the cause of the withering of hop vines and to save the latest harvest of Bergen Ale on which every inn and tavern in Pacifica depended was acted upon with haste. Tantilus gave his order to be sent by messenger to Inspector Carmichael, even as he shook his head, white hair flying, wishing he could—just once—catch that impossible man in one of his own traps.

Now, peering down at the item, which turned out to be an ancient book, Sandoval turned the brittle pages delicately, marveling at the characters drawn on the pages. He recognized them as musical notes, not unlike those currently in use. Not totally inept at reading music, he hummed along as his eyes scanned the page. He could decipher some of the words that were written over the musical notes, but others were lost to time, grime, or misuse. Hearing a grunt off to one side, he looked up.

Seated within two arms' lengths from him was Tronus Longbottom. The dwarf leader was sheltered from the hot midday sun by a makeshift canopy created from rough linen bags, cut and pinned together and propped on stakes. As the leader of the Dwarves of Thunderstorm Mountain, Tronus carried the simple title of Number One, designating him as the head of the High Council of the Dwarves. Sandoval wasn't sure of his age, as Tronus had been the leader of his people ever since Sandoval had known him, and that was too many years ago to remember specifically. Sandoval did know that other than his assistant, Hoagy Toogood, Tronus was one of the few persons he trusted implicitly.

As for Hoagy, his trust had been earned more than once since Sandoval had taken him as his intern ten years previous. Hoagy had then been a callow lad of thirty, just graduated from university and eager to become an assistant inspector. Though he wasn't a wizard, the young man was the son of Baron Toogood, a close friend of the crown, and there was no specific rule against assistants being of the common folk. Sandoval soon found that there were qualities that Hoagy had which were as impressive as the minimal power that most White Guild wizards could exert, the ultimate of which was his total recall of anything, whether it was a report he'd scanned briefly, a conversation he'd overheard, or something he'd seen. Along with that amazing characteristic, Hoagy also had a particular personality quirk that appealed to Sandoval—he was as adept at thievery as the most successful crook. Hoagy hadn't yet met the locked door he couldn't open (unless it was spelled) or pocket he couldn't pick, if need be. These were qualities that Sandoval naturally kept to himself and did not share with Director Tantilus, though word soon got around that it was wise to avoid playing cards with Inspector Carmichael's assistant.

Sandoval chuckled at this reminiscence, which caused another loud humph next to him. He looked up as Tronus fanned his heavy red beard, took a deep drink from the metal cup in his hand, and mused on the ignominy of a dwarf of his stature being subjected to the rigors of this heat.

"Don't know how you can stand sitting out there unprotected. This sun would cook the toes off a desert burro." Tronus grumbled loud enough to be heard by a number of Dwarves going about their work at the mouth of the cave.

They had set up the rough camp by a rocky outcropping overlooking the Valley of the Mists. He looked longingly down at the serene, grassy meadows that stretched from the foothills beneath their position on the eastern edge of the Thunderstorm Mountains to the small range of rocky hills that marked the borderline of the unexplored region. Beyond those low hills, he knew, stretched many days worth of travel through the barren, high desert before the cool waters of the Mordaen Strait marked the eastern edge of the continent of Pacifica. The thought of those deep, blue waters drew from him a resigned sigh. Not that he had that much of a liking for the sea and ships. *But it must be cooler than this oven*, he thought absently, *like the cool, dark interior of a great mountain hall.*

He frowned at Sandoval's lack of response, picked up a small map that lay on the table next to him, and fanned in vain at his rosy cheeks. With every few sweeps of the fan, he slapped at the dust that seemed to rise up, with or without a breeze, and attach itself to his shiny black boots and the new yellow vest he wore over his bright red shirt.

"I still can't see what's so damn important about this dig anyway. Those lads haven't unearthed anything but a few moldy old books. And I've got to pay them! With what? Can't get much coin for old books, unless we can find some old dolt foolish as you to pay the price!"

Sandoval's black eyebrows arched, and his riveting black-eyed gaze swung toward Tronus. It was a look under which many a criminal had paled, but Tronus merely regarded his old friend with a twisted smile.

"Orders from headquarters," Sandoval remarked tersely, turning his attention back to the book in his hands.

"Billypoop. We both know you're supposed to be discovering the source of the blight on the hop crop. And what are you going to say if Tantilus discovers where you've really gone?"

Sandoval's mouth twisted in a half-smile, but he kept his attention on the book as he carefully turned the brown, brittle pages and continued to study the rows of musical notes and accompanying words.

"You'd think that Tantilus would have brains enough to know you pull the wool over his eyes all the time. But then, you bureaucrats in the White Guild never had much imagination. Give me a Red Guild wizard any day! At least one of them would be drawing some rain, or a nice cool breeze our way. Or maybe a Green Guild wizard to put some fresh food on the table, instead of the week-old rations we've been forced to eat!"

"Oh, quit complaining, you dried up fossil," Sandoval said with a smile, "I thought you'd like the chance to field-train your men. Besides, we won't be here long. Not with Rendal watching me and making daily reports back to Tantilus in Sanctuary. Haven't you noticed?"

"That twit! Hoagy's got him running around after his shadow so much that you could steal away the whole damn mountain and he wouldn't know it. What's so special about these books anyway? And what purpose could they have in solving your current investigation?"

"I've informed the director that there is a particular mineral in this part of the Thunderstorm range that we will use as a soil additive to rid the hop crop of its blight. The boys have been very industrious and also very circumspect in what they are pulling out of the dig. Rendal has been assured that I brought these books with me merely to pass the time."

At that moment, five of Tronus' Dwarves, who had been helping with the digging, emerged from the cave mouth. The lead dwarf, Harald Brassbucket, marched in front as the other four, pushing a small cart loaded with rocks. Those other four were members of the Snufflebeam Company, given this honor because one of their number was the dwarf who had made the original find. Waldo, Milton, Tumpe, and Gort swayed as they pushed the cart, their voices raised in a chant.

"Hi ho, hi ho, it's off to work we go!" they intoned in time with their march.

"There they go again! Where in the demon's pit did they ever get that little tune? It's about to drive me nuts!"

"Just a little ditty I uncovered in one of these books. Pretty catchy, don't you think? Seems to have come from some legend of the old times, before the cataclysm. Tale of a young princess and some Dwarves who rescued her. Quite lovely, I think— she marries the prince in the end."

"What a lot of twaddle!"

"You have no romance in your soul, my friend. Actually, I find the ancient music touching. Simple, but effective. Now this book is completely devoted to songs, possibly ritual, though some of them appear to appeal to the more basic instincts. No, I think they were probably used more by the masses than for particular services. Strange combinations. I was hoping to uncover some of the instruments on which they were played. It would make for a nice musical diversion to play for the gathering of the five wizard guilds at the harvesting feasts."

Tronus sighed heavily and reached for his pipe as a horse and rider broke from the tree line above them and charged into camp. Heads turned and business stopped as the rider pulled his lathered horse to a halt near Tronus' sheltered canopy. The old dwarf sputtered as a cloud of dust drifted over him. He made a vain attempt to shield his mouth and beard as the rider strode up to him and snapped a salute.

"By your leave, sir, I seek Inspector Sandoval Carmichael."

Tronus leaped up with a roar and slapped at his dust-covered leggings and his yellow vest that was now indistinguishable from his brown pants. Before he could rain a string of expletives at the boy, Sandoval stepped past him.

"He's standing before you, boy. Make your report!"

The young man, his yellow tunic stained with sweat and dirt, looked up at the tall, legendary wizard of the White Guild, bowed quickly, and began to recite his orders in clipped tones that barely betrayed his weariness.

"Director Tantilus sends orders, sir." The young man looked around nervously, his gaze settling on Tronus. "For your eyes only, sir."

"Well, settle down, boy. Give me the orders. Go rest yourself and water that pony. It looks like the poor animal is ready to drop."

"Sorry, sir. I was instructed to make haste, and getting through the Grimwood wasn't easy. I was stopped several times. Almost didn't make it past the last group of elves that held me up. And I should have delivered this many days ago, but it took me time to find someone at the Thunderstorm Mountain hold who would tell me where you went."

The young man pulled a rolled parchment from the inside of his tunic and presented it to Sandoval, then sagged against one of the poles that held up Tronus' canopy. The flimsy construction immediately collapsed onto the old dwarf. Aghast, the young man pulled back the cloth and backed away as Tronus emerged, sputtering.

"What's going on? Get yourself to the food tent, boy, before I lose my temper!"

At that, the young man grabbed his horse's reins and scurried off to a large tent. Curious Dwarves already flanked him, eager to help him in hopes of getting information.

"This is interesting," Sandoval murmured, scanning the document quickly. "Better get Hoagy down here, Tronus. Tell him to meet us in my tent. Instruct the boys to take a break."

With that, Sandoval crammed the parchment into one of the large pockets of his robe and strode off toward his tent. Tronus stood for a moment, mouth open, whatever retort he had ready rendered useless for lack of an audience. Slapping his pipe back into the pouch that hung from his waist, he glared after Sandoval for a moment before heading up the hill toward the opening of the cave.

By the time Tronus entered Sandoval's tent, the White Guild wizard had unrolled the parchment and was scanning it. Sandoval nodded to himself, dropped the parchment into a bucket, and snapped his fingers. The parchment burst into flames.

"Good news, I hope," Tronus said sourly, peering down at the quickly disintegrating missive. "Perhaps you've been recalled to Sanctuary?"

"You might think so; then again, you might not," Sandoval answered, pulling a black, twisted cheroot from his pocket and lighting it with a quick snap of his flint.

His black eyes stared pensively at a point over Tronus' head. Recognizing the sure sign that the wizard's mind was distracted with a problem, Tronus moved to a rough wooden table in the middle of the tent and picked up a bottle of Truefruit wine and a metal cup. He hefted the bottle and checked the level, ignoring Sandoval, who had begun to pace the small space of the tent.

"Must be bad news, then. Might as well be prepared for it." Tronus filled the cup, took a sip, sighed, and set the bottle down. "Well, you going to tell me, or do I have to guess? If I had to guess, I'd say Tantilus is sending you someplace more disagreeable than this one for having trumped up this current *investigation*."

"We do have to break camp, I'm afraid," Sandoval said. He looked around the tent, as if gauging how long it would take him to pack up.

"And head home?" Tronus asked.

"Sorry, old friend. I'm directed to go to Queanell and speak to Nortenaine about the recent skirmishes between the Florian and Ileana elves."

"I knew it!" Tronus poured another healthy cupful of the wine. "I figured we were in trouble when I saw those elves on horses passing in and out of the Grimwood the other day through the pass below us. Going like the demons was after them when they came out."

"Those were the Ileana. Yes, I've noticed them, too; undoubtedly being chased, though Nortenaine's Florian elves wouldn't follow them beyond the tree line."

"So what does King Filemon care about two groups of elves arguing among themselves?"

"If it means disrupting trade between us and the Florian elves, Filemon would naturally be concerned," Sandoval explained. "There hasn't been all-out war between those two clans in untold years, though the skirmishes have been steadily increasing. Why now?"

"Oh, bless us! I can see your fiendish mind working already! Trade and Filemon be damned—you just want to get into the thick of things."

Sandoval smiled thinly, settled himself in a chair next to the table, and tapped the ash of his cheroot into a small metal bowl. He took a deep draught off the cheroot and expelled a cloud of smoke just as his young assistant, Hoagy Toogood, entered the tent, dropping the flap behind him.

"Rendal is strutting around outside, demanding to see you," Hoagy announced. "Seems he's talked to the emissary from Director Tantilus and is a little upset that the director didn't let him in on the message sent to you." Hoagy failed to suppress his smile.

"You can tell Rendal that his services will no longer be needed," Sandoval told him. "He can report back to his boss. We're breaking camp."

Hoagy's eyebrows rose over round blue eyes that had fooled many an interrogator into believing him the gullible young man his appearance would indicate. "No kidding? You mean we're off on a case?" Hoagy couldn't hide the excitement in his voice.

"Looks like it, boy."

"I'm surprised the twit didn't force his way in here anyway." Tronus dropped his round body into a chair next to Sandoval.

"Oh, he started to, but Harald took up his post right outside the door, with a battle hammer." Hoagy's voice dropped to a conspiratorial whisper. "You should have seen his face! Got redder than I've seen it yet."

Tronus laughed heartily, slapping his round stomach. "I always knew that boy had it in him! That's why I made him my lieutenant. Not that the members of the High Order of Dwarves haven't given me fits over it. They consider the Brassbuckets beneath any station, ever since his great-grandfather Shamut—"

"Tell Harald he's relieved, Hoagy," Sandoval said, gently cut off his friend—if he hadn't, he knew that Tronus would have started recounting the adventures of every family of Dwarves. "And ask Rendal to come in."

Tronus glowered slightly before he pulled out his pipe and contented himself with filling it. Hoagy slipped outside, his exit followed quickly by the blustering entrance of a small, dark man with eyeglasses perched on the tip of his nose. Rendal halted before Sandoval, waved his hand at the smoky air, then placed his fists firmly on his hips and glared down at the wizard through his glasses.

"I demand to know what orders Director Tantilus has given you."

"By those orders, I have burned them," Sandoval responded, slowly crushing his cheroot in the metal bowl.

Rendal's face sagged as he followed Sandoval's pointed gaze to the bucket, which was still smoldering. "This is highly irregular," Rendal sputtered, "I must communicate with Director Tantilus."

"Then I'd suggest you get together with the young lad who brought those orders before he leaves. Maybe you can accompany him."

Rendal gaped at Sandoval and then stiffened at Tronus' low chuckle. "I hope you know this calls for a formal complaint to be filed with the RBI upon my return. And don't think I didn't notice *items* in those carts being pulled out of the caves." His eyes narrowed. "I've not seen any so-called minerals being excavated either!"

"Do as you consider best, Rendal, which may or may not irritate your boss, if I know him. All depends on whether your report suggests that Tantilus hasn't followed protocol in letting you know what's going on. Could humble him if he's in a good mood. Maybe you'll even get an apology."

Sandoval studied the contemplative look on Rendal's face, followed by the slow dissipation of color in his cheeks as he indeed contemplated his boss' reaction to his accusation. Without another word, Rendal spun around and exited the tent.

Tronus waited until the tent flap bounced back behind the little man, then emitted a loud guffaw. "Serves that pompous fool right. You know he'll worry all the trip back to Sanctuary whether he's to be brought up on charges that he let you pull a fast one on him."

Sandoval smiled slightly. "Just following orders, my friend. The message did say to keep my destination secret. Didn't say from whom."

"You're a sly one, for sure. So ... are the Dwarves of Thunderstorm Mountain to follow you, or do I get a vacation?"

Sandoval turned his black eyes, softened now, on his old friend. Tronus knew the answer before he spoke it. "I would appreciate your company, Tronus. Somehow, I have a feeling I'll need all the help I can get. In fact, I think I'd better send word to Ferrel and Jade to meet me in Queanell."

"Assuming they can get that close. If Nortenaine's got his wind up, even your invitation might not help them reach that far into the Grimwood."

"Curious," Sandoval mused. His eyes carried a faraway look as he reached for the bottle of wine, pulled out another battered metal cup, and poured a healthy draught. "I have a feeling this could be an interesting case, indeed."

"You're perverse," Tronus said as he watched Sandoval sip the golden liquid, his black eyes glowing. *Here we go again*, the old dwarf thought.

CHAPTER 2

THE HERMIT

By the next day, the company had traded the direct glare of the summer sun for the sheltering shade of the Grimwood. Though the sunlight was muted now, filtered through the lush trees of the forest into dappled spots of gold and green that played upon the senses, the closeness and moist air competed with the heat.

Hoagy plodded along behind Sandoval, having long since peeled off his tunic and stuffed it in his backpack. Even without the additional layer of clothing, his sweat-stained, sleeveless undershirt and coarse cotton pants stuck to his skin. He could hear his feet squishing in his boots with each step. He pulled his soggy handkerchief from his pocket, wiped it across his face, and glanced over at Tronus, who thumped along beside him. Ahead of them, even Sandoval had taken off his wide-brimmed leather hat and stuffed it into the large leather bag he always carried slung over his shoulder.

Tronus was faring no better than Hoagy, dragging his steps over the narrow path they had followed for what seemed like hours, his head bobbing over his long red beard. That luxurious beard now lay limp against his barrel chest, a distinctive curl at the ends due to the excessive moisture in the air. Everyone was too exhausted to speak. Just a few short hours into their trek through the forest and already the magic of that place, which had been stimulating at other times, felt oppressive. On numerous occasions, Tronus and Hoagy found it necessary to halt the procession to run off in different directions to retrieve a dwarf who had become mesmerized and strayed off the path Sandoval had taken. Yet, even with everyone in the party showing signs of strain, Sandoval only stopped occasionally for short breaks.

On each successive break, muted grumbles could be heard as the group lay scattered about, taking small sips of water to wash down the nut rolls they had packed for the journey. Sandoval ignored the whispered concerns of the others and concentrated on the map he had made of the Grimwood during previous expeditions. As on previous stops, it seemed they had spent only enough time to catch their breath, ease their stomach rumblings, and count noses before Hoagy and Tronus were curtly ordered to pack up and begin again. Even Harald, proud of the faith that Tronus had placed in him, would stare off into the dense forest on occasion, his round eyes transfixed as he stroked his long brown moustache—he preferred a moustache to the long beard commonly sported by most male Dwarves. A sharp slap on the ears from Tronus would bring him back to order.

Hoagy longed for his horse, Bully, though he understood why Sandoval had Bully, along with his own black stallion, Menopet, following behind as they trudged on foot. Tronus did have a pony he occasionally rode, but he kept only a few of those animals in the mountain hold. There were by no means enough to mount even a small troop of his Dwarves—and that was assuming they could be trained to ride, since Dwarves weren't fond of that mode of transportation.

So they all walked in deference to the hearty Dwarves. At least Bully and Menopet could carry all the gear they had packed, while Hoagy and the Snufflebeam Company carried the food.

By the time the shadows had lengthened, the landscape still looked foreign to him. Hoagy moved up to step in time with Sandoval and placed his hand on his master's arm. The path now had narrowed to a point where their shoulders almost touched as they walked side by side. "Sir, I'm sure we've taken a wrong turn somewhere. I don't recognize this part of the forest. Maybe we should set up camp while it's still light. I could go on ahead for a while and try to find a familiar path."

Sandoval looked down at the young man, not breaking his stride. "You won't find a familiar landmark, Hoagy," he said. His black eyes swept the forest that continued to enclose them tighter in its grip.

Hoagy's gut tightened. "You mean we're lost, sir?"

"I'm afraid so."

"Shouldn't we stop now, then? Gather our forces, so to speak?"

Sandoval touched Hoagy's arm lightly, slowing his stride. "Look to your left."

Hoagy swept his gaze casually over the path in front of him and caught a slight movement out of the corner of his eye—nothing he could pinpoint; just a little rustle and parting of the underbrush by a nearby tree. In the gathering dusk, he thought he saw a flicker of light blinking in and out. His senses, more than sight, sent him a warning. "We're being watched."

"Just so," Sandoval said, his long stride not faltering. "And have been for some time. No matter how many times I've aimed us straight and true for Quelean, we seem to find ourselves going in the opposite direction."

"Do you know where we are?"

"Never been in this part of the forest before … assuming we're in any part of the forest."

Hoagy stared up at Sandoval's calm face, missed his footing, and stumbled. Sandoval's hand caught his arm and pulled him upright. That action caused the Dwarves who were following in close formation, two by two, to halt uncertainly. A thump and a sharp curse came from the back of the row.

"What's going on up there?" Tronus called.

Before Sandoval could answer, the forest around them came alive with rustling and sharp bursts of high laughter. A tree branch hanging over the path near Hoagy's head brushed his face. Hoagy ducked and slapped at it. Tronus pushed his way past the Dwarves, who were now huddled closer to Sandoval. He pulled his battle hammer and glared menacingly at the tree branches dipping close in on them.

"I don't like this, Sandoval," Tronus said. "I don't like it one bit."

At Tronus' words, sharp dots of light appeared in the darkening forest on both sides of the path. The dots danced and sparkled in erratic circles and swirls of light. Tinkling laughter followed the lights. Hoagy fumbled in his pack and pulled out his flint, striking a light to the lamp that hung at his side. A warm halo of lamplight enveloped them in a tight circle. Tronus' Dwarves gathered in closer, huddling in the safe glow of the lamp. The round, frightened eyes of the young Dwarves looked up at Tronus for comfort and assurance. Tronus tried his best to look the confident figure of a leader, cursing himself silently for bringing these young boys on this mission in the first place.

Harald pushed his way through the crowd and saluted his leader smartly. "I've been hearing some strange sounds coming from the trees on either side of the path, Number One, sir. Say the word. and I'll take two of these lads to reconnoiter."

Tronus looked at the young dwarf. His mouth twisted in a sour smile, but he only said, "I don't think so, Harald. At least, it wouldn't be my first choice."

Sandoval tapped his long fingers on the medallion on the top of his polished wooden staff. The blue gem in the carved eye of its center gleamed, and Sandoval's own black eyes scanned the forest on either side. Moving past the tight group around Hoagy, the wizard stopped next to Menopet and stroked the black stallion, speaking softly in the big horse's ear. Menopet nodded vigorously with a brief snort, as if he understood what his master was telling him. Satisfied, Sandoval returned to the group, handed Menopet's saddle bags to Hoagy, and called out in a booming voice, "Take me to your leader!"

Immediately, the forest came alive. Tree branches rustled and a low humming rose from the dark depths surrounding them.

"Oh, good idea, wizard!" Tronus said, his alarm showing. "How the devil do you know their leader isn't a flesh-eating demon?"

"He's right, sir." Hoagy looked at his boss as he was shoved up against Sandoval's side by the insistent nudging of the Dwarves, who closed in on their leaders for protection. "I vote we continue on as quickly as ..."

His voice trailed off as a pervasive hum grew suddenly in intensity, vibrating painfully in their eardrums. Several of the young Dwarves threw their hands over their ears and cried out. Hoagy pulled out his own short sword as Harald stepped out to the edge of the path, his battle hammer clasped in both hands in front of him. A number of the lights, like erratic little stars, spun into a circle in the path just ahead of them. As Harald threw back his arms to heave his hammer in their direction, a single dot of light separated from the circle and began to dance about the stout dwarf's head. Harald backed up, uncertain, his head swinging sharply back and forth in an attempt to follow the jittering point of light. The others watched, mesmerized as the spark of light stopped just above and in front of Harald's head and shimmered into the form of a young female.

Large, amber, almond-shaped eyes sparkled from an angelic face framed by wispy blonde hair, through which poked tiny, pointed ears—the only obvious physical clue to her true origin. A delicate little dress with a draping over one shoulder glistened like a leaf touched with morning dew. The scalloped edges of the hem barely covered her knees.

Entranced, the group stared at the ethereal apparition before them. A wide smile touched her mouth.

"Sir," Hoagy said breathlessly, "is that a faerie?"

Before Sandoval could reply, the apparition spoke. "My name is Tillie. You'll come with me now."

With that pronouncement, the air about them wavered and glowed. Hoagy looked up at Sandoval, who nodded, then back at the faerie, who had disappeared. In her place stood an old man in a rumpled brown robe. A heavy cowl draped over his shoulders, not unlike the pictures Hoagy had seen in some of Sandoval's old books. The old man's gray hair was cropped close about his head in a straight line, running from the bangs on his forehead and around over his ears. His soft blue eyes gazed steadily from a face upon which were etched more wrinkles than any of them had ever seen. It took all of them a few brief seconds to realize that the man hadn't appeared in the path before them. Instead, they had seemingly appeared at his lodgings. At least that's what Hoagy assumed, as they were now gathered in a room that contained several comfortable-looking stuffed chairs with accompanying tables set before a fire blazing in the hearth. Off to one side was a rectangular table with two long benches on either side. Even after the stifling heat and humidity of the forest, the fire did not add to their discomfort but seemed to blend with the homey feeling of the room and give off little heat.

As the recognition of change in their circumstances hit them, each reacted in his own way. The Snufflebeam Company shrieked in unison and clung to each other. Harald spun around, his hammer sweeping the air and almost putting a dent in Tronus' bushy thatch of red hair. Tronus cuffed his young lieutenant on the side of the head, shook his head in resignation, and sheathed his own battle hammer. Hoagy stared in fascination, stepping forth to peer into each corner and nook in the room. Sandoval merely picked the largest chair and settled himself with a heavy sigh, leaving the other two for Tronus and the old man to occupy.

The wizened old man nodded at each in turn, as if counting them to make sure he'd gotten the lot, then took the chair next to Sandoval. His hands, like claws, curled over the arm rests. As soon as he had seated himself, a young child scurried into the room, balancing a tray laden with steaming cups. He passed through the crowd, offering drinks to all. The child was dressed in loose, plain, linen leggings that looked homemade, judging by the large, erratically spaced stitches. He wore a shirt of the same coarse material, and his head was topped with a floppy wide-brimmed straw hat, of the type Sandoval had seen gardeners use to shade their heads from the sun.

The young Dwarves looked to Tronus, who nodded, took a cup, and seated himself in the overstuffed chair on Sandoval's other side. Given permission, each young dwarf grabbed delightedly for a cup and spaced themselves on the benches. Hoagy continued to survey the room, followed closely by Harald. Hoagy touched items on shelves and thumbed through the books scattered on a table in one corner.

The old man's blue eyes followed Hoagy's progress, then frowned as he turned to Sandoval. "He's a thorough young man, isn't he?"

"I've always thought so," Sandoval responded, taking a cup offered by the serving boy and sipping the warm broth contentedly. "Great stuff. You make it yourself?"

"From the herbs in my garden and a broth of my own concoction." The old man sampled his own cup and nodded at Sandoval, his blue eyes seeming oddly penetrating. "Name's Will Wiggins."

"You're a monk of some order, from your robe and the simple way you appear to live," Sandoval judged. "But I haven't heard of any order that would be allowed to inhabit the Grimwood—not if the elves knew about it, that is."

"Oh, they fussed about it many years ago when we first set up this place. But I suppose when they saw we had no intention of attempting contact with them or interfering in their lives, they decided to just ignore us. The rest of my order soon decided they did not care for the monastic life and left me."

"Doesn't sound like Nortenaine to me." Out of the corner of his eye, Sandoval saw Hoagy taking a cup of broth that was offered to him, and the young man's eyes followed the serving boy as he disappeared into the back of the cottage. Hoagy glanced quickly in Sandoval's direction and then seated himself on the corner of the hearth. "He tolerates few humans invading his forest and has no liking for the more extreme religious beliefs of humans, Dwarves, or any other kind," Sandoval added with a smile.

"What *kind* do I appear?" came Will Wiggins' curt response.

"Genuinely human," Sandoval chuckled.

Will studied Sandoval, his clear blue eyes meeting the piercing black gaze of the wizard without flinching. Then Will looked again to the Dwarves and Hoagy. As if making up his mind about something, he settled back into the chair and waved a hand at Sandoval. "You may smoke one of your cheroots, if you like, wizard. I don't mind. Kind of reminds me of the pipe I used to enjoy."

At the word pipe, Tronus' ears perked up, and he slipped his own pipe from his pouch, along with a little pick. Listening without intruding, he set about cleaning the bowl.

"You know who I am, I take it," Sandoval said, pulling a dark cheroot from his voluminous pocket, along with his flint case. He lit the long, thin cheroot, expelling a puff of smoke with a pleased sigh.

Will nodded. "You're a legend. I may be a monk, but I don't always cloister myself. Actually, I get around a lot. And I take a particular interest in the goings-on of the humans that share this corner of the world with the elves, Dwarves, faeries, and the like. You are known to have an exceptionally sharp mind and a soft spot for the underdog, so to speak. I've taken a particular interest in your Bondonai wizard guilds. Actually …" Will blushed, looking down at his hands clasped in his lap. "I've made a study of them. You're of the White Guild. The administrators, you're called; the least powerful of the wizard guilds. At least, that's what the common populace and the other guilds believe. But I'm sure you know a few tricks they haven't guessed yet."

Sandoval's black eyes narrowed but didn't move from Will's face, even though he relaxed his tall frame into the chair and stretched out his long legs closer to the fire. "It's been many years since I've seen monks in this part of the world," he said. "I thought all of your order had disbanded long ago, after the Bondonai guilds grew in number."

"Ah, yes, the guilds. Well, the Blue Guild wizards did sort of make us obsolete, since they enjoy the functions of caring for the health of the body, mind, and soul of the people on our world. But we monks were never really in the business of converting the masses to any particular belief. Actually, we guard our solitude and seek only the contemplative life. I have no quarrel with the Bondonai guilds, though I think the elves may be wary of the Gold Guild wizards because their power is similar."

"Not really," Sandoval responded casually. "Though the power may be equivalent, the elves' power is more constructive. They do have the ability to *make* things; to create forms from other matter and even transform themselves, when need calls for it. The Gold Guild wizard's power is more destructive. A Gold Guild wizard can pull apart and transform but not necessarily create something from nothing."

"A terrible power."

"Could be. Some of them consider it a benefit to apply that power to protect and serve their fellow beings."

"Sort of preventive, as opposed to inventive," Will suggested. "I hadn't thought of it that way. Actually, it's probably a blessing for humans, having had to survive in this changed world."

"And you've watched it all unfold from the safety of your little home in the woods." Sandoval's tone sharpened slightly, but it was noticeable only to Tronus, Hoagy, and the old man, whose mild blue eyes became suddenly shadowed.

"You give me more credit than is my due," he said evenly.

"I doubt that," Sandoval argued. "Though I'm curious where you came upon the boy. I won't presume to judge your age, sir, but I doubt the youngster belongs to you."

Will's blue eyes didn't flinch, though his mouth twitched in a slight smile. "As I said, a legend. As sharp a mind as I'd ever hope to come upon. And you're correct; the boy is not my child. He's a ward of mine, abandoned on the edge of the Grimwood and given to me by the faeries, actually. The creatures of the Grimwood can seem heartless in their simplicity, but they know the value of life, as this world makes it and takes it away."

"What's her name?"

"Flo …" Will hesitated, then barked a laugh and shook his finger in Sandoval's direction. "You are a trickster, aren't you?" He rasped out the words in a rough tone.

Hoagy jerked to attention, setting his cup aside and slipping his hand toward the sword sheathed at his side. He cast a sharp look in Tronus' direction as he held his pipe suspended before his mouth. He almost choked on a mouthful of smoke before he forced himself to expel it as casually as he could. With his other hand, Tronus stroked his long red beard, letting the hand drop to his battle hammer and calculating the positioning of his troop. The Snufflebeam Company had long since lost interest in the conversation of the old man and wizard and were chatting among themselves—all except Harald, who had remained alert, close by Hoagy, watching all. He saw the sudden stiffening in his commander and Hoagy. Lacking their subtlety, he read a warning and leaped to his feet, his hand already pulling his own battle hammer from its sheath. Shooting a warning look in Hoagy's direction, Tronus yelped, "Harald!" which caused everyone in the room—with the exception of the old man—to jump as if shot.

Harald stared at his commander, uncertain, his eyes darting from the old man to Tronus to Hoagy. Finally, as all eyes settled on him, he managed to bleat out a strangled reply. "Sir, yes, sir!"

"Set up a perimeter guard around this place, boy. What's the matter with you? Have you forgotten your duties? Those frisky faeries might still be after our hides."

Hesitating, Harald looked to Hoagy, who nodded solemnly, turning his attention quickly back to Sandoval. Hoagy saw the sparkle in his black eyes and forced himself to relax. Not really knowing why, he sensed the wizard was not alarmed, and that calmed him, though his nerves still twitched, as did Tronus', from another surreptitious glance at the red-headed dwarf, who gripped his pipe as if he would snap it in two.

"Oh, that won't be necessary." Will waved his hand at Harald, who relaxed immediately and dropped back down on the hearth next to Hoagy, his face reflecting his confusion.

"Flora," Will called out. "Come in and meet our guests. I guess we've been discovered."

The "boy" emerged from what Sandoval assumed was the kitchen area and walked over to stand next to Will's chair, head down.

"Take the hat off, girl. They won't bite you," Will said quietly.

Flora, her eyes still glued to where the floor met her feet, reached up and pulled off the floppy hat. Her dark brown hair popped from confinement, framing her angular face. Her hair settled in soft, short curls with a glint of reddish highlights in the candle glow. An intake of breath came from Hoagy as she lifted her chin and looked in his direction. Her large brown eyes settled on the young man for a moment before redirecting them to Will and Sandoval.

Sandoval took another drag from his cheroot and expelled a cloud of blue smoke, snuffing out the stub. The wizard's black eyes narrowed slightly as he took her in from head to toe until, noticing that she was trembling, he drew his gaze back to Will. "A fine deception. But why, I may ask? Did you think we were mercenaries? And, if so, why bring us into your home?"

"Oh, I didn't doubt your honest intent," Will answered. "I'm afraid it wasn't me who drew you here. I have no such power. The faeries do, and they are sensitive to people wandering in their homeland. There are sacred places in the Grimwood where none except the faeries and elves may venture. If they feel humans coming too close, they send them here. I expect they consider my acceptance a stamp of approval, so to speak."

"And you are not afraid?" Sandoval asked.

"Only for Flora, which is the reason for the fumbling attempt at disguise. Strange things have been going on in the Grimwood lately—armed elves slipping through the trees. The faeries keep me well informed. I think they dote on both Flora and me, as the elves pay them little attention these days. I listen to their stories, and they watch over us. Certainly keeps them out of trouble, though they've been too distracted by what's happening lately in the Grimwood to think up any new tricks to play on unsuspecting travelers."

"Ah, so you have heard of the elves' activities?"

"I haven't a choice. It's got the faeries all in a dither, that's for sure. They chatter about an impending battle between the Florian and the Ileana. Sad." He shook his head.

"Have you seen any of them in this part of the wood?" Sandoval asked. "And by the way, what part of the wood are we in?"

"You're near the northern border. Actually, the Dwarves' kingdom is not far from here. But, no, we stay close to home here. We have heard sounds and seen lights in the forest at night, though. I've got quite a good view from the tower."

Sandoval looked around curiously and spotted a draped doorway off in one corner of the room. "I'd like to take a look, if I may," he said.

Will sighed and rose slowly from his chair. He patted Flora gently on the shoulder, whispered in her ear, and proceeded toward the draped doorway. Sandoval stood and followed him, giving a quick nod of his head at Hoagy's questioning look. When he had slipped through the doorway, dropping the drape behind him, Flora addressed their guests in a light, musical voice.

"Will wishes me to provide food for you. I've some bread, cheese, and fruit, if you like. I'm sorry there's no meat, but there's honey to sweeten and nuts to chew." Flora spoke to the group, but her brown eyes were directed at Hoagy.

He smiled at her, entranced, feeling himself become lost in the dark depths of those eyes that now he noticed had touches of gold flecked through the brown irises. Flora, a red blush rising in her cheeks, pulled her eyes away and slipped silently from the room. Hoagy stared for a moment at the spot where she had stood, then turned to find the Dwarves studying him.

Tronus chuckled, his shaggy red beard bobbing. He leaned toward Hoagy, his voice low. "A pleasant enough place, don't you think, boy-o? But I'd like to get a look at just where we are. Not some poor old monk's cottage, I warrant."

"You're always suspicious, Tronus. They appear to be nice people who choose to live away from others. What's wrong with that?"

"Hmm." Tronus scraped out his pipe, shoved it in his pouch, and stroked his beard. "With faeries for friends. Well, I've been around the mountain a few more times than you, Hoagy. And this old nose smells trouble."

High above them, Sandoval followed the old monk up a narrow, winding stairwell that seemed to be carved of a piece out of solid rock. At the top, they stepped into a circular room, lit only by moonlight. Sandoval's keen eyes scanned the room and picked out the fine seams of the stones that formed the tower. Will walked to the nearest casement and drew a deep breath of cool night air. Sandoval stepped up beside him and looked out upon the treetops of the Grimwood. The opening spanned the circular tower, broken only by an occasional buttress. Below them, the forest was dark and silent, except for the sporadic chirping of birds and the mournful hoot of an owl.

As Sandoval swung his gaze around, he spotted several dots of light bobbing in and out of the trees. "I find it curious that the elves pay you so little attention. From our perspective, I would say this structure stands out conspicuously."

"An old ruin, for all they can tell," Will answered.

"Like its inhabitant—deceptive."

Will's narrowed eyes settled on Sandoval. "They know I'm here but pay me no heed. Flora has spoken to them on occasion. But you should be careful, young man. These elves are fierce fighters."

Sandoval smiled down at the wizened old man. "Actually, at 175, I'm considered middle-aged for a wizard.

"But I am curious about your report from the faeries. An *impending battle*, the faeries say? Did they tell you the reason for the sudden increased animosity between these two clans?"

Sandoval nudged at the old man, mentally. Will turned slowly and gazed out at the peaceful, moonlit treetops. Sandoval could see his bony shoulders moving up and down as his mouth opened in a silent chuckle. He sighed and wagged his knobby finger at Sandoval.

"Don't try your wizard tricks on me, *young* man." His eyes seemed to shadow over, and his face drooped in sadness. "There is much hidden in the hearts and minds of those involved in this conflict, and the bitterness drives to their very souls. It will take all of your sharp wits to solve this puzzle, my dear inspector." With that, Will turned and shuffled down the circular stairs, leaving Sandoval staring at the monk's stooped back in silent contemplation.

CHAPTER 3

A HISTORY LESSON

The travelers awoke the next morning to find their host and his ward absent. Sandoval was a little disconcerted at having slept through their departure, particularly as he had set his staff on a spell to wake him at any movement. After checking the tower for any sign of Will Wiggins or Flora, he resigned himself to the fact that they had somehow managed to nullify the spell, even though he was sleeping close by the main doorway, his staff clasped tightly against his side. *I should have known, after what happened last night,* he thought with chagrin. *I must be slipping.* Fortunately, the rest of his company were unaware of his pensive distraction, having discovered the breakfast of milk, fresh bread, and butter laid out on the table for them. After filling themselves and packing up for the final trek to Quelean, they were eager to set out.

All is right with the world, Sandoval thought as they marched briskly down the now broad, clearly marked trail through woods. Dappled sunlight sparkled through the tall trees. Not a sign of faeries or any odd sound disturbed their pleasant walk. If Sandoval was inclined to discount his own sense and memories of the previous night, he could almost convince himself that nothing odd had happened and that the company had simply bedded down, as usual, for a night's rest. But he knew better and kept his awareness sharpened while also watching closely for an uncommon reaction from any member of the group. It wasn't until the sun was at its apex and stomachs had begun to growl for a midday meal that Hoagy slipped up next to him and tugged his sleeve. Sandoval looked down at the young man, whose brows had drawn together in perplexity. Hoagy held up Menopet's saddle bags, which he still carried, along with his own.

His round blue eyes were questioning. "Sir, this may seem an odd question, but wasn't there an old man and young woman with us last night?"

"Certainly, Hoagy. Have you just now remembered?"

"It was like a gap that suddenly filled itself. One minute we were on the trail at night and the next, waking to a tasty breakfast. I was just so happy to get back on the road that … I guess I forgot. Funny. Seems to me she was a nice girl at that."

"And you rarely forget a pretty face," Sandoval said, smiling down at him. "Actually, you *never* forget anything. Doesn't that seem odd?"

Tronus' head swung around and his eyes narrowed, looking back at them. Hoagy's voice dropped to a whisper. "Did it happen then?" Hoagy's blue eyes rounded in shock. "Someone's wiped me, sir! The last time that happened was—"

"Yes, I know; our last case. But this has a different *feel* to it—not just a powerful force, but something alien, even to me." Sandoval paused for a moment in silent contemplation. Then his voice rose to grab the attention of the Dwarves marching ahead of them. "Let's have some rest and a noon meal, boys!"

Immediately, Tronus, Harald, and the Snufflebeam Company halted and stretched. Tronus shucked his pack and handed it to Harald, motioning him and the others to a small clearing just off the trail, where a broad shade tree beckoned. The dwarf frowned, waited for Sandoval and Hoagy to follow, and then sidled up to them, grasping Sandoval's sleeve.

"I've been keeping an eye on you, wizard. What's up? And don't try to tell me nothing. I know that look in your eye."

Hoagy's mouth twisted in a wry smile as he turned to follow Harald and the others to the tree, where they dug into Hoagy's bags and began assembling a communal meal.

"Seems we've been spelled, old friend," Sandoval murmured, picking out a spot in the soft grass beneath the tree and settling his long frame with a sigh. "Do you recall where we camped last night?"

Sitting down next to Sandoval, Tronus dug his pipe from his pocket and stared at it, his bushy red brows drawing together. Getting no immediate answer from his pipe, he pulled out his packet of tobacco and looked up at Sandoval as he primed his pipe. "I think … no … come to mention it, last thing I remember was some dancing lights." Tronus' face reddened to almost the bright color of his hair. "Damn! We were witched by faeries!"

"So it appears. Hoagy remembers an old man and young girl. But it would be hard to fool him without a strong mind-wipe, considering his amazing memory recall. Particularly when there was a female of almost any age involved."

"Old man and girl, you say? No … can't say … well, that really puts a fuzz on it! I don't like that one bit. Nobody messes around with Tronus Longbottom's mind and gets away with it! Are we possessed then? How do we know we're not in some black pit, just walking around like a bunch of fools?"

Tronus' angry retort caused heads to turn in their direction. Sandoval's steady hand on his arm calmed Tronus, as did the wizard's soft chuckle.

"Quelean is within an hour's walk from here. I've been in this part of the Grimwood. No, friend, we're not possessed; merely redirected, so to speak. A neat trick, if I must say."

"Well, good for you. And I expect a full report when we get to the elf city, or I pull my boys and head for home. You know I'll back you whenever you say, Sandoval, but I don't like all that magic stuff. Makes me nervous."

"You and me both, Tronus. Particularly since we couldn't possibly have gotten as far as we have today, starting from the point we did."

"Only you'd know that, since I sorta can't remember where we were to begin with. Besides, you said we'd been spelled. We could've been put down anywhere."

Sandoval had pulled out a cheroot and was contemplating the twisted, dark, roughly wrapped shape of it. He snapped his flint and lit the thin cigar before looking back at Tronus. "No, there was no interruption in the continuity of our journey. I would have noticed. It's been a smooth transition since starting out at that tower this morning. The faeries possess a greater power than I would have expected to move us around like pieces on a chess board."

Tronus' bushy red brows drew together again, and his eyes narrowed at Sandoval as he drew slowly on his pipe and expelled a puff of smoke. They both watched it as it drifted upward on the light breeze, dissipating. Sandoval mused on the previous night's events, and Tronus calmly judged the wind direction. Neither spoke again, even when Hoagy brought them food and drink. Tronus tapped out his pipe and munched on his bread and cheese absently, so engrossed in his contemplation of the folly of hanging around with wizards that he didn't even hear the soft footfalls on the surrounding leaves until Hoagy leaped up and pulled his sword.

At a yelp from Harald, Tronus' head came up, and he found the entire group surrounded by elves armed with longbows, several of which were aimed in his direction. At the other end of the bows stood a contingent of tall elves, with long blond hair framing smooth pale faces, clad in loose-fitting green trousers and matching sleeveless tunics. Their clothing had the odd effect of blending into the surrounding forest. Even the faces and arms of each elf appeared painted with a pale green tinge. Only the various blue, green, or hazel eyes, if looked at directly, stood out against the backdrop of the trees. Tronus leaped up, sadly gripping nothing but the pipe in his hand. The company of elves stood silently, heads swiveled to look down at Sandoval who, having taken notice of the elves, merely nodded in confirmation to an unspoken thought.

"Emissaries of Nortenaine, I gather," Sandoval spoke to the elf aiming his bow at Tronus.

The elf lowered his bow, unnocked his arrow, and turned his pale blue eyes toward Sandoval. "You are Inspector Sandoval Carmichael, the wizard?"

Sandoval rose in one smooth motion, brushing the grass from his soiled white robe. "Of the White Guild. At your service."

"You will follow me," the elf said.

Without further word, the elf nodded to his men, who surrounded the company and waited as Hoagy and the Dwarves hurriedly gathered their meager foodstuff into their bags. With a brief glance at the group now assembled in a circle around Sandoval, the elf started off into the forest. Sandoval waved his hand at his company and stalked off after the lead elf. The others fell in line behind him. Tronus and Hoagy exchanged worried glances.

The travelers marched silently for the next two hours, locked within the encircling troop of elves, along a well-worn hunting trail. Not even Tronus ventured a motion or word in Sandoval's direction—he remained silent as the group moved steadfastly forward. Harald, who had taken a liking to Hoagy, managed to move into a position next to the young man and, at first opportunity, nudged him with an elbow in the hip. Hoagy glanced down at Harald, cracked a small smile and winked. After that, Harald was content to plod along with the rest of the company. After all, if the wizard's right-hand man wasn't worried, why should he be? Having gained that advantage, Harald communicated it to the rest of the Dwarves through a simple sign language they had developed. By the time the afternoon was waning, a flickering light could be seen through the dense closeness of brush and trees.

Sandoval's company was exhausted and apprehensive as the elves closed in around them, forcing them through a narrow tunnel of trees. None of them, except Sandoval, could see over the bodies of the tall elves in front. Hoagy, taller than Tronus and the other Dwarves, pranced along on his toes and craned his neck to peer over the shoulder of the elf marching in front of him. To his surprise the contingent of elves suddenly spread apart as they all passed from the darkening green tunnel of trees and were immediately confronted with a dazzling display of colored lights and soft music.

Huddling together around Sandoval, they stared in dumb fascination at the amazing array of lanterns hung in the trees and on the eaves of wooden houses and larger dwellings, which blended their architecture with the shape of the enormous trees that surrounded the large open area in which they now stood. Some buildings were merely single-story affairs, but there were several that rose in delicate levels, blending with the arching branches of the trees at the far end of the Quelean central common. Each lantern on the common was made of gold, with sections of tinted glass that gave the effect of a rainbow of colors. In the exact center of the common stood a fountain, spewing what Hoagy could only think was magically colored water—or maybe the different hues of lamplight were affecting it. The water rushed upward from a single tall stone in a spray that fell gently on a circular stone pool, around which were built smoothly polished wooden benches. Seated on one of the benches, surrounded protectively by several tall male elves, was another elf so regal in bearing that Hoagy decided he could be none other than Nortenaine, high lord of the Florian elves.

Sandoval stepped forward as Nortenaine rose, lifting his hand in greeting. One of the young elf warriors stepped up beside him. Hoagy thought that the elven lord looked to be a man in no more than his thirties, though he knew Nortenaine must be well over a hundred years in their reckoning. Even wizards like Sandoval, who were the only truly long-lived humans by virtue of the power in them, often looked advanced in age; though most all humans had life spans of over a hundred years. Hoagy glanced sideways at Sandoval. His boss did hold up much better than most and looked no older than a normal man in his sixth decade.

Nortenaine, on the other hand, appeared to have suspended time in the physical sense. He was even more statuesque than the other elves, clothed in a long robe of soft fabric that seemed to change colors as magically as the lamplight. The robe was simple in its scoop-necked, long-sleeved design, drawn loosely about his waist by a gold cord. His head was bare of crown or other ornament. His long golden hair was drawn back from his face over his delicately pointed ears and left to hang loose, like spun gold on his shoulders. It was the light that surrounded him that drew one's eyes to him in awe, that light being reflected in his dark blue eyes. But now that Hoagy centered his attention on the elf's eyes, he saw more than the beautiful, brilliant leader of a race. There was sorrow in those eyes and a hardness that spread to the elf leader's taut jawline. Here was a creature who could condemn with clear conscience and little afterthought.

"Well, Sandoval!" Nortenaine's voice was robustly melodic with only the slightest edge to it. "What do you have to say for yourself?"

"I wasn't aware making excuses was a necessity," Sandoval replied, standing relaxed but diplomatically at a distance from Nortenaine.

"You have been commanded by your leader to intercede in a dispute between the Florian and Ileana without request or permission from us. Wouldn't you humans call that presumptuous?"

"Only to observe the lay of the land, so to speak, considering the impact an open war between elven factions could have on the humans that inhabit this world with you. If that appears presumptuous, my dear Nortenaine, so be it."

Hoagy controlled his reaction by clamping his teeth tightly together, though from the sound of the gasps behind him, the Dwarves didn't do as well.

Nortenaine's pale face reddened, his mouth opening in reply, as another elf suddenly appeared on his open side. Hoagy stepped back involuntarily, feeling a lurch in his gut.

The elf standing next to Nortenaine was as unlike the high lord of the Florian as sunlight was unlike cold shadow. Long brown hair framed a dark-skinned, angular face, the main distinguishing features being the cold brown eyes. His skin looked more like the Ileana elves that he had seen in paintings in the capital; similar in coloring as well as war-like demeanor. Hoagy opened his mouth to speak in an aside to Tronus but checked himself, as those hard eyes turned on him for a brief moment. The elf was clad completely in gray, his robe drawn at the waist by a same-colored sash. Maybe it was the color of the robe that hid his entrance. At any rate, the cold stare gave Hoagy's gut another twist, unnerving him. Maybe he had simply appeared out of thin air.

Nortenaine stiffened visibly at the elf's appearance, even though his eyes never moved from Sandoval's face. The young elf that stood at his side glanced at the new arrival, his eyes barely concealing his wariness. Of the entire group, only Sandoval showed no outward reaction. He merely turned his steady black eyes on the elf and nodded respectfully.

"Maelthor," Nortenaine said, "how good of you to join us. But excuse my lapse; I should make a formal introduction. Inspector Sandoval Carmichael of the Royal Bureau of Investigation, I present Maelthor, vessel of the Florian elves and brother to Gaelen, my revered father."

Sandoval put his hands together, touched them to his lips, and nodded again in Maelthor's direction. "Gaelen was king to me as a young boy. I revere his name and memory. I am pleased to meet his kin and one who holds such high honor in the Florian clan."

"We shall speak later, wizard. Lodgings have been prepared for you and your man. Your dwarf guard will have to house themselves outside of Quelean." Maelthor's lip curled in a slight sneer. "We cannot allow them to stay within the confines of our city."

Tronus stiffened and lurched forward, as if to protest, but his movement was halted abruptly by the young elf warrior who stepped in front of Nortenaine and stuck out his arm.

"Your friends don't have much in the way of manners," Tronus sputtered, but Sandoval shot him a warning look, and he clamped his mouth shut, only able to satisfy himself with a hard glare at the young elf, who ignored him. Maelthor turned and walked quickly away.

"You must forgive my son, Bruel." Nortenaine said, indicating the elf that had intervened—a strong hand on his shoulder restrained him further. "We have reason to be ... careful, I assure you, Sandoval."

Sandoval nodded slowly, turned, and spoke quietly to Tronus. "We will confer in the morning. I want to take this slowly."

Tronus pulled himself erect as the outraged Dwarves gathered around their leader. Tronus' red beard bobbed as he nodded curtly to Harald, then turned and stomped off. The other Dwarves followed closely. They were herded unceremoniously by armed elves toward the tunnel from which they had entered.

Gesturing to Sandoval, Bruel directed Sandoval and Hoagy to their quarters, his hard blue eyes trading glares with Hoagy. Sandoval and Hoagy did not speak until they were alone inside the small hut and had closed the door behind them.

"I can't believe that!" Hoagy growled, throwing his bag on one of the two large beds that crowded the small room. Along one wall was a dresser that Sandoval was inspecting. Two wooden chairs with leather-laced seats were placed at a small table in the remaining area, next to the only window at the back of the room.

"I'm afraid the situation is graver then I surmised when I received Director Tantilus' message." Sandoval shut the bottom drawer, straightened, and studied his reflection in the ornately framed mirror that hung over the dresser. "I'd never met Maelthor before, but I had heard that he was a rigid believer in elven separateness, not only from humans and Dwarves, but even from other elven clans—and the Ileana in particular, for some reason. "

"Are there other elf clans?" Hoagy asked.

"Some would count the faeries as elves, since they are certainly similar physically. Legend has it they were all created as one and didn't branch off until later. But don't ever let an elf hear you say that. At any rate, they have decidedly different social orders."

"Interesting. I'll have to bone up on my history." Hoagy flopped down a bed and tossed his bag on the floor. "You and Nortenaine grew up together, didn't you? Weren't you here often, many years ago?"

"Yes, but we were quite young at the time. I remember hearing about his uncle Maelthor, but he was always out with the elven warriors, protecting the borders of the Grimwood against Ileana incursions. Actually, Maelthor was Gaelen's half-brother. You notice Nortenaine did not introduce him as his uncle. There may be bad blood between them, figuratively as well as literally."

"Well, Nortenaine didn't seem too happy to see you, either," Hoagy pointed out. "At least he covered it better than that Bruel."

"I think there is more to this *diplomatic* mission than I expected. Though I have not seen Nortenaine in many years—decades, actually—I have kept up on the news coming out of the Grimwood over the years. I would not believe that the young elf I knew in my youth could be so bitter. But I have not seen him since I heard about the death of his aunt Lilliana, and that was many years ago."

At that moment there was a light knock on the door. Sandoval opened it to find an elf maiden holding a serving tray, on which she carried a bottle and two delicate pewter cups.

Hoagy rose from the bed and stepped forward before halting, mesmerized by two large, almond-shaped, melancholy brown eyes—

eyes that glowed in warm, bronze skin, surrounded by waves of reddish-gold hair, out of which peeked dainty, pointed ears.

"Uh … my … well, this is …" he stammered.

Sandoval's black eyes softened as he took the tray. "An unexpected treat," he finished, covering Hoagy's lapse.

Hoagy's mouth moved into a crooked grin as he recovered himself. "Oh, let me, sir!" His blue eyes sparkled as he placed the tray on the dresser top, turned, and bowed toward the striking elf maid. "My name is Hoagy. Oh, and this is Inspector Carmichael … uh, my boss."

"I am pleased to meet you both," the maid responded in soft, honeyed tones. "I am Trelaine, the sister of vessel Maelthor. And actually, I have seen the famous Sandoval Carmichael before."

Sandoval's black brows rose slightly and Hoagy's almost reached into the curly blond bangs that fell across his brow.

"We are honored to be attended by one with your status." Sandoval bowed solemnly, his sharp eyes not leaving the young maid's face." You must excuse me, but I don't recall having met you."

"We never actually met. You were a young man who was allowed into Quelean for Nortenaine's coming-of-age celebration. I helped my half-sister, Lilliana, and my mother handle the gathering. But you need not be concerned about my status; I have none here." Trelaine's beautiful brown eyes lowered, giving her face an even more melancholy look. "I was merely concerned that you had not been properly welcomed and thought to bring some drink to ease the weariness of the road. I'm afraid my brother may have been abrupt with you."

"Oh, no, don't even think it!" Hoagy laughed lightly and waved his hand as if to brush aside her comment. "We're fine!"

She bowed, turned, and slipped away into the gathering night. Sandoval closed the door after her, his long face pensive.

"Now that adds another dimension to this mission. I recall seeing Lilliana on that rare visit, but not Trelaine. Lilliana was beautiful and doted on her nephew. She was also gracious to me—the gangly human boy that I was, even though Gaelen, her brother, wasn't fond of humans. Lilliana's beauty would overshadow any other. Everyone loved her, from what I was told. But I know little of her death. It's funny I've not thought of it in all these years, and the events surrounding it are unclear to me."

"A mystery, sir?" Hoagy's round blue eyes widened and a smile creased his boyish face.

"A lapse on my part, at any rate. I must wrestle the cobwebs from my brain and try to recall those days of our youth, when all we were concerned with was learning sword play and rudimentary magic. I do now recall Nortenaine's mentioning Maelthor's twin sister, another aunt, though not one he was close to—which means that elf maiden is old enough to be your mother, Hoagy." Sandoval turned to the bottle on the dresser. "Elven wine—like ambrosia. No, it *is* ambrosia. But careful, Hoagy, this delicate brew can make you a stumbling fool in no time."

Sandoval poured a small portion in two cups and handed one to Hoagy who continued to stare at the door through which Trelaine had exited, a look of wonder on his handsome young face. Sandoval smiled grimly, shook his head, and sipped some of the liquid, rolling it around in his mouth before swallowing. At Hoagy's resigned sigh, Sandoval poured another few drops into his cup. Hoagy sank back onto the bed and absently sipped from his cup. His eyes widened, and he drank more eagerly, savoring the cool, clean taste of the clear liquid as it warmed his insides and made its way to his already fogging brain.

"What do you know about this Maelthor?" Hoagy slurred the words slightly, looking up in surprise. Then he smiled, pulled off his boots, and propped himself against a pillow, his arms behind his head.

"He is the vessel of the Florian elves and has been for more years than I've been an investigator in the Royal Bureau of Investigation."

"What's a vessel? And what's his problem?" Hoagy asked. "I can't believe that pretty lady that served us is his *twin*. He's so ... dark."

"Curious choice of words."

"Scary, might be better."

Sandoval pulled a cheroot from his pocket and snapped it alight with his flint. He pulled contentedly upon it and settled himself on a chair opposite Hoagy, prepared to feed the young mind of his assistant. Sandoval knew that even in a sleepy state, Hoagy's total recall would absorb every word given to him.

"A vessel is the spiritual leader of an elven clan. They are the custodians for the clan lore and the keepers of their faith. Sort of like historians but more. The job of a vessel is to hold all of the clan's physical history and to be the sole possessor of its spiritual legends and teachings. In the human world, he—or she—would be a combination of a civil judge, teacher, and master of the wizard guilds. In any disputes, whether civil or spiritual, the vessel's word is paramount. It is through that very powerful person that they educate and dispense justice in an elven clan. In some ways, the vessel is more important to the people than the high lord. The vessel *speaks* the law; the high lord *keeps* the law, as elves would say."

"Not very warm and fuzzy, is he?" Hoagy smiled crookedly.

"Maelthor needs to have that effect on his kin as well as outsiders. His power depends on not letting his guard down with anyone." Sandoval was pensive, staring into his empty cup.

"Doesn't leave much for Nortenaine to do, does it?" Hoagy asked.

"Oh, Nortenaine still has the final say. As most elven lords, he'd most likely defer to his vessel on spiritual matters, but civil disputes are a different thing. Though the vessel can suggest the final outcome, it's up to the high lord to mete out the verdict. There have been some, in long times past, who were so subdued by their vessels that the power of leadership, in effect, lay in that person's hands. Not unlike a king of ours putting too much power into the hands of his personal wizard and liaison with the High Counsel of the Bondonai. And we have our own history to tell us what can come of such an event as that."

"Like Threll Justain, you mean?" Hoagy leaned forward, always eager for replaying a good tale.

Sandoval smiled and took another pull from his cheroot. "Quite," Sandoval said, "and that almost would have been King Haldren's undoing, if it hadn't been for his son, Julius."

"I love this one." Hoagy nodded quickly, and his blond curls bobbed. "Had the Dwarves and elves really nervous for a while, thinking they were going to war with the humans in those early days. He took the Walk of Death, as I remember."

"You always remember correctly, my boy. And he was the only Gold Guild wizard to have done so. But it was for the good of all, as the whole situation created the Royal Bureau of Investigation and strengthened the arbitration powers of the High Council of the Bondonai wizards. It always pays to have a people's civil powers apart from its spiritual laws. Seems I've read that somewhere."

"Well, so this Maelthor doesn't really have as much power as he thinks?" Hoagy said.

"We're not talking about human political divisions, Hoagy. The elves have never had the problems we men have, and their vessels have only been extensions of their high lords. None of them, in the past, has really aspired politically. Until now, that is."

"You think Maelthor is power-hungry?"

"I do love your choice of words, Hoagy. Get right to the point, don't you? But no, I don't think *personal* power is an aspiration for any elf. They are more connected with the natural—say, spiritual, if you will—life of the world. Unity with nature and attaining a pure entrance into their afterlife to walk with their gods is their prime goal. I don't even think there's been an incident of an elf of power attempting to equate himself on a level with one of their gods. At least, not to my knowing. I'd venture to say Maelthor is more interested in control than power."

Hoagy sighed, as if disappointed there wasn't more to chew on. He slumped back on his pillow, eyes drooping. Sandoval smiled thinly, knowing that, given a choice, Hoagy would love nothing better than to battle an evil in any form, as opposed to carrying out what, so far, was a mundane diplomatic mission.

"So, what about these Ileana elves?" Hoagy asked.

Sandoval's black eyes shone in the glow of the oil lamp on the table as he expelled a small cloud of blue smoke and crushed out the remains of his cheroot. "We've all heard stories about the Ileana elves for as long as I can remember. My mother used to scare us with tales of wild, dark-skinned elves, riding on horseback, stealing young humans and eating them—the usual twaddle."

"Oh, sure, mine, too. I think they figured it would keep us out of the Grimwood."

"Not much help for you, I'm sure," Sandoval said. "But few humans have even seen them, since they make their home far from the Grimwood. Only the Lestrami maintain a trade relationship with the clan. That's not hard to understand, as little surrounds their main settlement in Mt. Thorn other than the foothills, deserts, and savannas of the unexplored region. Swift horses became a necessity. Baron Wentland tried to develop some kind of diplomatic ties with them, since Mt. Thorn is close to the northern border of his barony, but he failed, as all of our ruling monarchs have. So myths, stories, whatever you want to call them, have drifted back about the few contacts we humans have had with them.

"The Ileana are to the Florian elves of the Grimwood as moonlight is to sunlight. In my youth, Nortenaine told me the elves were all one people, but there came a split between two powerful elven factions. Klevian, Nortenaine's grandfather, broke off from the other faction, led by an elf named Iledan. According to the Florian history, Klevian believed the elves should remain within the confines of the Grimwood and maintain their way of life without taint from the outside world. Iledan wanted to go beyond the forest and was enamored of the wild horses he had seen in his youth that roamed the grasslands beyond the eastern border of the Grimwood. Iledan took those with him who sought adventure, and a separate clan as born that took the name Ileana.

"Led by Iledan, they tamed some wild horses and eventually made their way to Mt. Thorn. According to a historian from the Wentland barony, who wrote extensively about them, they literally carved out a city within the mountain; one that Tronus and many other Dwarves would give their beards to see. They have also become expert horsemen, riding swiftly, in tune with the desert and the lowlands, and are quick with their bows."

"It may be that their darker coloring developed over the years with exposure to the merciless sun," Hoagy said absently.

"There are both Florian and Ileana with color variations. You may see some elves with dark hair and eyes as you wander around the city."

"But to just write them off—to cut off communication with them? That's harsh."

"The Florian elves contented themselves with maintaining a close contact with their gods, who, according to them, live in the heart of the Grimwood in a secret place. The Ileana, on the other hand, are considered outcasts, separate from the source of the elven being, their gods. There are some questions that Nortenaine wouldn't or couldn't answer."

"So, this has gone on for who knows how long, and all of a sudden, the Ileana have gotten ticked off and have decided to take over the Florian clan?" Hoagy yawned in spite of himself.

"I'm not sure, but something has driven them back to the Grimwood—and with a vengeance, it seems. They seem intent on forcing their presence on the original elven homeland ...maybe"

"In other words, you're as much in the dark as the rest of us—though speaking of *dark* again, Maelthor seems to carry that to extremes."

"You are correct, Hoagy. Actually, Maelthor's mother was one of the Ileana who chose to remain in the Grimwood. She fell in love with Klevian and married him after his wife, Idelia, passed on."

Hoagy's blue eyes widened once and then began to droop again.

"Early to bed and quick to rise." Sandoval corked the bottle of wine, blew out the lamp and, in one fluid motion, slid down on the other bed and stretched out with a sigh. "We all have work to do on the morrow and not much time to do it."

Hoagy's eyes closed as he murmured. "I'd rather investigate the mysterious lady Trelaine."

CHAPTER 4

SEPULCHER FOR AN ELF MAIDEN

Sandoval stepped outside into the dawning light of a morning filled with the heady scent of flowers and the chattering of birds. The one-room dwelling where he and Hoagy had spent the night appeared to be a sentry's hut, as it was situated before the broad steps that led up to a larger, more imposing dwelling. The shining wood surface of the larger structure was decorated with lovely, flowing carvings in an elfish script. Without a second thought, Sandoval turned and started up the wide stairs, sure that this imposing residence had to be Nortenaine's. He was not disappointed, for as he reached the wide veranda that ran around the entire structure, the front door opened and Nortenaine stepped out. The tall elf lord's head was bowed in contemplation, and he would have walked right into Sandoval, had the wizard's boots not appeared in his line of sight. His head snapped up, a look of affront on his face as he came to an abrupt halt. Nortenaine's blue eyes softened almost immediately upon identifying the person who was attempting to enter his house. It was the *almost immediately* that intrigued Sandoval, for there was still a wariness behind that steady gaze that he would never have thought to see in the eyes of his boyhood friend.

"Sandoval, I had not expected you to rise this early. I will summon your breakfast immediately," Nortenaine said in a clipped, business-like tone.

"I've always been an early riser. Don't you remember those days in our youth when we used to beat the sunrise to hide in the woods and see if we could catch faeries?" Sandoval's mouth quirked as he smiled, and his black eyes sparkled.

Nortenaine frowned, and Sandoval thought he noticed a slight darkening of the elf's coloring, though it could never be said that an elf blushed. Nortenaine finally spoke, his lips twitching also with a surpressed grin. "I suppose I deserve that, Sandoval. I was not much of a host when you and your party arrived last evening. I apologize for that, though I will not relent and allow the Dwarves to be quartered within the city. We have reports of some Dwarves assisting the Ileana in their raids."

"I find that hard to believe. Dwarves generally prefer to stay out of the troubles of men and elves. And certainly none of Tronus' from Thunderstorm Mountain would do such a thing."

"Nevertheless …" Nortenaine's voice trailed off as he surveyed his surroundings, his blue eyes hardening again.

"We will certainly abide by your wishes," Sandoval said. "In the meantime, I would like to discuss the matter of my mission with you. Have you broken your fast yet this morning?"

There it was again—that wary look as Nortenaine glanced around too casually.

"I will order us something to eat and drink to refresh ourselves, if you will join me over here," Nortenaine said, gesturing toward a small table and chairs on the veranda that was beneath an overhang of vines with large pink trumpet flowers in abundance, their sweet scent filling the air.

As if a mental command had been sent, the moment they seated themselves, a servant appeared and stood stiffly at attention, awaiting orders.

"I will have porridge and water. Sandoval?"

"Some bread and cheese would be nice, with a small pot of cherok brewed to go with it, if it's not too much trouble. I do have some of the ground cherok with me, if that would help." Sandoval smiled warmly, which carried to his black eyes.

"I think we can accommodate you, Inspector Carmichael," the elf said, bowing formally before turning and disappearing back into the residence.

Nortenaine smiled and shook his head. "You haven't changed much, have you? You always were a charmer. I never could quite figure it out, as you don't *look* that charming. Oh, I know, *charming* is part of your particular power. But I've not seen it work that well on a male elf."

"The key is honesty. Even most humans can identify phony charm. Also, believe it or not, my dear Nortenaine, I didn't use an actual *charm* on your servant."

Nortenaine nodded, and the two old friends slipped into a silence broken only by the return of the servant with a large tray. The elf spread the food before them, poured a steaming cup of cherok for Sandoval. He then turned and disappeared again without a word.

Both Sandoval and Nortenaine ate in respectful silence. Sandoval enjoyed the crisp, fresh-baked herb bread—a specialty of the elves that no human was able to duplicate—along with the soft, delicately flavored cheese. As soon as they had finished with the food and Sandoval raised a cheroot with a questioning glance at Nortenaine, he received a nod in response, and a servant popped up, as if from nowhere, and took the plates away. Sandoval snapped the flint and lit his cheroot, studying Nortenaine's pensive gaze at the brightening sunlight—the light caused the water bubbling from the fountain in the common to glisten like liquid diamonds.

"I am reluctant to break this beautiful solitude with matters of diplomacy, but I would not be carrying out my orders if I did not request a meeting with you, Maelthor, and whomever you choose to discuss the escalating troubles between the Florian and the Ileana," Sandoval said softly.

"I understand your king's need to be reassured about the problems we have in the Grimwood, but I don't believe there is much that you humans can do to rid us of the threat to our borders," Nortenaine said, his tone clipped.

Sandoval looked at his old friend intently. It appeared that the elf lord had reverted to the cool, businesslike manner that he had adopted upon Sandoval's arrival in Quelean. But Sandoval saw something else beneath his demeanor. The clear blue eyes slid away from the wizard's steady gaze and a frown of apprehension settled over Nortenaine's otherwise smooth brow. Sandoval crushed out his cheroot in a small metal dish, which Nortenaine's servant had placed on the table upon his lighting up.

"Let's be honest, my friend." Sandoval said.

He leaned toward Nortenaine, his large hands clasped together on the table, his black eyes intent. He knew from past experience that to make overt efforts to influence his friend's thinking would be useless. The mental *nudge* he directed at Nortenaine was not strong enough to direct a particular response from the elf lord; it merely applied a soothing effect on the mind. There was a sadness—a dark memory, like a physical obstruction—that Sandoval felt was acting like a mental barrier. It must have been with Nortenaine for some time to be so resilient to intrusion.

Nortenaine inhaled deeply and exhaled without comment, though his blue eyes cleared and he looked directly at Sandoval. "The dispute between the Florian and Ileana involves more than issues over borders. Those disagreements have been going on for untold years, ever since the sundering of the original clan and the segregation of the Ileana. Had it remained merely a situation of their violating our borders to seek the sacred center of the Grimwood—or even retrieve artifacts—I think, eventually, we could all have come to some diplomatic resolution. Unfortunately, any hope of that collapsed when my aunt Lilliana was murdered at the hands of an Ileana lord, Rolf Andelar."

Sandoval had been staring intently at his own hands while concentrating on Nortenaine's words and the roiling emotions that welled up in his friend's mind, but at the word *murder*, his head jerked up. "Ah, much makes sense now." Sandoval saw the open pain in Nortenaine's hard blue eyes. "I wish I had known. I was posted to the Grode barony at that time, I believe."

"You don't have to apologize, Sandoval. Had you come, you would not have gained access to Quelean. Maelthor succeeded in shutting the outside world out of the Grimwood for some time after that. The

Florian blood was up, and it was only cooled by the death of Ileana. Little has satisfied our lust for revenge since that day, not in all the years. It was only by force of my will that Maelthor relented and allowed all but the Ileana to enter the Grimwood without retaliation. Since then, Lilliana's bier has become a sacred shrine for many Florian."

"I'm sure your common sense also averted any reaction from the local baronies. I sense that you would not be averse to ending this blood feud. Did you capture this Ileana lord?"

"Maelthor killed him that day." Nortenaine's voice was heavy with sorrow.

"But the battle continues and grows in vengeance as time passes. It will do so until the end of time or until either the Florian or the Ileana have their fill of bloodshed. You may have been young in your duties as high lord at that time, but you have grown into it now. I would like to support you in saving the Florian from further destruction."

"I will discuss it with Maelthor and my lead warriors. I can't promise more than that, Sandoval. It is … a precarious situation."

"I would like to visit her while I am here, to pay my belated respects, if that is acceptable."

Nortenaine winced, physical pain crossing his face. "I'm afraid I can not accompany you, but you may visit her bier." Nortenaine rose and touched a small bell that hung from the vines above them. A light, high tinkle brought the same servant who had served them. Nortenaine spoke quietly with him, bowed his head quickly in Sandoval's direction, and left.

Sandoval's black eyes were contemplative as he watched Nortenaine until he disappeared through the front door of his lodgings. Sandoval rose and nodded toward the elf, who turned and stepped briskly down the stairs. Sandoval had no trouble matching the long strides of the tall elf, and they were soon passing through cultivated areas with flower gardens and what looked like herb beds being tended by young elves. The workers didn't raise their eyes or turn their heads as Sandoval followed his escort past them, but the wizard could feel the curious gazes aimed at his back as the elf led him among sculpted shrubs until they passed from sight. They moved deeper into the forest surrounding Quelean proper and finally came to a halt in a small glade. In the center of the glade stood a wooden bier; carved ornate flowers and vines encircled the base. The limbs of huge oak trees bent over the glade protectively, leaving an opening only in the center, which directed beams of sunlight to illuminate the dome of glass over the sarcophagus. An old elven female knelt beside the base, her head bowed.

The servant halted, as did Sandoval; they stood silently, respectfully waiting. The old elf had heard them, for her head half-turned toward them. She appeared to dab at her eyes before rising and turning full on them. Sandoval was shocked by her appearance. She looked more like a bent, wizened old crone than an elf. Even in advanced age, elves retained their delicate stature and proud bearing. The only distinguishing mark of her race was a pearly pointed ear protruding from fine gray shoulder-length hair. Her pale blue eyes appeared washed out from tears that had drained them of color and clarity, but they met Sandoval's without wavering. There was strength still within that body twisted by grief. Sandoval knew without asking what had caused this woman to wither physically.

He bowed his head. "Forgive me for intruding."

Her voice was steady and melodious. "You are the wizard. I have heard of your arrival. My name is Noona. I was Lilliana's handmaiden. I am maiden no longer, as you can see. My pain has all but broken me."

Sandoval was taken aback by the open honesty she displayed. Even the elf servant beside him gave a spasmodic jerk, his eyes widening. Elves were not openly emotional, even to their own kind; to open their hearts to strangers—and this one a human—was almost an affront to their sensibilities.

Evidently, Noona realized the effect upon the elf, for she waved her knobby hand in his direction in dismissal. "You may go, Lenlael. I will take this man back after he has answered some of my questions."

Lenlael bowed quickly, turned on his heel, and left. Sandoval moved forward and stood gazing down at the glass-enclosed casket. Within was the body of a young woman whose beauty still took Sandoval's breath away, even after all these years. She lay in repose, clothed in a pale rose gown, as if merely sleeping, the pale skin of her oval face framed by long silver-blonde hair, her hands folded peacefully across her chest. Sandoval had not been conscious of his intake of breath, but Noona had, for she lightly touched his hand as it gripped his staff. When he turned to look down at her, she smiled slightly.

"I remember you now. Sandoval Carmichael. The young human who raced about the forests with Nortenaine and was stricken by the beauty of our Lilliana. She loved you young ones. But it was another love that killed her; another love that tore the heart from her and left her broken and forever silent."

"Tell me about this love." Sandoval's voice sounded rough in his own ears. "Who was he?"

Noona turned without a word and walked away. At the edge of the clearing she turned, raised her hand, and crooked a finger at Sandoval, motioning for him to follow her. After weaving through the trees for a short period of time, Sandoval emerged behind Noona in a small clearing, where there was a little cottage surrounded by colorful, flowering shrubs that exuded a sweet smell. Once inside the cottage, Noona sat wearily on a small couch, motioning for Sandoval to sit down next to her. She came right to the point.

"His name was Rolf Andelar, and he was a lord of the Ileana who was captured and held by Maelthor's men in a faerie hill."

"Nortenaine said it was he who killed Lilliana."

"So it is said. I only say she loved him. Now tell me, wizard, how you can do what no other has been able to do and make peace between the clans?" Noona's old voice was grating.

"I'm not sure yet. But maybe Lilliana will tell me." Sandoval watched Noona's reaction.

Her head came up, and she gave him a narrow-eyed gaze. "You commune with the dead?"

"You might say so … indirectly," Sandoval said.

Once back at the common, Sandoval spotted Hoagy talking to an elf maiden, one that seemed closer in age to his own—although she didn't seem to be in danger of swooning at Hoagy's charm.

"Oh, there you are sir!" Hoagy broke away and walked over to Sandoval.

"So, have you been gathering information that may be helpful for me in my mission?" Sandoval asked.

"Not much so far." He lowered his voice as he said, "I don't think they like humans much."

"Stick with the older elves who can give you some background on the death of Lilliana," Sandoval instructed. "Especially Trelaine, if you can get her to talk. Maybe they have a central library of some sort where they store their history. I'm afraid this is more complicated than I first thought." Sandoval turned to go, then swung back around as Hoagy stood mulling over his orders. "But be discreet!"

Nortenaine's reaction was one of anger and disbelief. "Why would you want to visit the spot of her terrible death? What could that possibly hold for you, Sandoval?"

"I do not want to deepen your sorrow, Nortenaine, but I feel that Lilliana's death may have a direct bearing on my understanding of the war you currently are waging with the Ileana."

Nortenaine's face clouded over, his brows drawing together. Sandoval was grateful that elves didn't show open displays of emotion on most occasions; otherwise, he was sure that Nortenaine wouldn't have hesitated in raging at him or storming off. As it was, Nortenaine controlled himself, his voice steady and cool.

"I see no reason to allow this. The *murder* of my aunt at the hands of Rolf Andelar did not cause the troubles with the Ileana. Obviously, that had been going on for some time, as it was during a skirmish with the Ileana that Rolf Andelar was captured."

"I agree that the animosity between your two clans had been going on for a long time, but has it always involved the ruthless bloodletting it has become?"

Nortenaine nodded briefly, once. His steady blue eyes stared into Sandoval's. "No. But I—"

"The only way I can help in this matter is to have a clear understanding of all the history between the Ileana and Florian clans. And Lilliana's death, though tragic and bitter to revisit, is right at the core of that escalating war. If you have any real hopes of resolving the matter, I must be allowed to continue as I see fit."

Nortenaine sighed, and his face seemed to draw in as he looked out over the peaceful panorama of Quelean below the slightly raised veranda of his home. "It has been going on so long, I sometimes wonder if we can stop. Maelthor would say no, not until they all perish or give up."

"Would the Florian give up?"

Nortenaine stared at Sandoval, his lips pressed tightly together. "You may go. I will have a small troop of elves accompany you. And please do not trouble Noona further. Her mind is held in check by no more than her own will. To expose her to more distress could cause it to snap completely."

"I will wait outside the city with Tronus and his company." With that, Sandoval nodded, turned, and left Nortenaine gazing after him.

After Sandoval had enjoyed a cheroot, ignoring Tronus' constant questions, he brought Tronus up to speed with the events of the day, until a group of four elves arrived. Glaring at Sandoval's terse explanation that he had to view a historic site, Tronus ordered Harald to gather his men. Sandoval bowed gravely to the lead elf, whom he was not surprised to see was Bruel. Bruel nodded curtly in return.

"We will take you to within a short walk of the green pool, but we will not enter there. That place is cursed and unclean."

Sandoval nodded as Harald and the other Dwarves stomped up and came to attention. Bruel's mouth twisted in a sardonic smile until he turned back to Sandoval and saw the steady, contemplative look in the wizard's black eyes. The young elf's display of contempt was a lapse for which he knew his father and any other elf elder would have admonished him. As if he had been chastised openly, he covered himself by quickly motioning to his elf warriors to precede him, and they moved off, followed silently by Sandoval, Tronus, and the rest of the troop. Only a glance was exchanged between Sandoval and Tronus, and the old dwarf's answering smile was acknowledgment of what had occurred.

It did not take them long to arrive at a rise above a broad stream. A twisting track had led them through an exceptionally dense part of the forest. Sandoval knew they had covered a good distance and felt a great deal of pleasure in the fact that Tronus and his Dwarves had marched along, keeping up with the long strides of the elves and Sandoval, without breaking a sweat. Even Bruel seemed to appraise them, a new respect growing in his blue eyes. Sandoval could see the path of the stream below them as it disappeared to plunge down the falls to what appeared to be a pool, glistening below the mist.

"That is the green pool beyond," Bruel said softly. "This is as far as we will go."

Did he shudder? Sandoval wondered.

"We will rest here and take some food before continuing," Sandoval said. "Thank you for your assistance. I realize you have orders not to proceed further."

The elf standing beside Bruel quickly cast his eyes downward, and Bruel smiled bitterly.

"It used to be considered a rite of passage to go to the pool and pluck a leaf from the spot where Andelar died—but no more. Some of us were lucky enough to take on that foolish test and succeed; two did not. After a challenger did not return, his friend went to find him. When that elf did not return, a party was sent out. We found their bodies beside the pool. Their blood had been drawn from them, leaving nothing but a ghostly shell." Bruel's gaze took in the entire group standing with Sandoval. "You have been warned. Death lives there, and it is thirsty."

With that, Bruel and the other elves slipped into the woods and disappeared. Tronus' eyes narrowed at Sandoval, while behind him, Harald and the lads shuffled their feet and mumbled among themselves.

"I will go alone," Sandoval said.

Tronus opened his mouth to protest, but Sandoval raised his hand, and the retort died as Tronus clamped his mouth shut, glaring angrily up at the wizard.

"You settle in here and post a watch," Sandoval instructed. "I will be safe, but the protective spell I am able to cast can not encompass us all. Don't worry, old friend, I will be alert."

"You damn well better be," Tronus blurted out, sputtering, his face as red as his beard. "If we hear the least yell from there, we'll come in, armed and ready."

Sandoval smiled warmly as Harald and the rest of the troop nodded sternly, in agreement with their leader. Sandoval knew these were brave boys, but he also knew that bravery is stronger when danger is not imminent. He raised his staff in salute; then he started down the narrow path that curved around the outcropping and down the slippery slope beside the falls.

It was a clumsy climb down, but eventually, he found himself stepping through the trees into a small grassy clearing. Before him was a glistening green pool, the water bubbling below the falls and spreading ripples to lap the edge of the pool not far from where he stood. Sandoval concentrated his senses intensely and felt a slight flutter in the air to the left of his shoulder. He didn't move but let his lowered eyes follow the round red stain that covered the grass next to the pool. As if distracted, he moved to step to that spot, then spun rapidly and snapped his hand up to grasp at a bright light. A high squeal answered him, and a figure shimmered before him, still gripped by his fingers tightened on its wing. It was Tillie, the same faerie who had assisted in their transfer to Will Wiggins' tower two days before.

"Ow! That hurts me, wizard! Wings aren't totally without feeling, you know." Her bright amber eyes flashed at him, and then she froze, held by his steady black eyes.

Sandoval released her wing, but continued to hold her with a quick mesmerizing charm. "Tillie, nice to see you again. I promise to release you if you will tell me what you know about the death of Rolf Andelar."

Tillie's little eyes welled with tears, and her hands flew to her face. "Oooh, it was terrible! Poor Miss Lilliana fell from the ledge and died in his arms, even as he discovered her lie. I think his heart died with her. And then the terrible man chopped off his head! But his spirit rose and cursed the man. It will not rest. And I tremble because the spirit that guards this place may kill me for the lie. But I didn't know! Oh, we must flee—*now*!" Her thin little voice raised to a shriek.

"Is that Rolf Andelar's spirit?" Sandoval persisted, even though Tillie was thrashing her head from side to side and flailing her arms.

"Yes, but he shares this place with his avenger. Men shall not survive a female that feeds on love! She will not release you, once she has you in her grip!"

Tillie wailed even louder, and Sandoval broke off the charm that held her to glance quickly around the clearing as sounds of thrashing came to his ears. He raised his staff to ward off any intruders as Tillie, now free, shrunk to a bright glow and shot upwards through the trees. As Sandoval braced himself, the brush parted near the path, and Tronus charged into the clearing, with Harald and the Snufflebeam Company tumbling after him. Sandoval sighed with relief and shook his head at Tronus' battle stance—his hammer raised.

"There is no urgency, Tronus. It was only Tillie, the little faerie. She's fled now."

"Oh, that pretty faerie girl?" Harald sputtered, twisting his head around to scan the clearing.

Tronus brought his battle hammer down and slipped it into the loop at his waist, brushing twigs and leaves from his vest.

"Get anything out of her?" Tronus grumbled, glaring hard at Harald, until the young dwarf backed away with his eyes downcast.

"She was too terrified to be coherent. But I think I'm getting a clearer picture of what happened here. And I don't think Rolf Andelar killed Lilliana. And I think there is one who knows that too well."

CHAPTER 5

HOAGY REPORTS AND A COUNCIL OF WAR

Sandoval left Tronus and his company at their temporary bivouac outside of Quelean and went straight to the hut he shared with Hoagy. The young man was pacing nervously as Sandoval stepped into the room.

Hoagy whirled on him. "Sir! I'm glad you're back! Something is definitely up here. That Maelthor came back with a group of elves, and it looked like some of them were injured. I wasn't sure whether I should look for you, or—"

Sandoval held up his hand to halt Hoagy, tossed his leather case on the bed, and poured a glass of elven wine from the bottle on the dresser. As Hoagy watched him, he danced from one foot to the other in anticipation.

Sandoval lowered himself into a chair and set the glass on the table beside him. "Now, calmly, Hoagy. Please report."

"Well, I'm not sure where to begin."

"At the beginning would be good. Or at least from the last time we spoke." Sandoval raised the glass for a sip before snapping his flint to light a cheroot.

Hoagy nodded. "I decided to have breakfast this morning in the communal dining area, and it was there I saw Trelaine again. All of the elves were giving me the cold shoulder, but she took pity on me—though the reaction didn't change much; they just ignored both of us. When we finally left the dining area and walked about the grounds, she told me that the elves are always that way with her now. The community blames her for Lilliana's involvement with Rolf Andelar.

"Trelaine's story was that Klevian, their father and the high lord at that time, wanted to kill the Ileana lord when he was captured. He was still bitter about the defeat and the wounding of a number of his warriors at the hands of the Ileana during a previous skirmish. A council was called to decide the Ileana lord's fate. In the meantime, Andelar was placed in the enchanted faerie hill. Maelthor set Trelaine to see to his needs and ordered that none were to go near him, except for Trelaine and the faeries that took his meals and tended him. Trelaine said that her mother, Maeleana, believed the Ileana had a right to have access to the sacred center of the Grimwood as much as the Florian did. She was the one, according to Trelaine, who urged her daughter to take Lilliana to meet Rolf. Maeleana thought that if Lilliana believed in his quest, she would speak to her father, Klevian, about a compromise treaty with the Ileana. Evidently, Maeleana knew that Lilliana, as her father's favorite child, would have more chance of convincing him than she would herself.

"It may have been a good plan, but Trelaine said that as soon as Lilliana and Rolf met, Lilliana knew what their destiny would be. Trelaine tried to convince her half-sister not to see Rolf again, but she knew Lilliana was already under his spell. It was Trelaine who charmed the faerie, Tillie, into spying on Lilliana and Rolf. But it was all brought to a head when Lilliana went to her father, Klevian, and begged him to spare Rolf Andelar. She succeeded in getting Klevian to waive the death penalty in favor of continued imprisonment in the faerie hill.

When Maelthor found out, he went into a rage, but neither he nor Nortenaine could convince the old elf leader to change his mind. He had been swayed by his daughter's good heart and also by Maeleana. His wife told him they could use Rolf Andelar to bring about a cease to the fighting with the Ileana. Once that clan knew Iledan's son was still alive and being held captive, Iledan and his vessel, Vaester Shee, would agree to such terms.

"Hmm, I wonder if Maeleana knew Iledan, to be so confident?" Sandoval said quietly, his black eyes intent on a spot on the wall as he slowly puffed on his cheroot.

"Trelaine didn't own up to that. But I did get her to let me view the archives the clan keeps—and I discovered you are right."

"Oh?" Sandoval's interest was piqued.

"Yes, and they were very interesting. But I was only allowed to look at some wall hangings and a few pictures. So after I left Trelaine, I sort of wandered back there and took a second look."

Sandoval leveled his narrowed eyes at his young assistant. Hoagy gave him a crooked smile in return.

"Don't they have someone on duty at the archives?" Sandoval asked, even though he knew the answer.

"Well, no. They really don't expect any *elves* to enter without permission. They don't even keep it locked! As for humans, they probably figure we can't read their language anyway."

Sandoval smiled. "Shocking. I guess we had better keep it quiet that you speak and read several languages fluently."

"I thought so. As Trelaine was taking me around, I spotted some journals written by the clan historian, who is like a scribe and keeps their records of all notable events. I told her how disappointed I was that I couldn't read them. But one wall mural was especially interesting. It depicted a tall, dark-haired, blue-eyed elf warrior, standing in the middle of a forest clearing, his arms raised to the heavens. Behind him, I could see the mountain range to the east and … guess what else?"

"Enlighten me, you scamp," Sandoval said.

"A horse!" Hoagy cried triumphantly. "Trelaine said that this elf in the woven wall hanging was Queleastor, the first warrior and father of the elves."

"Interesting. I'd like to see that, too. So, tell me about the journal you read. Scan it for the good parts," Sandoval said, stamping out his cheroot and taking another sip of wine.

Hoagy's eyes took on a faraway look, then he closed them and leaned back in his chair. His eyes beneath his closed lids moved back and forth, as if he was again scanning a page that appeared in his mind's eye.

"The old records told of Queleastor and his bringing the elf races together and setting a sacred spot for them in the Grimwood, which the old records call Thelestorian and which would be the source of their spiritual energy and power. Mmm, let's see … more about Queleastor and his lady elf. It also tells of the elves being the guardians of all the creatures of the forest *and plains*. And lots of stuff about the early elves and their city, which was named Quelean after him … and so on." Hoagy's eyes continued to scan the document.

Sandoval broke his concentration. "Let's move ahead. Is there anything about the sundering?"

"Oh, yes … okay, I found a journal that told of the departure."

Hoagy began reciting:

The Exile of Iledan.

It was upon the first rising of the full red orb in the time of planting that it was found Iledan and his family had taken to the plains on the eastern border of our forest, Thelestorian, and had captured swift animals for their pleasure. They rode these animals and gave them names. Our lord Klevian, angered that Iledan had turned against the common rule and had taken others outside of our homeland, called Iledan before a council. Iledan, in his pride, stood before the council and challenged them by saying there was no such rule brought down by the god Queleastor, and therefore he would not abide by this edict. The council found him unbending in his arrogance and sentenced him to exile. Into exile with Iledan went his wife, Helaneth, and their children, along with his brother, Raester, and his family and all of the other elves who had spurned the teachings of our vessel, Kithael, from

the early spoken words of the god Queleastor. Alone of
those of Iledan's family, his sister, Maeleana, withstood
him and paid her fealty to Klevian unto death.

"Whoa!" Sandoval sat up. "Maeleana was a sister to Iledan, it said?"

Hoagy opened his eyes and smiled. "Yes, I hadn't really read it until now, just scanned it. That's a good bit, isn't it, sir? There's more of this particular era that tells of some of the early run-ins, when the Ileana tried to penetrate the forest to the sacred spots to worship the gods. The Florian tried to chase them to the plains but couldn't, because they didn't have the horses as the Ileana did."

"So the Florian couldn't mount an offensive battle. Getting stuck on the defensive all the time has lengthened this age-old conflict."

"Sure seems so."

"*My kingdom for a horse!*" Sandoval mused, shaking his head at the confusion on Hoagy's face. "An old book," he explained.

Enlightenment spread over Hoagy's face and his blue eyes twinkled. "Are you sure the gods didn't create all those old books you keep finding? They certainly seem to help you solve a lot of cases."

"It's a distinct possibility, my boy. Some of them do speak of ancient spiritual wars and hatreds between peoples caused by such minor things as which hand to eat with or whether music was the work of evil spirits."

"No!"

"Just so … but to our current problem."

"I also found some journal entries for the capture of Rolf Andelar and Lilliana's murder."

"Let's go to those then," Sandoval said.

Hoagy leaned back in his chair again and closed his eyes. Sandoval watched the young man's eyes beneath his lids moving back and forth, as if scanning a document. It never ceased to fascinate Sandoval to watch this particular oddity that Hoagy displayed. Again, the young man began as if reading:

The Capture of Rolf Andelar and the Murder of Lilliana of Quelean.

Learning of the maiden Lilliana's being enamored of Rolf Andelar, Maelthor, our honored vessel, increased the observation of the faerie hill. Our vessel also had the maiden Lilliana watched closely at that time, even with the acquiescence of the great Klevian, who loved his daughter to the extent of placing a veil upon his eyes and heart that masked any criticism of her actions. Yet, being convinced that the observations of her actions were for her own safety, he agreed, as his daughter had been demure and kept to her own house for some time, with only her handmaiden, Noona, for company. Klevian was sure that his precious daughter had lost her first flush of admiration for the Ileana lord.

It was thus that on the fateful day, Maelthor relaxed his acolytes' observance of Lilliana and would have been ignorant of her movements, had he not been preparing for a celebration of the gathering of crops. He was to review the preparation of the site when he saw the maiden slip out of her house and into the forest. Filled with anxiety for her safety, Maelthor sent word to Nortenaine, son of Gaelen, and followed the maiden to the faerie hill where Rolf Andelar was imprisoned. He waited, watchful and filled with doubt, until he spied them both exiting the faerie hill. Alarmed, he followed them as they slipped into the dense forest growth. On a winding path, Rolf and Lilliana drew to a clearing that held a large pool fed by a falls from the wendthril stream, the living vein than runs through Thelestorian, to its living heart in Gaelen. At that place, Rolf, having discovered they were being followed, accused Lilliana of deceiving him. When she pled her fealty to him, he pressed his advances upon her, but the maiden refused. In a rage, Rolf threw the maiden down beside the pool, where she struck her head upon a sharp rock and died. Our vessel had not been close enough to save her; but in a rage, upon seeing her corpse, he battled with Rolf Andelar and succeeded in sweeping off his head.

When Nortenaine came upon the scene with his warriors, he wept and called to the heavens in his anguish to curse the Ileana. It was his father, Gaelen, who took upon himself the agonizing chore of breaking the news to Klevian, our high lord, who could not be consoled. Before the interment of Lilliana in her bier in the forest, Klevian left Quelean, slipping quietly into the forest, never to be seen again. He chose to take himself to the everlasting forest and join the gods in his grief. Afterward, it was Gaelen who took on the mantle of high lord and demanded the extinction of any Ileana who would defile the homeland of Thelestorian and its sacred center, where the god Queleastor dwells. Thus came to an end the sad tale of Lilliana, most bright maiden of the Florian.

Hoagy opened his eyes, blinking at Sandoval. The wizard stared at the ceiling, a faraway look in his black eyes. Hoagy rubbed his own eyes and poured some wine into his cup, sipping slowly until Sandoval finally turned to him.

"An interesting tale."

"You don't believe it?" Hoagy's blue eyes became rounder.

"Let's just say I think it was embellished for the record. Scribes do that. The tale of Baron Quincana in his travels around the world told of his almost super-human powers, and the battles—well, they were magnificent. Not that there actually were any."

"Oh, right. But the folks loved it, especially the plays put on afterwards."

Sandoval didn't respond to Hoagy's enthusiasm. His mind was chewing on the information just given to him. Hoagy sipped on his wine and waited.

"It must have been difficult for Maeleana after Klevian left. Did you find any mention of her in the records?"

"Some records indicate she still held a position of honor and was often consulted by Gaelen, as he still revered her as his stepmother. But that changed after Gaelen's death in a battle with the Ileana some years later. The account I read said that Maelthor and Nortenaine both blamed Maeleana for Gaelen's death, as he rarely went on raids with Nortenaine and his warriors and was only on that one because Maeleana had urged him to lead them—she'd told him that Nortenaine was too untried in leading the warriors. After that, Maelthor refused to see his mother. It was also the cause of her being banished and ousted from the Grimwood to wander in the plains."

Sandoval's black eyebrows arched and his eyes narrowed. "So Maelthor would want to separate himself from suspicions of being a party to his father's death. And without obviously separating himself from the Ileana and their beliefs, he would never have achieved the position of vessel for the Florian. How else could they trust him to be their spiritual guide? Anything further?"

"That's it, sir." Hoagy leaned back and felt the wine ease his body.

Sandoval tossed down the remainder of his wine and then rose, brushing off his slightly soiled white robe. "I must see Nortenaine. Make sure we are packed and ready to go at a moment's notice and stay close."

With that Sandoval grabbed his leather pouch and his staff and left. Hoagy pursed his lips, his blue eyes scanning the room for anything to occupy his time while waiting. They settled on a book Sandoval had left on the dresser, beside the wine. Smiling, Hoagy picked up the wine, poured himself another goblet full, and then took the book and settled in the chair.

The blue moon of Horus shone down on a square devoid of activity, except for the bubbling water of the central fountain. Lower on the horizon, the red moon of Khensu blinked ominously, as if to remind the citizens of Phoenix, who might turn their eyes skyward of an evening, that life was not without diversity between hope and fear, blessings and dire events. With those heavy thoughts, Sandoval reached Nortenaine's dwelling, and after knocking, requested entrance. Lenlael, the same servant who had escorted him to Noona, answered the door, silently motioned for him to follow, and led him down a long hallway to a closed door. Sandoval could hear the murmur of voices within the room and paused while the servant slipped into the room. A few moments later, the door opened, and Sandoval stepped through.

Sandoval was not surprised to see Bruel, Maelthor, and a group of elf warriors sitting at a large round table. Nortenaine sat on the far side, his face more pale and drawn than when Sandoval had seen him earlier in the day. The stately lord rose with what appeared to be an effort.

"Inspector Carmichael of the Royal Bureau of Investigation," Nortenaine announced to the room in general. "The inspector has been given the unfortunate mission of attempting to mediate peace between the Ileana and Florian clans."

"Unfortunate is correct," Maelthor snapped, rising also, as if imposing his superiority over his lord. Even Bruel frowned slightly at his action. "I wonder that this human hasn't also been on a mission to Mt. Thorn for instructions before coming here."

A gasp escaped from someone, and Nortenaine raised his hand immediately, his blue eyes hardening as they turned on Maelthor.

"That is not necessary, Maelthor. Suspicions alone do not prove cause. Inspector Carmichael is welcome to put forth the case of his superiors. We should at least allow them the courtesy of listening."

With that, Nortenaine resumed his seat, ignoring Maelthor, and waved his hand toward an empty chair opposite him at the table. Maelthor stood stiffly for only a moment before seating himself.

Sandoval took the proffered chair as his black eyes slowly scanned the table. "I would like to express my gratitude to Nortenaine for allowing me to speak before you. Am I correct in recognizing a council of war?"

Stony silence was the only response, but he did not miss the twisted smile on Maelthor's lips. Finally, Nortenaine's soft voice broke that silence.

"It is true we are meeting here to decide the fate of the Ileana."

"And the Florian?" Sandoval queried, not missing Nortenaine's downcast eyes.

"The Florian will triumph in the war to come!" Maelthor's rough voice rose above scattered murmurs of protest.

"Perhaps, but without unnecessary loss of life?" Sandoval asked. "There has already been loss of life on both sides. I wonder if a minor delay of your plans to arrange a meeting with a contingent of the Ileana would hurt those chances."

"Out of the question!" Maelthor thundered, his fist striking the table. Even the other elves appeared shocked at the vehemence of his response. "We know what they would say, and it is blasphemous. Their very presence in Thelestorian has placed a taint upon it. I suppose this is the plan they have given you?"

Sandoval was taken aback by Maelthor's use of the sacred elven name of Thelestorian, rather than using the common name of the Grimwood that the humans had placed upon the forest.

"Maelthor—" Nortenaine began, but he was cut off as Maelthor rose angrily.

"You know I speak the truth, Nortenaine. Even your son, Bruel, and these representatives of all our people agree. The Ileana will not budge. So this Rolf Andelar told us before murdering *our* Lilliana!"

Voices rose, adding to the cacophony caused by fists pounding the heavy oak table. Sandoval gazed calmly across the table at Nortenaine. The elf lord's face seemed to drain of life.

"Father, I believe Maelthor speaks the truth." Bruel's voice cut through the noise, immediately silencing the others at the table. "We have to regain our honor. The body of Welmoen's son lies outside, tended to by handmaidens even as we speak. There has been enough talking. The delay of years has not diminished the fighting. Should we sit, undecided, while the Ileana infiltrate our sacred wood and take us in our beds?"

Voices rose again, but in a high-pitched trill, like a discordant chord of music. It cut through to Sandoval's soul; it was the battle cry of the Florian that had not been heard in this world for ages. Nortenaine's eyes met Sandoval's, and the wizard knew from the spark of pride and resolution in those now-clear blue eyes that his cause was lost.

"If you mean to meet the Ileana on the plains, you will be at a distinct disadvantage." Sandoval kept his voice steady.

"The majority has approved our course. We thank you, Inspector Carmichael, for your king's concern, but there is no point in your continuing on your course. We will allow you time to gather your things before leaving Quelean."

Sandoval nodded solemnly and rose, leaning heavily on his staff. He bowed to Nortenaine and the others before turning, without another word, and walking from the room. When it closed silently behind him, he allowed himself a heavy sigh and brushed his hand through his gray-streaked black hair. He hardly noticed Lenlael standing at his side until the elf spoke softly.

"I will escort you out, Inspector."

Sandoval had expected to find Hoagy pacing impatiently back at the room they shared, but when he returned, he instead found Hoagy snoring softly in the chair, the open book on his lap. Sandoval glanced at the empty wine bottle and shook his head, at the same time giving Hoagy's knee a sharp rap with his staff.

Hoagy yelped and popped up, his hands raised defensively. "Oh, sir, I must have dozed off. It was so warm in here and I—"

"Get your things together, and let us be away."

Hoagy scrambled about, scooping up what few things he carried and shoving them in his knapsack. When Hoagy was ready, they scanned the room one last time before stepping outside. As expected, a contingent of elves was waiting for them, standing at attention, their bows held ready. Hoagy peered at them suspiciously, but Sandoval merely turned without a word and headed for the entrance tunnel.

Waldo Snufflebeam, who had been put on guard, saluted them as soon as they appeared, then dashed to get Tronus. By the time Tronus came running, still pulling up his suspenders, the elves had gone.

"I think they will not bother to roust us for spending the remainder of the night here, as long as we are gone before the sun is up," Sandoval said wearily. "We have much ground to cover, and I don't mind saying I'm tired. Have you got room for Hoagy and me, Tronus?"

"I think we can manage that," Tronus said as they walked back to the small fire that was still glowing. "And glad I am that we're leaving this place. The peacefulness was beginning to get to me. Leave it to you to get us booted out of paradise."

CHAPTER 6

ENTER A DRAGON

Sandoval had everyone on the road with the first rays of the morning sun. They were already near his cottage on the outskirts of Darren's Choice by the afternoon, when a huge dark-skinned man stepped onto the path in front of them. His thick brown hair was plaited in scattered rows that hung down to his shoulders, and he glowered at Sandoval. As the man spread his arms causing muscles to bulge on his glistening brown skin, Harald pulled out his battle hammer and thrust himself in front of Tronus, yelling a warning. Tronus cuffed him on the ear and sent him dodging, as Sandoval chuckled and called out to the big man.

"Ferrel Lovelace, it's about time you showed up! Where's your boss?"

A tall woman in leather pants and vest stepped out from behind a tree. Her long brunette hair was pulled back and tied at the nape of her neck, accentuating her high cheekbones and large brown eyes. She winked at Sandoval and smiled. A big buckskin mare nickered and trotted out from behind the same tree that had hidden the woman, followed by another even larger bay stallion with a blaze down his face. The buckskin nudged the woman's shoulder with its muzzle.

"Nice horse flesh," Sandoval called, moving ahead to meet them. "The Lestrami still excel in breeding magnificent running stock; Menopet is proof of that. The Sholeens produce the best of them all. Welcome, Jade."

Jade nodded her head in greeting and slapped Ferrell on one of his big arms, her husky voice softened with amusement. "What are you doing, scaring unsuspecting people like that?" She motioned toward Harald. "This warrior could have split your head in two."

Ferrell opened his mouth almost as wide as his eyes, but no sound came out, as Tronus cut him off with a loud guffaw. Harald scowled at them, and Hoagy put his arm around the young dwarf.

"Don't listen to them, Harald. You did right, not knowing who these menacing strangers were," Hoagy said, but he couldn't suppress his wide grin.

"Aw, okay." Harald smiled uncertainly. "Just doin' my job."

"Your timing is perfect," Sandoval laughed. "Pack your horses with our bags, and we can trek the last bit to my cottage with lighter bodies."

Ferrel and Jade did so, slapping the horses on the rumps and watching as they trotted off—they knew where to go, as it was where they had reluctantly left their stall mates and welcome bags of oats.

"Have you got lunch ready?" Sandoval said, his long strides eating up the trail.

"As a matter of fact, yes." A broad grin split Ferrel's wide face. "I was just about to light up a fire and enjoy the first hot food and a good, steaming cup of cherok we've had in days. We had to make some time to meet you here. I hadn't settled my bum into a chair before she was shoving me out the door to meet you."

"Sorry about that. We were somewhat *rushed* out of Quelean."

Sandoval smiled as they turned the last bend in the trail and the sight of his cottage filled his view. Harald and the Snufflebeam Company needed little encouragement to double-time it and even made a race of it, with Harald winning. Hoagy was right behind them and heading for the water trough to wash his face and hands in anticipation of a meal, when Jade snapped him on the ear. He popped up as she moved him to let the horses drink their fill.

"I could use your help bedding the horses down, if you don't mind, Hoagy. There are also some oat bags already waiting in the barn, and you can give some to Menopet and Bully, also. When you're done, I've got a special treat for you."

She winked, and Hoagy smiled in return. He knew Jade probably had a cask of Bergen ale cooling in Sandoval's larder. He took the reins, and when the horses had drunk their fill, he led them toward the barn. Harald followed. Hoagy smiled at the young dwarf, then hurried as he heard his gelding, Bully, nickering. By the time Hoagy and Harald had fed and bedded down the horses and stepped into the cottage, everyone had settled around the fire with their food, and the sun was dipping behind the tall trees.

Jade handed Hoagy and Harald tin plates filled with stew and biscuits and a cup filled to the brim with ale. Sandoval and Tronus were already settled in comfortable chairs with cheroot and pipe and steaming cups of cherok. While Hoagy munched happily, Sandoval brought everyone current on the war council he had witnessed.

"Sounds pretty bad," Ferrel said roughly. "Jade's kin south of the unexplored region are said to be trading heavily with the elves of Mt. Thorn for the Sholeens' finest running stock. The Ileana seem to be preparing a pretty large army. How can the Florian compete with them? If the Ileana get them out on the grasslands, they'll be exposed with little to help them."

"The Florian seem unconcerned. I think it's going to be a cat-and-mouse game. The Florian will try to lure them into the woods where they will have the upper hand. And the Ileana will do hit-and-run skirmishes into the Grimwood. Nothing good will come of it at any rate. King Filemon may need an army of his own to stop them from slaughtering each other."

"Aren't elves supposed to be peace-loving, communing with nature and all that?" Tronus grumbled. "Now they're willing to kill each other off … for what? Revenge? Sounds dippy to me."

"Men will fight and kill over borders, material goods, or just plain power. But this is more complicated than that," Sandoval mused. "They perceive this as a lofty aim that justifies the cost."

"In lives?" Jade shook her dark brown mane of hair, which now hung loose about her shoulders. "We Lestrami revere our horses, but our people are of far greater worth to us. I don't believe we would put them in harm's way so carelessly."

"There's more that drives them. Hoagy found some revealing documents in the elven archives that shed some light on the age-old separation of the clans. He also found a chronicle of the murder of the elf maiden Lilliana, supposedly at the hands of an Ileana elf lord, Rolf Andelar."

"Ho! That puts a new twist on it," Ferrel said.

"You said *supposedly*, wizard." Jade eyed Sandoval with a grin. "Does that mean you have uncovered evidence that does not support the story?"

"See, this isn't just a diplomatic job anymore, friends. Our Inspector Carmichael is on a murder case!" Tronus blurted out, slapping his knee. "That's why we went to that place in the forest, eh, Sandoval?"

"So Hoagy got into these archives, eh? I'll bet he wasn't invited to look at that stuff." Jade said, winking at Sandoval.

Sandoval smiled tightly. "Not quite."

"This murder has overshadowed any mere border disputes for the elves on both sides, it seems," Jade said.

"Trelaine told me the spiritual fire of the elves burns fiercely. I don't think they take it lightly," Hoagy said. "She said those who have gone before are always with them in spirit." He wiped his mouth with his napkin and set his cup down with a sigh.

"Maybe that answers the fear of the faerie, Tillie, to be exposed in human form at the green pool. She was terrified that the spirit of Rolf Andelar would take revenge upon her," Sandoval said, crushing out the last of his cheroot.

"But she wouldn't say what she thinks she did to earn his vengeance?" Tronus asked, tapping the last of his pipe tobacco into the dying fire.

"No, but I don't give up so easily," Sandoval answered. "I mean to visit the hermit, Will Wiggins, again and see if I can find out what information he holds so close to his chest. Maybe it will draw out the faeries, as it did before. There seems to be a lot of faerie activity in the Grimwood, more than I have ever seen. I'm wondering if that crafty old hermit has something to do with it. If nothing else, maybe he will assist me in interrogating Tillie.

"And while Hoagy and I are on that mission, I want you, Tronus, Ferrel, and Jade to visit the Ileana at Mt. Thorn. See if you can find out from them what they are planning and whether they are more agreeable to open talks with the Florian. We have to measure the tempers in this matter, on both sides. Only then can I report to Director Tantilus, and he to King Filemon. If the humans must become involved, we'd better know it as soon as possible."

"And how to do we get to Mt. Thorn quick enough for that?" Ferrel said. "It will take us two to three days at least, with our horses running flat out and few rests. And I'm not willing to kill them to stop a war with the elves."

"Oh, I have a quicker way for you to travel without your horses even breaking a sweat." Sandoval's mouth twisted in a crafty smile and his black eyes twinkled.

Jade and Ferrel glanced uncertainly at each other and back at Sandoval. Tronus shook his head and chuckled.

"And Tronus doesn't like riding horseback that much, anyway," Sandoval added.

A sudden gust of wind outside of the open window blew in dust, leaves, and Moonbeam, Sandoval's lurecat. He cleared the windowsill in one leap and spun around, hissing and arching his back, black fur standing up all over his body, and the long, thin tail with a small tuft at the tip whipping around to snap Hoagy's leg.

"Hey!" Hoagy backed away from the bared fangs of the large cat, but he needn't have worried. With one angry growl at the open window, Moonbeam's paws scrambled against the fire hearth as he leaped toward the interior rooms.

Hoagy was on his feet, as were the rest, with the exception of Sandoval, who gazed out of the window from the comfort of his chair. He only pulled himself back when the huge green snout of a dragon appeared without, and a large green dragon eye specked with gold peered in at them.

Sandoval chuckled at the horrified looks that Tronus, Ferrel, and Jade gave him as he rose and headed for the front door. "I do believe your ride has arrived."

"You can't expect us to—" Ferrel started.

"I think you've gone over the bend, boy!" Tronus sputtered.

"You must be mad!" Jade added.

Sandoval waved his hand dismissively at their protests. "Now, come and meet one of our dragon friends. I've been assured by Taimat that this means of transportation is quite safe, and we've been given permission to attach a sort of saddle affair, just to make you more comfortable, though I've been told no dragon would ever allow anyone riding it to fall off."

"Oh, I feel better all ready!" Tronus snorted, glaring at Sandoval. "You won't get me up on that thing. I just won't do it."

Sandoval ignored the agreement from the other two and motioned to Hoagy, who was sputtering with barely contained laughter, to follow him. Hoagy bounded out of the door after Sandoval and then came abruptly to a halt as the head of the dragon loomed over him, its open maw stretched in what truly looked like a smile. Sandoval bowed before the huge beast.

"Thank Taimat for the speedy response," Sandoval said to the dragon.

"King Taimat sends his greetings and tells the inspector the dragons will always come when he calls. Moitha is at your disposal." The dragon's voice was almost melodious, evoking joyous song.

"Thank you, Moitha," Sandoval responded; then he turned to Hoagy. "Please bring those straps hanging on the hook just inside the stable door. And stay away from the horses. I believe they are spooked."

Hoagy glanced around surreptitiously, the hope on his face fading to reflect his disappointment. "I just thought …" Hoagy clamped down on his unspoken thought at the sharp look and shake of the head from Sandoval.

"Hurry now, Hoagy. Don't let's keep this lady waiting."

By now, three heads had poked out of the front door of the cottage. After the exchange in greetings, Jade stepped forth, her chin high. She bowed nervously before the dragon.

"Greetings … Moitha, did you say? Aren't you afraid the elves surrounding this cottage will see you and report this to Nortenaine?"

"Not likely, miss. All creatures for some ways around this cottage are sleeping comfortably. They will awaken sometime later, none the worse for wear, as you humans would say. We dragons are not without some *magic* of our own."

Jade chuckled and motioned for Ferrel and Tronus to come out. The large man stepped out first, following closely by Tronus, who still had a look of anguish on his face.

"If we must do this, we will do it with the courage of warriors, not whimpering like little pups." Jade pulled her long brown hair back from her face and tied it with a woven cord, specifically fashioned for containing her long locks while riding or in battle. She slapped Ferrel on the back and gave him a grin of encouragement that only slightly wavered at the edges.

Hoagy came running up, skidding to a halt, leather straps hanging from his arms. He gave Sandoval a questioning look, but before the wizard could answer, Moitha spoke.

"Now, young man, those should do nicely. If you could, run the long lines under me, then step up on my front leg and put them together over my shoulders. Shorter straps can be run underneath the main straps to secure on the waist straps—those shorter ones." Then, to Tronus, the dragon said, "I will not let you fall."

Tronus looked as if he was ready to faint, but Sandoval put his large hand on Tronus' shoulder and spoke quickly in his ear, so low that the others could not make out what he said. Tronus reached under the neck of his vest and pulled out a round piece of silver with a heraldic crest etched in the center. The dwarf pressed it to his lips and then dropped it back inside his vest. Sandoval smiled and rose up, placing both hands on Tronus' shoulders.

"You'll be fine, old boy! Why, I'll bet Harald and the boys would love to take the trip with you."

Tronus stared up at him, momentarily stunned, before shaking his head as if to clear it. He looked back toward the cottage door, which was empty of any Dwarves.

"Not likely, *old boy*. I just want you to remember this one, Sandoval Carmichael. You owe me."

Hoagy had run the lines under Moitha, and Jade straddled the dragon's shoulders and pulls the lines together. She caught the shorter lines that Hoagy threw up to her, belting one on her waist and slipping the others under the lines that braced the dragon's shoulder. When she was finished, she took the spot closest to the dragon's head, pulling up the shorter straps and securing them to the wide belt at her waist. She looked down at Ferrel and Tronus, who were putting on the belts Hoagy had given them, her grin now broad and steady.

"I'm ready boys. Let's do it if you want to get there this evening."

"So just how long will this take us?" Ferrel asked.

"I am capable of reaching the coast of my homeland by nightfall with a strong upper wind current," Moitha answered, "but we should be able to arrive at Mt. Thorn by the setting of the sun, as I must travel on the lower current. Higher up would make breathing uncomfortable for my passengers."

"Higher up …" Tronus gulped, shaking his head and running his fingers nervously through his beard.

Ferrel shrugged, and with a look of chagrin, he took Tronus' arm. The old dwarf stiffened suddenly, but when Ferrel shot him a look that undoubtedly meant *Either you step up, or I lift you up*, Tronus relented and allowed Ferrel to boost him aboard the dragon. Settled behind Jade, Tronus' attached the straps to his belt as Jade had done. Ferrel hefted himself up behind the dwarf and secured his own straps to duplicate the other two. Thus ready, the three of them gazed down at Sandoval, their faces flushed with anticipation and fear.

Hoagy emerged from the cottage with their packs and hefted them up to each. Stepping back, Sandoval nodded, as if satisfied with the results.

"They will be safe on me, Inspector," Moitha assured him. She backed away from the cottage to give herself room to lift her massive wings, and she brought them down in one swift thrust as she bounded skyward. She seemed to hover briefly—only for the space of a breath—before she winged rhythmically higher, soon disappearing from view over the treetops. Sandoval turned back to the cottage to see Harald and the other Dwarves huddled around Hoagy. Everyone gazed skyward, their eyes wide.

Harald turned to the others now under his command. "Number One is a brave dwarf. We will earn his respect by carrying out his orders without question!"

The young Dwarves nodded solemnly, turned, and went back into the cottage, followed by Hoagy. Sandoval went toward the stable. He could hear the soft nervous nickering and stamping of the horses as he stepped into the dim coolness of the stable. He moved to pat each of them in turn, finally running his hands lovingly down Menopet's strong neck. The large black stallion blew out his breath and shook his head in protest.

"I know, my friend. Such carryings on. But you must stay behind this time. We'll be quieter on foot through the forest."

Menopet nickered softly, rubbing his big head against Sandoval's shoulder. Sandoval gave him a final pat and headed back to the cottage. Once inside, he began taking stock of the contents of his leather pouch. Everyone, including Hoagy, stood at attention, staring expectantly at him.

"Harald, you are in charge of keeping up a good front for the elves who are watching this cottage. It's an easy duty for you. You boys could even practice your skills in mock battles for their benefit. Keep close by. If need be, I will send a message ball. Hoagy, pack up and let's get going before the sleep spell wears off those elves. I want to be at our destination by nightfall."

"And that would be the hermit's tower, sir?" Hoagy asked as he grabbed his cloak and pack.

"Yes, that is our destination."

"Do you really think we can find the tower again?"

Sandoval pulled on his cloak, shouldered his leather pouch, and grabbed his leather hat. "Probably not, but I don't think we'll have to."

With that, he snapped a salute to Harald and the Snufflebeam Company and stepped out the door. Hoagy followed, turning to wave at the expectant faces that peered out the front door of the cottage. Within minutes they had disappeared into the brush and trees of the Grimwood.

CHAPTER 7

MISTRESS OF THE GREEN POOL

Sandoval and Hoagy slipped through the lush green depths of the Grimwood. The area was heady with the scent and moisture of dew on the leaves, and the summer sunlight dappled the animal trail they followed. Striding quickly, their steps were muffled by a gliding spell that Sandoval had created to elevate them a few inches above the forest floor. They soon found themselves through the elven lines that encircled Sandoval's cottage before the late afternoon sun had dimmed the forest that surrounded them. His ears alert, Sandoval glanced back at Hoagy, gauging for any reaction from Hoagy to the sounds only his wizard hearing could separate from the normal bird and small animals sounds of the forest. He had noticed those sounds as soon as he and Hoagy had cleared the elven lines hours earlier—the wispy flutter of faerie wings and the occasional snicker of faerie laughter. But he noticed no reaction from Hoagy as the young man trudged along behind him, his head bobbing in time with his steps.

Feeling comfortable enough for a brief rest stop, Sandoval spotted a small clearing off to his left. He motioned to Hoagy, and they stepped into a cathedral formed from the heavy boughs of the trees that bent to create the leafy dome. It was even dimmer in that enclosed spot than on the meager trail they had been following, but Sandoval was leery about starting a fire.

"We'll only be here briefly, Hoagy. Just a quick snack and some water. I can hear a stream nearby. I'll check that out while you dig into your pack for some cold biscuits."

With that, Sandoval slipped through the trees that surrounded them and followed the faint sound of a bubbling stream. The hillside angled downward, and it wasn't long before he came upon the stream, sparkling clear in the last rays of the afternoon sunlight. Sandoval bent to lower his canteen to the water, his ears pricked for the slightest sound. It came before he'd finished filling the canteen, which he dropped, even as he swept up his hand in one move to snatch the faerie, which was hovering just over his right shoulder.

He ignored the squeal of indignation and the frantic flutter of wings against his loosely held fist. Putting his mouth to his fist, he blew gently before he opened his hand. The faerie dropped to the ground like a stone and shimmered momentarily before becoming a full-grown faerie maid—none other than Tillie, kicking her toe into the grass and glaring up at the amused wizard.

"You'll just never learn, will you, Tillie?" Sandoval smiled, his black eyes sparkling, holding her in their spell.

"That's not fair!" she cried indignantly. "You're not supposed to hear us, and I made sure to stay behind you, so you couldn't see."

"But I *can* hear you—all of you. Now, what I want to know is whether you and your mischievous little group are misdirecting me again. And I want a straight answer, or I'll bind you to me for eternity!" he finished with a flourish.

Tillie stared at him, horrified. "You can't do that, wizard!"

"Do you want to test me, Tillie?" Sandoval said softly.

Tillie stuck out her bottom lip and glared at him silently. Sandoval picked up his canteen, not worrying that he didn't have his eye on her. He knew she couldn't leave just yet.

"You are near the place where I saw you last," she piped in her little sing-song voice. "Your path has been laid out. I can not alter it. But I can give you something to help you." With that, she pulled a small vial from the pocket in her dress and handed it to him. Sandoval took the clear vial and looked at her questioningly. "You must put this oil on the eyelids of the young human who accompanies you," she instructed him. "It will protect him. This is very important! Without protecting him, you will perish!" It was her turn to finish with a flourish, and her arms raised dramatically as a smirk curved her little mouth.

"I appreciate that, little Tillie. And what will this do for Hoagy?"

"It will make the young man able to see beyond a faerie *glamour*. There are some faeries in these woods that are not as honest as Tillie is." She poked out her chin proudly.

Sandoval contained his laughter and only raised his black eyebrows, his mouth twisted in a sardonic smile. "Well, I did wish to visit the green pool again, but I'm not too happy about doing it in the dark."

"You may use the light of your staff, wizard. The elves are far from here and will not come even this close to the pool at night. They are not as foolish as human wizards who choose to tempt the fates."

Sandoval gazed at her solemnly, then tapped the little faerie on the head. With that she shimmered into a dot of light and shot off through the trees. Sandoval turned back toward the clearing just as Hoagy popped out from behind a tree.

"There you are, sir. I was beginning to worry about you. Oh, good, you found water." Hoagy pulled out his canteen and filled it.

Back at the clearing, they ate silently and quickly. Sandoval told Hoagy they would be stopping at the green pool, and he pulled out the vial Tillie had given him.

"Close your eyes, Hoagy. I've got to rub your eyelids with this."

Hoagy stiffened and looked at the vial suspiciously. "What is that?"

"It's something that will protect you against faeries who may wish to do you harm. I promise you, it will not interfere with your mental capabilities. Actually, it may sharpen them, I'm told." Sandoval lied gracefully, his black eyes guileless.

"Aren't you going to use it, too?" Hoagy asked, after Sandoval had dabbed some of the oil on Hoagy's eyelids and put the vial back in his pouch.

"I don't think I will need it. I'm going to be depending on your alertness to protect us both."

"Oh, that is scary, sir. Me, protecting you?"

"We'll be fine. Now, onward to the next stop." Sandoval mentally chanted a benediction.

By the time they reached the green pool, the blue gem in the eye medallion carved on the top of Sandoval's staff was casting a broad aura of light around them; it extended over the entire area of the pool. Beyond the gem's illumination, Sandoval could clearly see and hear the falls cascading over the rocks to the pool below. Hoagy's blue eyes glowed in the artificial light of the staff, but Sandoval noted that his eyelids were already drooping sleepily. Dropping his bag and jamming his staff in the soft soil, Sandoval settled on the grass as far from the dark stain next to the pool as he could get; he motioned for Hoagy to do the same. Within minutes of easing himself to the ground and shucking off his pack, Hoagy was snoring softly. Sandoval muttered a spell that caused the gem on the top of his staff to flare momentarily. Satisfied, he lay back and closed his eyes, keeping his mind alert, even as he rested his body.

It was the *presence* that Sandoval sensed, even before the soft sound of footsteps on the grass brought him upright. He opened his eyes, brushing his gray-streaked black hair from his face, and looked up into the glowing green eyes of a beautiful woman. She was clothed in a long, flowing green gown that rippled about her and brushed softly against the grass. He knew this vision was not a woman but the faerie that Tillie spoke of, even as he noticed the tip of a pointed ear separating the flowing blonde hair that drifted about her head. Her red lips parted in a smile, and his responded. He felt a warmth permeate his body, starting from his head and moving down to tingle in his booted feet. It had been many years since a woman had stirred lust in him, but he could feel it now, burning in his loins. As he pulled the power from deep within him to clear his head and shake the physical grip of yearning, he heard a whisper of melodious tones coming from the red lips.

Mesmerized, even while his mind warned him of danger, he rose, drawn toward her outstretched arms. Almost as tall as he, her fingers touched his shoulders, gently tugging him toward her. With no other wizard to support the power he'd drawn upon, Sandoval could not maintain the barrier he had thrown up to bar the intensity of primal emotion that emanated from the woman. Yet as her face drew closer to his, her lips parted, and Sandoval saw clearly the fangs behind those red lips.

Sandoval braced himself and halted her forward momentum with his hands upon her shoulders. The enticing gleam in her eyes and the smile on her lips froze. Her fingers dug into his shoulders, and for a moment, he and the woman seemed to be having a tug-of-war, with him pushing and her pulling. Reaching again for his core of power, Sandoval won, shoved her backward, and reached for his staff—only to find his fist enclosed on empty air. It was then that he realized he was tied to the spot with a magical web of faerie ropes. The green creature laughed a low, bubbling-liquid sound.

"You are not used to being bested by anyone, are you, wizard? Least of all a faerie." Her dulcet tones were chilling.

"I expect you are much more than just a faerie, my lady. Since you appear to know who I am, perhaps you will introduce yourself."

"I know *what* you are, wizard. *Who* you are is not of importance to me. But I've had wizards before, and you aren't a very satisfying bunch. Bitter, I'd say. Now, this boy who lies at your feet—I believe he would be a tastier morsel for me. What would you say if I spared your life in favor of him? Would you give me your approval?" Her voice slid up an octave, and she ran her finger over her lips in anticipation.

Sandoval shuddered inwardly but kept his face immobile and passive. "First, may I know who you are?"

The green lady moved to circle Sandoval, licking her lips as she looked down at Hoagy. Sandoval stiffened, breathing in and out slowly, willing himself to be calm.

"I am the Glaistig. I am the mistress of this pool, and you tread here only with my blessing. Your magic can not match mine, wizard, so don't think you can muster your energy to battle me."

"I wouldn't think of it," Sandoval said, smiling tightly. "I will give you my approval on condition that you tell me what you know of the death of Lilliana, the elf maiden, and Rolf Andelar."

The Glaistig's glowing green eyes widened, and she chuckled softly, the sound slithering down Sandoval's spine.

"The elf maiden fell from the ledge above. It goes back underneath the falls. It is a good hiding spot. I can watch the entire pool from up there. But the maid wasn't watching for the man who came. She meant to toss herself into the pool. He came and tried to stop her."

The Glaistig paused and gazed at Sandoval, waiting for him to accept her story. He met her gaze with hard, black eyes. Sandoval could recognize the truth there, beyond the gloating, twisted smile on her red lips.

The Glaistig's eyes broke away first. "She fell."

"Fell?"

She shrugged. "Mayhap she was assisted in that fall."

"By you?"

"No. I have no interest in maidens of any sort. This maiden had just given birth to a child—over there." She pointed to a sheltered spot at the bottom of the falls. "I assisted her."

Sandoval felt his pulse quicken. This was the missing piece! A child! Did Maelthor know of it? Had he taken it those many years ago?

"And what of the child?" Sandoval asked quietly.

"It died in my arms. Now you must pay for your part of the bargain."

"How did she get up to the ledge in the falls?" Sandoval pressed. "Why did she go there?"

"She was despondent and crazed over the loss of the child. She climbed up there to die." The Glaistig moved closer to Hoagy, who was still sleeping on the grass at their feet.

"You said she may have been *assisted* in her fall. Was someone, other than you, here at the time? Within the falls, as you said—a good watching spot?"

The Glaistig pulled her eyes from Hoagy's sleeping form to look at Sandoval. Her cold green eyes and the slow movement of her tongue over her red lips caused his stomach to lurch. He knew he had precious little remaining time.

"I saw only a shadow—shortly before the man burst through the trees and called to her. That is all. You will allow me to take my payment now."

The Glaistig brushed Sandoval aside and touched Hoagy lightly on one knee. The young man's blue eyes fluttered open, and he looked around, his brow furrowing. He shook his head slightly to clear his sight. Then he saw her. Immediately captivated, Hoagy rose, his eyes not leaving the glowing green eyes of the Glaistig. She backed up and opened her arms for him. Hoagy moved closer to her, barely aware of Sandoval, standing close by. The wizard's body was stiff with apprehension, every muscle tightened and ready to spring. He watched as the Glaistig's lips parted slightly, her tongue flicking out to wet her red lips.

Then Hoagy spotted the tips of her pointed fangs and froze. His eyes moved over her frame, down the flowing gown. The faerie oil that Sandoval had dabbed on his lids did its work and with his sight cleared of the illusion in which the Glaistig had covered herself, Hoagy saw her lower limbs beneath the dress that covered her body—twisted limbs covered with speckled brown fur, the legs of a goat ending in cloven hooves. Horrified, he gasped and staggered backward, the mesmerizing spell broken momentarily.

"Run, Hoagy!" yelled Sandoval, leaning as far to his left as he could to reach for his staff.

Jolted into action, Hoagy spun away, neither looking back nor pausing to wonder at the terror that shot through him, urged upon him by Sandoval's desperate mental thrust. Tearing through the undergrowth of brush as he dodged trees, Hoagy heard behind him the furious shriek of the Glaistig.

The Glaistig turned on Sandoval, her face red with fury. "You will not escape me, wizard! I may not taste your blood, but I will have my revenge!"

The Glaistig lunged at Sandoval, just as his hand grasped his staff. Quickly muttering a protective spell, Sandoval pulled the staff from the soil and brought it up across his chest, both hands braced for the onslaught of the faerie's blood lust, while the lower part of his body was still encased in the web of faerie ropes. But he knew his magic had weakened from the combination of the faerie holding spell and the power of the mental thrust he had directed at Hoagy. The Glaistig tore the staff from his hands and raised it above her head.

"Your answers have been false, Glaistig!" Sandoval's voice was harsh with exhaustion. "As false as the beauty that covers the hideously twisted animal body beneath your gown!"

The Glaistig hesitated, the staff still gripped in her raised hands.

"Oh, yes, the clearing of the young man's sight also cleared mine. I've seen you as you are."

"If you didn't clear his sight, who then?" The Glaistig lowered the staff. Her eyes narrowed and she leaned in toward Sandoval.

"Do you think all the faeries do your bidding?" Sandoval taunted, playing for time so he could regain his strength and clear his head, even as he considered his next move. "You did not live up to your part of the bargain, either. Therefore, no reason for me to give you what you want."

"The deal is off, human." The Glaistig threw the staff on the ground, out of Sandoval's reach. "I may not taste your blood, but I can invite you to join me in my beautiful home. It may be a little damp for you, but that can't be helped. I've always wanted company." With that, she grabbed Sandoval by the hem of his robe. The faerie ropes dropped away, and she drew him after her as she slid backward toward the cold green water of the pool.

Sandoval fell to the ground and began to chant:

"Harken to me ye gods that hold,
over dale, forest, and rocky knoll,
faeries first, then elves that dwell,
awaken justice and break this spell!"

Still, the Glaistig's grip remained, and she pulled him with her into the chill water. Sandoval drew a last great gasp of air as the water closed over his head, and he disappeared beneath the green surface.

CHAPTER 8

WATER, ROCK, LEAF, AND BOUGH

Though stoutly determined to stay alert upon the back of Moitha as they flew over the fields and towns of Pacifica, Tronus was soon lulled to sleep by the rhythmic movement of the up-and-down sweep of dragon wings. Jade stared at the patterns laid out below, fascinated for as long as she could see them, but it was becoming difficult with the increase in altitude of the dragon and the fading daylight. She could hear Ferrel's throaty chuckle at the loud snores coming from Tronus. Twisting her head backward as far as she could, she saw the old dwarf's head bobbing in beat with the body movement of the dragon, his long red beard splayed out and fluttering in the wind on either side of him. She smiled and winked encouragement at Ferrel. For a while, Jade had been unsure they would be able to reach Mt. Thorn in the time limit set by Moitha, but they still had the benefit of the last rays of the setting sun as the huge dragon began her final glide downward.

Below them, Jade could see the dormant volcano of Mt. Thorn, its dark hulk outlined in the last rays of sunlight. As Moitha banked for her descent, Jade could make out the lower slopes covered with brush that ended in a wide, grassy plain. She barely had time to wonder whether the dragon had placed a sleeping spell upon any elves that might be wandering in the foothills as Moitha began to back-wing for her landing. The jolt of that movement and the change as Moitha angled slightly backward brought Tronus fully awake with a startled yelp.

"Quick, boys! Grab hold of anything to save yourselves!" he yelled in Jade's ear.

"Wake up, Tronus." Jade rammed her elbow into his gut. "We're landing."

Tronus shook his head, his grip on Jade's shoulders loosening.

Ferrel spoke softly in Tronus' ear, so only he could hear. "Shook me up, too, when she made that sharp downward turn, and I was awake. Well, here we are, thank the gods!"

Moitha landed delicately, to the surprise of all, as they had braced for a jolt. Tronus, with his eyes still closed, prayed to his ancestral gods. Ferrel quickly unlatched his straps, tossed his leg over, and slid down Moitha's side. Tronus fumbled with his straps, muttering angrily. Jade caught a couple of curse words and Sandoval's name.

"When you get unhooked, sit still until I can unhook myself and help you down," Jade said, turning her head to look back at him.

Tronus, free now from his straps, looked down at the ground below and cut off his retort. Before he could admonish her for slowness, Jade had thrown her leg over Moitha's neck, her legs dangling over Moitha's side. She took Tronus' hands and swung him out over her legs, into Ferrel's waiting arms. Tronus dropped to the ground and walked a few feet, his legs wobbling under him until he sat down, expelling a *whooff!* Jade pushed off and dropped into Ferrel's arms. They turned and saluted Moitha.

"Farewell, and thanks for the ride," Jade called as the dragon walked awkwardly away from them for clearance to leap skyward.

"It has been a pleasure. I see no one to halt your progress. The trail to the entrance on the side of Mt. Thorn is behind you," Moitha said as she bounded upward, the gust of wind from her wings almost blowing them over.

Within several sweeps of her massive wings, Moitha was almost out of sight, driving for a cloud layer that had moved in. Even without those clouds, the closing dark of night made following her progress impossible. Ferrel grabbed Tronus by the back of his vest and pulled him up.

"Up and at 'em, Tronus. It's already darkening, and we've got to find that trail before the full black of night closes on us, or we'll be fumbling around the bushes for hours."

Jade was already following the direction Moitha had indicated. Low in the eastern sky, the yellow light of the crescent moon, Horus, gave them little enough help to keep from stumbling. But they were urged on by the prospect of the rising of the smaller red moon, Khensu, for that additional illumination could expose them. By the time Ferrel and Tronus trotted up to Jade, she had spotted the trail. It was dirt and rock, hard-packed and smooth from years of travel. It was just narrow enough for a single horse and rider but wide enough for them to walk two abreast. Ferrel took the lead, with Jade and Tronus behind him. Ferrel kept his big hand on the hilt of the sword that hung at his side, but it remained sheathed. Since they were going on a diplomatic mission, it wouldn't be good form for them to march up with their weapons at the ready, Jade had reasoned. Both Tronus and Ferrel had reluctantly agreed, though not without casting an uncertain glance at each other.

As darkness closed in on them, even the weak light from the crescent of Horus didn't reveal a clear path, and the trek up the trail became difficult, with occasional stumbles on the uneven surface, as well as mumbled curses.

"Their ponies must have a time with this," Tronus grumbled.

"They ride Lestrami-raised horses," Jade responded proudly. "And our stock has fine night vision and a delicate step. They'd have no problem with this trail."

They moved on in silence until they reached a turn in the trail and saw that it ended at a heavy wooden door across an entrance in the mountain side. They'd halted, unsure of the next move, when an arrow whizzed out of the air and landed in the ground at Jade's booted feet.

Jade looked up as Ferrel slowly pulled his sword from its scabbard. Above them, on a terrace overlooking the entrance, stood two elves clad in leather pants and tunics, bows drawn and arrows nocked.

Jade raised her arm to signal Ferrel to lower his sword. Reluctantly, the big man slipped it back in the scabbard. Tronus had pulled his battle hammer and held it in front of him, but he, too, lowered it at Jade's nod.

Women! Tronus thought. *Always careful about raising dust.*

But he knew the wisdom of allowing Jade the upper hand in this mission, as the Ileana were familiar with her people and would be more likely to allow their little diplomatic delegation access to those in charge.

"We come in peace to speak with your leaders. I am Jade Sholeen of the Sholeen Lestrami. These are my friends, Ferrel Lovelace and Tronus Longbottom. We have been sent by a representative of King Filemon to discuss the ongoing dispute between the Ileana and the Florian clans."

Ferrel and Tronus shot looks at each other at Jade's slightly twisted truth. A rough laugh answered her speech, and another elf, slightly stooped with long gray hair, looked down upon them. His bright hazel eyes reflected the light of the fully risen crescent moon, accompanied now by the red orb of Khensu. Though his face was not lined with age, Jade knew he was an elder, as much by the gray hair as his imposing figure that was robed in a fine cloth of white, stitched with threads of gold throughout. Though his body was bent with age, this elf carried power. The other two elves backed off to stand slightly behind him on either side.

"May we know to whom who we are presenting ourselves?" Jade asked, her voice steady.

"You are speaking with Vaester Shee. Are you acquainted with that name?"

"We are," Ferrel interjected, ignoring Jade's sharp turn toward him. "You're the vessel of the Ileana."

"And it's only leader since the death of Iledan and his son, Rolf Andelar, at the hands of the Florian!" His voice rasped out the words.

"We're also having that incident investigated fully." Tronus pulled himself up to his full height. *Might as well lay it on thick,* he thought, as Jade turned her flashing brown eyes in his direction.

Vaester Shee silently regarded them for a moment before nodding to one of the elves and disappearing through the opening beyond the terrace. The two elves followed him. Jade swung around to Ferrel and Tronus.

"I thought I was handling it pretty well."

"And you were, my love. But it doesn't hurt to let them know we're equals here, on the same errand. Even though you are Sholeen, some males might not like dealing with … strong women."

"Aye," Tronus added. "It doesn't hurt to show them a united front."

Jade seemed placated, though her brown eyes narrowed as she studied each of them in turn. Ferrel had just about decided that Jade wasn't going to accept his explanation when the heavy wooden door swung open. A tall elf, with brown hair bleached in blond streaks and skin bronzed from the merciless sun of the plains, stood with one hand on the door and the other on his bow. He nodded to them and swept his arm wide to allow Jade inside, followed by Ferrel and Tronus.

As soon as they had cleared the entrance, the heavy door swung shut with a thud that was discomfortingly final. Other elves stepped up to flank them, with two more behind. Silently, they allowed themselves to be moved along through a tall tunnel. The area was dimly lit by candles in delicate metal lanterns attached to the walls of the rock tunnel. Tronus attempted to stop to study the lanterns but was gently nudged ahead by one of the elves who followed them. When they finally cleared the tunnel, they were stunned to find themselves in a massive cavern, the depths of which faded into dim, indistinguishable features—vague shapes of rock-carved habitats as high up as they could see. A soft light came from high above them, and Tronus decided that there were more glow lanterns above, as even if the crater of the dead volcano did allow light within, it was dark outside.

They continued on, down what appeared to be a main avenue, with structures that looked like living quarters on each side. As they passed another lane that led off to their left, Jade's nose detected the familiar scent of horses, and her acute night sight, though nothing like a wizard's, could still make out lines of stables running off into the distance. As they neared a central park-like area, with trees growing from excavated areas in the rock floor, they saw male and female elves gathering wood and lighting bonfires in open pits. Most of the elves were dressed in leather pants and vests, but some of the older ones wore long robes in delicate pastel colors, gathered at the waist. Jade, Tronus, and Ferrel craned their necks as they walked by to get a good look at the Ileana citizens of Mt. Thorn. They were tall and lithe in movement, as were all the elves, though these had skin bronzed from the sun. The coloring of hair and eyes varied somewhat, though few were as blonde as the Florian elves and most had a mixture of dark to light brown hair, and there were more brown-eyed elves than would be seen in Quelean.

Before the travelers could observe more, they were moved deeper into the farther recesses of the mountain, where the avenue widened and angled upward. Ahead of them, they could see tall lanterns flanking a walkway that led up to wide steps before a huge edifice. This structure blended into the sides of the cavern and looked to be at least three stories high, as that was the count of open-air balconies and the windows above them that stood out from the walls of the cavern. Unlike on the utilitarian lodgings of the people, the wide wooden doors at the top of the stairs were intricately carved and polished to a high sheen. As they walked up the steps, those tall doors were swung open by the two elves that stood on either side of Vaester Shee.

The vessel of the Ileana gripped a tall staff in one knobby-fingered hand. The staff was ornately carved in a twisting vine and leaf motif, and using it for support, Vaester Shee didn't appear as bent as he had when looking down on them from above. Still, the fellow travelers guessed that had been a careful illusion for their benefit. Vaester Shee's hazel eyes glittered in the firelight from the lanterns on either side of the huge doors, and his mouth spread in a wide grin. Jade felt a jolt of warning tighten her stomach.

"Welcome, emissaries from the good King Filemon," Vaester Shee said, gesturing toward the interior of the edifice. "Come in, please."

None of the three missed the sardonic tone in the old elf's voice. Tronus glanced worriedly at the other two, but both Jade and Ferrel stared directly ahead. Their guards dropped back as they followed Vaester Shee into his dwelling, but they now were flanked by the two elves that had stood on either side of the vessel. The fact that the vessel of the Ileana walked with a sprightly step, his staff clicking lightly on the stone floor in time with his step, also belied the previous impression of advanced age he had projected.

I've got a feeling we're in for it now, Tronus thought gloomily. His hand rose to lightly touch his chest where the silver amulet hung from the chain around his neck, creating a small bump under his yellow vest. Anyone looking at him would think he was simply stroking his luxuriant red beard. Before he had a chance to formulate a quick prayer, a door opened down the hallway, and another elf stepped out, as if mentally commanded by Vaester Shee before they'd even reached the door.

They followed the vessel into a large room and heard the door close quietly behind them. The room was not unlike a comfortable study in the castle of a baron or even King Filemon. Large, soft, woven rugs in bright sunny colors covered the floor before the large fireplace, and opposite that was a grouping of two large stuffed chairs with accompanying small tables. On the rug before the fireplace sat a smaller, round table, surrounded by three hard-backed chairs and one larger chair with a soft cushion in the seat and well-worn arm rests. The vessel of the Ileana went to the arm chair before the fireplace and lowered himself with a sigh. He moved his hand to indicate they should each take one of the chairs.

"We thank you for having allowed us an audience," Jade began.

The vessel raised his hand, palm open, before she could say more. "Let us dispense with your rehearsed speech, and tell me where the Florian are massed to begin their attack, and when that attack is to take place."

Tronus' mouth dropped open, as did Ferrel's. Jade reddened and stared back at the vessel for a few heartbeats, before all three of them started to speak at once.

"That's a dangerous accusation—" Ferrel boomed.

"What is this—?" Tronus stammered.

"I beg your pardon!" Jade shushed the other two with a violent jerk of her hand in their direction. "The Sholeen have been allies of the Ileana and trading partners for years. I find no reason to insult us in this manner."

"You haven't been home in a while, have you, Jade Sholeen? According to the leader of the Lestrami, who, I believe, is master of *all* of your tribes, your people wish to stay out of the business of the elves. Anyone violating that is considered to be without the diplomatic protection we would otherwise offer to your kind."

Ferrel leaned forward slowly, both large hands on his knees, his eyes narrowed menacingly. "Seems like you're forgetting me and Tronus here aren't members of the Lestrami. You going to toss out that diplomatic protection for one of King Filemon's citizens, too?"

Jade raised her hand to forestall any more eruptions from Ferrel. "You are correct that we are not aware of much that has transpired between the Ileana and Florian over time. That is one of the reasons we have come here. We do know that the situation between your two clans has accelerated within this last year, after many years of minor skirmishes."

"And you wonder for the cause?" Vaester Shee's voice rasped. "I can give you that much, Lestrami woman. We Ileana knew Rolf had been captured but did not know of his *murder* at the hands of Maelthor until about a year ago. Our prior attempts to contact the vessel of the Florian were met with silence over the years. Having finally decided to free his son, Iledan took a party and swore they would either return with Rolf—or his own dead body. We got Iledan's dead body in return!"

At that moment, an armed elf appeared at Ferrel's side, as if he had emerged out of the wall.

"Now wait a minute, boy-o," Tronus said, his hand on Ferrel's arm. "We're drifting from the problem here. Seems like the revered vessel here thinks we're spies. That's what you're saying, isn't it?" Tronus saw that he had taken the vessel by surprise. "Maybe you'd like us to holler to the heavens and make enough of a ruckus so you could have a good reason to slap us in irons. We'd make some good bargaining pieces for you, wouldn't we?"

By now, Jade's hands had tightened into fists, and her chest heaved as she sucked in a gulp of air. Her wide brown eyes turned from Tronus to Vaester Shee, as the realization of the truth behind what Tronus said dawned on her. She shook her head to regain more clarity, her face taking on the smoothness of a practiced calm in battle, for which the Lestrami were famous. When she spoke, her husky voice was soft and controlled.

"I'm afraid the vessel of the Ileana is mistaken in his assumptions or has been getting incorrect information from some quarter. We three are not part of any Florian plot, and we weren't hired by them. We were, in fact, sent by Inspector Sandoval Carmichael of the Royal Bureau of Investigation. We are on his orders from King Filemon to attempt some kind of agreement between the elven clans to meet and make peace."

"Enough of this!" Vaester Shee slammed his fist on the arm of his chair and rose quickly. Jade, Tronus, and Ferrel all jumped up at the same time, uncertain, their hands automatically going to their weapons. The other elf stepped up next to Vaester Shee, the spear in his hands aimed in Jade and Tronus' direction. The elf next to Ferrel placed a vise-like grip on Ferrel's elbow.

Ferrel's reaction was immediate. He twisted and spun away from the elf, pulling his arm free, and grabbing the elf. Ferrel twisted the elf's arm up and around his back, lifting him as he did, and threw the elf to the ground. Before he had completed the movement, Vaester Shee stepped forward and lightly touched Ferrel's arm. A mark appeared immediately, a drop of blood visible upon that pinprick. Ferrel's dark eyes glazed over, and his body crumbled slowly, even as he turned a confused, questioning gaze toward Jade. Neither Jade nor Tronus had the opportunity to take action, for as soon as Ferrel moved, the elf covering them grabbed Jade around the neck, pulled her head back, and pressed his knife tip against her jugular vein. Tronus stiffened, his small knife in his hand raised defensively. He watched as both of his friends were pulled away from the vessel of the Ileana.

Having been Number One of the Thunderstorm Mountain Dwarves for many years, Tronus knew the wisdom of caution, even as he cursed himself for not having attacked the vessel directly before he could move against Ferrel. But reprimanding himself was not part of his mental makeup, so Tronus merely shrugged and placed his knife in Vaester Shee's outstretched hand.

"A wise move, dwarf." The Ileana vessel didn't attempt to conceal his contempt for his visitors. He turned his back on Tronus and flipped his gnarled hand at the two warrior elves to dismiss them and their charges.

"You won't get anything out of us but what little we know," Jade threw at him as the elf shoved her toward the door, following the other elf who carried Ferrel's inert body with little effort. "Protect yourself, Tronus," Jade called to him. "Tell him what you know."

She was pushed through the door that swung back and snapped shut behind them. Tronus gazed calmly at Vaester Shee. His hand reached up to grasp the amulet beneath his vest. Drawing his hand down, he stroked his luxurious beard, patting it against his chest as he resumed his seat. The vessel stood next to the fireplace, one hand resting on the mantel, his hazel eyes narrowed upon Tronus. The silence was beginning to make Tronus uncomfortable when the door opened, and another elf stepped across the threshold. Vaester Shee nodded to the elf, who stepped up to Tronus and, placing his hand on the dwarf's shoulder, pulled him upright and led him away.

The elf then moved Tronus ahead of him, nudging him whenever he hesitated, until they had gone down several stairwells that ended in a long, brightly lit hallway with doors on each side. Each door had a small square opening in it covered with bars, but they were too high for Tronus to see into the rooms. *More like cells*, Tronus thought. He glanced back at the elf behind him and stumbled, crying out loudly as he fell to his hands and knees. The elf was upon him immediately and pulled the dwarf up roughly.

"None of your tricks dwarf," he said tightly in Tronus' ear.

Huffing, Tronus glared at the elf warrior. "Our hallways in Thunderstorm Mountain are smooth, with nary a bump to catch an unfamiliar boot. Maybe we could give you boys some tips on how to accomplish that."

The elf leaned over Tronus, his eyes dark with menace. Looking up in defiance, Tronus saw Ferrel's face appear in the barred opening of the cell on the opposite wall. Tronus winked as the elf grabbed his arm and shoved him ahead. They stopped at the end of that hallway, and the elf pushed Tronus inside a cell and shut the door behind him.

It took a few moments for Tronus' sight to become accustomed to the dim light in the small room. The only light came from the window in the door, which cast a shaft of wavering, yellow light onto a small table. He saw there was also one chair next to a bedroll that had been spread on the rock floor. But Tronus hadn't spent his life within the confines of Thunderstorm Mountain not to be able to adjust his sight to dim, filtered light.

Listening for the fading footsteps of the elf, Tronus nodded, satisfied. He hefted the chair and took it to the door. Stepping up on it, Tronus peered out at the hallway. The flickering light made odd shadows on the rock walls. He cleared his throat loudly, then coughed. A faint chuckle came to his ears.

"I think they've left us for now, old fellow!" Ferrel called out.

"Quiet, you two!" Jade's rasping voice said. "If they think we're communicating, they'll move us. Just let me see whether I can salvage anything from this."

Ferrel's voice was low, and the note of sadness in it struck a stabbing pain in Tronus' chest. "Take care of yourself, dear," he said softly. "We will make it out of here in no time. Just don't tick off the old guy, okay?"

Jade's chuckle was cut off by the clang of a far-off door and the footsteps of someone coming toward them. Tronus jumped down from the chair and moved it back to its spot by the little table. He moved back to the door and put his ear to it, listening with every fiber in his body. Another door nearby slid open, and he heard Ferrel's rough voice.

"Watch it there, fellow. No need to shove. I'll come along nicely."

Then the slam of that cell door and the sound of Ferrel's clumping boots faded down the hallway. Tronus continued to listen but finally decided to rest a little. He had to keep his strength up. He unrolled the bedding and crawled inside. He meant to lie quietly and keep his ears open, but no sooner had he lay down than his eyes closed and sleep took him.

A howl awoke Tronus with a jolt. He was on his feet before his mind was even cleared of sleep. Moving quickly to the cell door, he pressed his ear to the rough wood. It was faint and far off but distinctly male in nature. Not an animal nor a female. It was the lusty howl of anger and pain—that of a man. It came again, falling off with a long wail and then silence. Tronus knew it was Ferrel. He could envision the huge man fighting with his last breath, crying out in defiance, even in the face of sure death.

Oh, my boy! Tronus groaned and slumped down on the bedroll. *May whatever gods you look to bring you peace and cease the agony in your final hours. Damn these Ileana!*

His ears pricked up at the sound of footsteps coming near, but the footfalls stopped before they reached his door. He heard another door open—and then Jade's voice, strong and clear.

"Don't let them break you, Tronus!" she called out and then uttered a sharp curse as, he suspected, she was probably yanked away. The sound of footsteps shuffled back down the hallway. Tronus didn't think he could take it. Not Jade! He tried to shut his ears to all sounds but knew it wouldn't do any good. All he could do was prepare for his own turn, which would come next.

Not allowing himself any more time to ponder the fate of Jade and Ferrel, Tronus pulled the ancestral amulet out from under his vest and pressed the carved family shield against his forehead as he chanted softly:

"Water, rock, leaf, and bough,

Revered ancestors hear me now!

Leaf, bough, water, rock,

My thoughts are clear,

My memory is locked!"

Sighing with the wash of calm that flowed over him, Tronus pulled open his vest and dropped the amulet back inside. He turned at a sound outside the door. Slowly, it swung open and the same elf warrior that had brought him to the cell motioned for him to follow. Tronus took a deep breath and complied.

CHAPTER 9

THE GHOST OF ROLF ANDELAR

With the Glaistig's hands gripping one ankle, Sandoval continued downward, deeper into the green pool. Even as his lungs were about to burst, his natural curiosity about his environment forced him to take in his surroundings. Not that he could see that much—clinging water vines drifting about him, obscuring his sight. But he could see the Glaistig below him, her mouth twisted in a rigid smile, sharp fangs bared in triumph. Oddly, he paused in wonderment that this peaceful pool beneath the falls could have such depth to it. Then, a bump of his head against hard rock shocked him into the realization that he was being pulled down a long tunnel beneath the falls. The shock took him by surprise, and he almost cried out in pain. He could imagine the Glaistig crowing with delight. And then, quite suddenly, she was jerked away, disappearing even as Sandoval felt his ankle freed. Desperate to reach the surface before his lungs gave out, Sandoval thrust himself upward out of the tunnel and broke the surface of the pool, frantically gulping for air.

Grasping the grass at the edge of the pool, Sandoval pulled himself from the water in rhythmic jerks, pulling out his legs and scrambling the final feet to give himself distance from the pool, in the event the Glaistig recovered and came for him again. Collapsing to the ground, he continued gulping in lungfuls of air, his hands still clawing the ground as he pulled himself toward his discarded staff, which was a short distance from him on the grass. On the edge of complete exhaustion, Sandoval felt something beneath his hand at the same time he became aware of a presence looming above him. Sandoval looked up to see a shimmering shape standing at the edge of the trees. As he rubbed the water from his eyes, the figure seemed to gain solidity, though still iridescent, as if standing behind a veil of mist. It was a headless specter, a muscular male in appearance, clad in brown leggings and tunic—and his right arm curled around a head, which was that of an elf.

"Rolf Andelar, I presume." Sandoval's voice gasped out the words as he wearily stood. "Do I have you to thank for my rescue?"

The ghost grasped its head in both hands and held it up for Sandoval to get a full view of the visage of what once had been a handsome, dark-skinned man with long brown hair. Beneath open eyes, clouded white in death, the cold blue lips of the phantom cracked apart in a smile. "My legacy must live!"

The air appeared to vibrate with the sounds that were almost a wail. The words appeared to emit from the gaping mouth, though the lips didn't move to form the words.

Sandoval felt a shiver run up his spine, assisted by the chill of his wet robe as much as the oddity of an unattached head becoming animated. Then, the spirit tucked its head back under its arm and stepped up to him. Sandoval could feel cold air bathe his face, as if a breath had been expelled by the specter. The ghost lifted his hand and pointed to Sandoval's clutched fist. Sandoval looked down at his hand in confusion, opened his fingers, and stared at the ring in his palm, silver gleaming through the mud that encased it. He looked up at Rolf's ghost and opened his mouth to speak, but the hand merely raised in a gesture of farewell as darkness enveloped Sandoval.

Sandoval heard the murmur of voices before his eyes snapped open. Sitting up, he blinked twice before he realized the reason his eyes seemed to be unfocused was that there was a face only inches away from his, blue eyes peering owlishly at him. Sandoval jerked back spasmodically, his hands coming up to ward off what could have been another specter, but it turned out to be merely the round face of an old man, framed in white hair that was cropped in an inverted bowl shape about his head. The old man emitted a high chuckle.

"Will Wiggins," Sandoval croaked out. "How did you get here, old man?"

"I live here, *young* man." Will Wiggins pulled himself upward and brushed his brown robes to straighten them. "I'd like to know just how you got here. I'm getting pretty tired of people just popping up around here without invites. My poor Flora has been running all morning, just trying to keep up with taking care of your friends. If it isn't a bowl of soup, it's a warm blanket or a cold compress, or—"

"My friends?" Sandoval grabbed the staff that lay next to him and scrambled to his feet, spinning around to take in the main tower room. "Where are they?"

"Sleeping by now, I hope," Will responded curtly and moved to settle himself slowly in an overstuffed chair with a sigh.

"How many?" Sandoval said, almost dropping the object he still clutched in his hand. Without taking his eyes from Will Wiggins, he slipped it in a pocket as he brushed the dirt and grass from the grimy robe.

"A man, woman, and dwarf. He was here before—the dwarf."

"Tronus," Sandoval murmured, grabbing the arm of a chair on the other side of the table next to Will's chair. He lowered himself heavily. "Morning … what time?"

"You do jump from one subject to another, don't you?" Will grumbled. "Earlier than I'm used to rising, I can tell you. But there's nothing that will get you up and running as quickly as two dragons alighting on your front lawn and demanding a response from within. Nearly knocked my front door off the hinges."

"Moitha."

"Huh?" Will leaned in closer to Sandoval, his hand cupped over his ear. "Was that a name? They didn't introduce themselves to me," Will growled indignantly. "Just dropped your friends and took off, spraying dust, leaves, and twigs all over the place and scaring the stuffing out of Flora."

"I'd like to speak to them, if I may," Sandoval said, his mind working over the latest news.

"Suits me," Will responded, "*Flora!*" the old man thundered in a voice that didn't seem weak with age at all.

The kitchen door swung open, banging into the wall, as Flora ran into the room, her eyes wide with terror.

"They're not back again, are they?" she cried, brandishing a large wooden ladle.

"No, young one, I'm sorry. Got carried away with myself. This man wants to see his friends. Guess he could use some cleaning up also. Do you have a change of clothes in that bag?" Will pointed at the leather bag that hung around Sandoval's chest.

Sandoval looked down at the battered bag, momentarily amazed that it had survived the events of the day—or the previous day, or whatever. "Yes, I do, thank you."

"You might want to let him clean up before he sees his friends. I suppose we should also put on some more vittles for the bunch of them. I'm getting kind of hungry myself, and I don't think you've eaten since yesterday, my girl."

Sandoval followed Flora through a doorway that led to a short hallway, off of which were four doors. He marveled at the economy of the tower. It was difficult to tell how much space was contained within it, but it seemed much larger than it had looked from outside. Flora opened the first door, and Sandoval stepped into a room with a bed, chest of drawers, table, and chairs. A wash bowl and jug filled with water sat on top of the chest. Sandoval poured the water into the deep bowl and began to wipe the remains of the green pool from his face and hair with a wet cloth and some sweet-smelling soap. He pulled a clean robe from his leather bag, shook it out, and muttered a brief spell, watching, satisfied, as the damp, wrinkled cloth dried and smoothed out. Taking off his soiled robe, he dug into the pocket and pulled out the object he had brought from the green pool. It lay in his palm—a dirt-encrusted silver ring, the wide band engraved with elven characters. He dipped it into the bowl and wiped it dry with a corner of his soiled robe.

Sandoval placed the ring on the dresser top and tossed the soiled robe onto the bed. Then he pulled on the clean robe and tied a sash around his waist. He tumbled the remainder of the contents of the bag onto the bed and left them there, taking only the comb to draw it through his hair. He inspected his likeness briefly in the mirror over the chest. Then, nodding, he picked up the ring and slipped it into his pocket. Taking up his staff, he stepped out of the room. Flora was still standing there, her hands clasped lightly together. Sandoval looked at her closely, marveling at the delicate beauty of her face, composed and glowing rosily with youth. Her wisps of curly brown hair framed a face dominated by large soft brown eyes with flecks of gold glinting in them. Her smile brought one in return from Sandoval.

"I hope I haven't kept you waiting, young lady."

"Not at all, sir," Flora said in a softly modulated voice. "Actually, I stepped away to check on our food and have just now returned. Your friends are in the other three rooms. That one next to you is occupied by Mr. Tronus."

"That would be Mr. Longbottom, actually." Sandoval smiled warmly at her, his black eyes softening involuntarily.

"Oh. When we picked them up off the lawn outside, he just stood at attention, said 'I am Tronus,' and collapsed. I misunderstood."

Sandoval chuckled, nodded, and stepped to the door. He turned the handle quietly and opened the door to the sound of Tronus' heavy snoring.

"He sounds normal from here," he told the girl, then slipped into the room and closed the door behind him.

Sandoval studied his friend for a few moments. It appeared that Tronus had been placed there, still unconscious and fully clothed. Sandoval shook his head, noting how horrified his friend would be when he saw the condition of those clothes, filthy and all one-toned grimy brown, rather than their natural bright colors. Knowing how particular Tronus was about his clothes—and cleanliness, in general—Sandoval was almost afraid to waken him. He reached down and lightly touched Tronus on the shoulder. The dwarf's eyes fluttered before snapping open and staring wildly at nothing.

"Who's there?" Tronus croaked in a rough voice, his body stiff and hands flailing before him.

"Tronus," Sandoval said quietly, placing a hand on the dwarf's shoulder to hold him down. "It's Sandoval."

Tronus did not seem to respond to Sandoval's voice, but he did drop his hands to his side, his round eyes still staring at the ceiling. Sandoval raised his staff and tapped it lightly on the floor until the blue gem in the carved eye at its top began to glow softly. He lowered the staff and touched the gleaming stone to Tronus' forehead, then briefly closed his eyes in concentration. When he lifted the staff, Tronus' eyes blinked twice, and then he looked at Sandoval.

"Where in blazes am I?" he said, sitting up and throwing his legs off the bed. "Damn that Vaester Shee! I hope you gave him a piece of your mind, Sandoval. He jailed all of us! I was afraid we were going to be mesmerized." Tronus' eyes became wild. "Ferrel and Jade—they may have been tortured to death!"

"They're here also. I don't know their condition yet. Don't you remember being carried here with them?" Sandoval asked quietly.

"Carried? How?" Tronus stared at him, uncomprehending for a moment. Then he looked down at his clothes and the dusty, scuffed boots still on his feet. His eyes widened in horror. "By the gods!" Tronus began to pat himself all over, frantically, as if to check for injuries or sore spots. He grabbed his shirt at the chest and sighed his relief when his hand closed over the slight impression beneath the filthy shirt—he still had his amulet. "I said the words, Sandoval. At least, I think I did … I remember …" He shook his head furiously, his dusty beard flying back and forth emitting a small cloud of grime. He slapped absently at it and held it up for inspection. At the sight of the tangled mess, he groaned. "I heard Ferrel crying out—a terrible sound. And then Jade was taken away. …" Tronus' shoulders sagged.

"A nice bath, and you'll be as good as new, Tronus." Sandoval patted his shoulder. "If you hadn't repeated the spell I gave you, you wouldn't have come around so quickly. Let's call Flora and see if she can draw you a bath. I am not sure about Ferrell and Jade. I have to check on them, but I think I will need her services there. I also must notify Director Tantilus that I am alive and well."

Sandoval left Tronus still sitting on the bed, shaking his head at his soiled and altogether useless clothes. Flora appeared almost immediately, coming out of one of the rooms opposite Tronus' as Sandoval stepped out into the hall.

"Sir … Inspector … the lady still sleeps. I think I have a draught that may help her. I suspect the same of the gentleman in the next room. Neither of them seems to have fared as well as your friend Tronus. I guess you may have helped in that quarter." Her gold-flecked eyes flashed as her grin widened.

"A last-minute thought. But I am still missing one of my party, and I must find him before we can proceed. Would Will mind if I went to the tower? I must send a message to my director. And Tronus could use some cleanup."

"Will Wiggins is in his room sleeping right now, but you may go up to the tower. I will see to Tronus and the other two," Flora assured him.

Sandoval nodded and left the hall to climb the stairs to the tower room. He was surprised to see the sun high in the sky and the day bright and clear. A warm breeze ruffled his hair as he opened his leather bag and rummaged around, finally pulling forth a bright ball. *Time to accelerate this situation*, he thought. Angelon wouldn't be pleased, but bureaucrats rarely appreciated action over analysis. He muttered a few words and spun the ball in his hands until it began to glow and rise from his outstretched palms. The small, glowing object hovered only momentarily, then shot out of the open casement and disappeared from sight. Satisfied, Sandoval started to retrace his steps to the rooms below when his eyes caught the gleam of sunlight off metal. Curious, he stepped over to a table covered with books. It was the metal clasp on one of them that had flashed at him. He lovingly ran his large hand over the ornate leather of the cover and flipped open the clasp. It was only for a little peek. Not like he was going to steal it or anything. But he still jumped involuntarily at a sound from below and chuckled to himself, shaking his head.

When he got downstairs, he found Jade sitting up, braced by Flora, who was sitting next to her on the bed, holding a cup to Jade's lips. Jade took a sip, screwed her beautiful face into a grimace, and emitted a gagging sound.

"Yaaah, that's foul!" Jade pulled her head back and looked up at Sandoval, her eyes narrow and wary. "What are you doing here?" she demanded in a gruff voice.

"Is that any way to welcome one of your rescue team?"

Sandoval couldn't help but notice how drawn and pale her face was. Yet, other than her being distraught and confused, he didn't notice any obvious physical marks on her from the severe interrogation Tronus implied. Her strong, tanned arms, exposed by the sleeveless leather tunic she always wore, were unmarred. His brows twisted in consternation before he hid his concern behind an appropriate smile.

Jade continued to glare up at him, but her countenance began to soften. A couple of shakes of her head, and her eyes appeared to gain clarity.

"What the blazes am I saying? How did we get here? Where are Ferrel and Tronus?"

"In their rooms. Tronus is cleaning up, and I expect you could use some cleanup also. But I think you'd better help me with Ferrel first. If he wakens as … upset … as you did, I may need your calming influence."

Jade nodded, still shaking her head as if to clear it. Flora rose and handed Sandoval the pitcher and cup she had carried in. After assisting Jade in rising to her feet, Flora left them at the door to Ferrel's room. When they opened it, the big man was sprawled on his back on a small bed, his long arms and legs hanging over the side. Jade rushed to him and inspected his body briefly. Sandoval, intent on the inspection as well, didn't miss the questioning look on Jade's face—his muscled body had not a scratch upon it. Sandoval gently moved past Jade, lifted Ferrel's head, and poured a good amount of the draught between his lips. With his eyes still closed, Ferrel gulped the liquid and gagged convulsively. His eyes flew open, wide and wild. He rose so quickly, he knocked Jade off her precarious perch beside him on the small bed. She hit the floor as he flailed his arms, striking out. Sandoval had the presence of mind to step back, outside of the range of Ferrel's fists. Jade scrambled back away from the bed and gained her foothold. Ferrel eyed Sandoval menacingly as he moved toward him.

"What are you doing here, wizard? We were warned about you!"

As Ferrel raised his fist, Jade grabbed his arm and wrestled him back to the bed. Ferrel turned and saw her, his face clouded with confusion.

"Easy, boy!" Jade laughed lightly, though her laugh sounded hollow. "Give yourself a moment to clear the cobwebs."

Ferrel grabbed his head with both hands, as if trying to squeeze the cloudiness away. When he lowered them, his eyes appeared clear.

Sandoval looked down at the cup in his hand, raised it to his nose, and sniffed. "I'm going to have to get some of this stuff."

"Gaaawd! It tastes like cattle dung!" Ferrel stuck his tongue out as if the air alone would rid him of the taste. "What's happened to me? I feel as if my head's been under water."

"You and me both, my man. I think we may not want to know, though the last thing I vaguely remember is being on the road to Quelean. We were instructed—" She shook her head again, her brows knitted in concentration.

"To kidnap Trelaine," came Tronus' gruff retort.

They spun around to see the dwarf standing in the doorway in clean pants and a clean, if wrinkled, red shirt. His cheeks gleamed and his luxuriant red beard and hair stood out from his head in curling wisps. Sandoval cocked an eyebrow at the dwarf, who seemed to be no worse for his ordeal now that he was clean.

"Your memory appears to have returned," Sandoval said. "Do you recall why Vaester Shee wanted Maelthor's sister kidnapped?"

"Vaester Shee was arguing with someone—they thought they'd knocked me out with some foul-smelling stuff. Vaester Shee said he wanted Maelthor and Nortenaine to suffer as they had. Another elf asked him if that would appease their gods and get them back to the sacred places in the Grimwood. Seems they're pretty desperate about it. I guess they figure they've been abandoned long enough. Vaester Shee said after we got Trelaine back to Mt. Thorn, he would make sure the Florians knew the *humans* had done it. Then the stuff must have started working. I don't remember anything else."

Jade and Ferrel both watched Tronus, their mouths open in astonishment. Jade recovered first.

"How did you—?"

"Remember all that," Ferrel finished for Jade.

"So how did he figure we could get to Trelaine? Do they have someone who is supposed to bring her to us?"

Sandoval cut off further comment with a sharp upraised hand. Jade looked around as if expecting someone to be hiding behind a curtain, but she nodded acknowledgement.

"Looks like Tronus had some charm on him." Ferrel shook his head in wonder. "How else could he have kept awake that long? Your work, wizard?"

Sandoval gazed at the affronted Jade and Ferrel's glowering stare.

"Tronus had a little protection of his own. I merely reinforced it. I expected Vaester Shee to have some tricks ready for us. I think you both know that his magic may have *turned mine off*, so to speak. As it was, that spell barely worked for Tronus. If he weren't such a cussed stubborn old guff, it may have failed. I'm more concerned with your miraculous rescue by dragons and the sound physical condition of both of you."

"I don't remember much after we were forced to drink the stuff Tronus talked about," Ferrel said. His eyes widened. "I think I remember Jade screaming and telling them to keep something away from her. Then everything went black."

"I don't remember screaming," Jade said softly.

"I suppose it's possible all the torture was mental and not physical. You were drugged. If you minds were pliable enough, you could have been made to believe you were seeing something—or someone—that wasn't there."

They stared at Sandoval, Ferrel's head nodding absently.

"So, what do we do now?" Jade asked.

Tronus humphed and glared at Sandoval. "Well, this old guff is starving. Can we get something to eat in this place?"

"I agree," Ferrel added, now mollified as he contemplated his empty stomach.

"Tronus and I will talk to Flora, and to Will, if he's awake. In the meantime, both of you need to clean up a little."

Tronus sniffed at them, wrinkling his nose, before turning and following Sandoval to the kitchen. Flora was already laying out small pies, hot from the oven, along with cheese and fruit on a large platter when they arrived. She shooed them into the main room and carried in a large carafe filled with beer and four cups. While Sandoval and Tronus poured and sipped the cool beer, Flora returned with the laden tray, as Jade and Ferrel emerged from the hallway. As if by magic, Will Wiggins arrived just as they sat down. Sandoval was beginning to think the girl and the old man had some kind of mental communication going, but he brushed it aside as the pleasure of food reaching his stomach wiped out all other thoughts. They all dug into the cheese, fruit, and spicy pies filled with mushrooms and tubers. It wasn't until they had finished that Jade looked around.

"By the way, where's Hoagy?"

"I suspect he's back at my cottage by now," Sandoval said. The hope in his voice wasn't lost on his companions. "Probably cheating Harald and the boys out of whatever they have in some game of chance."

"Your young man is being held by Nortenaine," Flora said quietly. "So the faeries have reported to me."

"At least we don't need to know where we're off to next," Ferrel said roughly, scraping the floor with his chair as he rose.

At that moment, all of the inhabitants of the tower heard sharp exclamations and high-pitched yells coming from outside. Ferrel, already on his feet, beat Sandoval and the others to the front door. When he threw it open, the big man's eyes widened in astonishment and a loud boom of laughter burst from him at the sight of Harald and all four of the Snufflebeam Company, jumping to the ground from the backs of two dragons. They all threw themselves on the ground of the courtyard and kissed it with yelps of joy. Everyone except Tronus seemed to find it funny.

"At attention, you ragamuffins!" Tronus yelled, stomping out of the door and standing in front of them, red-faced.

Harald recovered first and snapped a brisk salute to his captain.

"Oh, sir! It's so good to see you! We were commanded to accompany the dragons here and I was … not sure. … They are so imposing!"

"Never you mind! Just bring yourself and those lads to attention and quit acting like a bunch of boobs!"

Neither of the dragons was Moitha; both were shiny brown with glowing amber eyes. One of the dragons lowered its head and blinked an eye at Tronus, the size of which was at least as tall as he.

"Our most revered leader instructed us to bring your company of soldiers, as you may need them to extract your assistant Hoagy from the elf city," said the dragon in rumbling but precise speech.

"How did you know of our situation?" Sandoval stepped forward. "Are you the ones who rescued these three?" Sandoval motioned toward Ferrel, Tronus, and Jade.

"It was given to us to perform that deed also. But our most revered leader did not say who bespoke him."

Sandoval smiled and bowed to the dragon as the two huge beasts moved back to gain some wing room. Knowing what was to come, Sandoval and company moved out of the way, reaching the front door as the gust from the first down-thrust of their massive wings reached them. Will Wiggins, who was by now grumbling about the goings-on of creatures, elves, faeries, and humans in general, gave an irritated wave of his hand at the group and stomped off toward his tower. Sandoval bowed to Flora.

"I am afraid we must forego your generous hospitality and leave immediately for Quelean. Grab your knapsacks, everyone. We're off to rescue Hoagy."

"You do that a lot, don't you?" Tronus mumbled.

CHAPTER 10

FAMILY SECRETS

Sandoval gathered everyone together, and then, leading the group with long strides, he started off down the forest lane that went in the direction of where he determined Quelean would be. Ferrel and Jade kept an even stride with him, while Tronus and the Snufflebeam Company stepped lively to keep up. The tall wizard only kept the pace brisk for an hour before he stopped and motioned them all to gather around him. Tronus immediately turned to Harald and tapped the young dwarf on the shoulder.

"All right, Harald. It's safe to give us the details now."

Harald nodded eagerly, grinning with pleasure. "Oh, thank you, sir. I figured you wouldn't want me to blurt out anything in front of ... civilians, so to speak. Well, the dragons popped up at the inspector's cottage and told us we had to warn the inspector that the Ileana was making in force for the eastern border of the Grimwood. Seems the dragons have been keeping an eye on them."

"Lucky for us they were," Tronus said.

"I'm sure they went to check on the Ileana soon after dropping you three off at the tower," Sandoval said. "The dragons wouldn't want this war spreading out on this continent, even though their home in Mordaen is far removed from us. They are wise enough to know that instability on Pacifica may eventually spill over to their domain. And," he added, with a twinkle in his eye, "I think they like us."

Harald stared down at his feet, shuffling them nervously.

"There's more, though?" Sandoval asked him.

"They told us to get the horses outfitted. I'm sorry, Inspector, sir, but even that big black of yours stood calmly, right there under them dragons' noses, and let us saddle him. Hoagy's was kind of skittish, but the others didn't seem to mind much. Made the boys here really nervous."

"We weren't sure they wasn't going to have them horses for dinner!" exclaimed one of the boys. *Waldo*, Sandoval thought.

Harald glared at Waldo and continued. "But I figured if that was it, they wouldn't have wanted them saddled and all. Then those dragons up and told us to let them horses go. Then they said to get on their backs and go with them. I'm really sorry, sir ... and sir," he added to Tronus.

Tronus' face reddened and seemed to be ready to blow up, when Sandoval laughed.

"You're taking the loss of Menopet pretty good, I see," Tronus grumbled.

"I'm not as happy about that as you are," Jade said sharply.

Ferrel nodded solemnly, while Sandoval slipped off his leather bag and sat down, propping his back against a tree. Fumbling within the bag, he brought out his flint and a cheroot and lighted it.

"We might as well settle in for a little while and have a hot cup of cherok and a rest." Sandoval smiled up at them. "There's a bit of a morning chill in the air." *Unusual for summer,* he mused, *as if the forest is a sentient being that has reacted to the troubles within its borders.*

Tronus, Jade, and Ferrel looked questioningly at each other, as Harald directed the boys to take a break and found himself a nice spot to rest.

"So, what do we do now, wizard?" Ferrel asked, fists on his hips.

"We wait for Menopet and the other horses to arrive," Sandoval said through a puff of blue smoke.

"Well, I'll be damned. Do you think he'll get the others to follow him?" Jade wondered.

"I think all creatures have their own means of communicating, and those dragons wouldn't have gotten near Menopet or any of the others unless those animals knew they meant them no harm. How they would direct them to us, I don't know. But Menopet has always had a way of finding me, no matter where I am."

Tronus, Jade, and Ferrel nodded in wonder, and they relieved themselves of their burdens and settled down to wait. Tronus pulled out his pipe and his pouch of sweet weed and began his ritual of packing, tapping, and lighting up. Before long, the Snufflebeam Company had prepared a fire, and the cherok was bubbling. It was almost with a holiday air that they took the brief respite; an opportunity to relax and let the stress of the world leave them by enjoying a warming drink and—for Harald and the boys—a brief nap. Like all soldiers, the first lesson the Dwarves had gotten from Tronus when they were commissioned was to sleep at the drop of a hat when in the field. They could never get enough rest—as long as someone else was standing watch, of course. They all agreed it was the best part of their basic training.

But no sooner had Tronus' pipe and Sandoval's cheroot been extinguished than they heard a soft whinny from the woods. Moments later, Menopet's black head emerged from a stand of tall bushes. Sandoval whistled softly, and the big black stallion came trotting across the clearing, followed by Bully and then Jade's and Ferrel's mounts. Both Jade and Ferrel's horses shied nervously until Jade walked up to them and placed a hand on the soft muzzle of first one, then the other. Ferrel quickly checked the saddlebags, packing what they had brought with them, while Jade checked the gear to make sure the saddles had been cinched properly.

Tronus kicked the boot of Tumpe Snufflebeam, who just happened to be the dwarf nearest him, causing him to jerk upright. As if choreographed, Harald and the other three popped awake also.

"Up and at 'em, boys!"

Sandoval finished packing his leather bag on Menopet and gave Bully a brief pat of reassurance after the small gelding had head-butted him for attention several times. Then he turned to Tronus, Ferrel, and Jade.

"I'm afraid you three must head for the Valley of the Mists on the eastern border and keep an eye on the Ileana. You'll have to stay ahead of them. I don't want you caught again."

"Caught?" Harald croaked.

"They'll be fine," Sandoval assured Harald, turning a reassuring smile on the younger Dwarves. "And you must come with me. I'll need your support."

Harald saluted Sandoval smartly.

Tronus shook his head. "I don't think they'll be much help to you, boy-o. They're still green, you know."

"I think you'd be surprised how much help they can give me," Sandoval said cryptically. "Now, keep to the woods until you get to the forest break, then head for the dig. If you can make it back to that spot without being seen, you'll have a great view of the Valley of the Mist and even the plains beyond. That's the route we saw the Ileana taking into the Grimwood before."

"And close enough for me to quickly slip around any party of elves as soon as they've passed. I want to get as much information from my people as possible and alert them to what's happening." Ferrel said.

"Well, let's get going then," Jade said, slapping Ferrel smartly on a heavily muscled arm.

Ferrel swung himself up on his mount easily. Jade assisted Tronus up behind her with a strong arm, and without another word, they trotted off through the trees with reins slack. They knew that their horses would automatically aim for home if given their lead and would find the quickest route to the well-traveled easterly entrance to the Grimwood.

Sandoval helped the Snufflebeam Company up on Bully. Though smaller than Menopet, Bully could easily handle carrying all four of the young Dwarves. He mounted Menopet and lifted Harald to sit behind him. Harald and the others looked askance at each other, then down at the ground, as if judging how far they would fall. Sandoval nudged Menopet lightly with his heel, and the big horse trotted off. Without waiting for the same encouragement from the boys on his back, Bully followed, trotting briskly down the narrow forest lane behind the big black, the young Dwarves bouncing on his back. Sandoval smiled to himself at the sound of startled voices behind him.

"Let go of my neck, you twit!"

"I think I'm slipping!"

"I can't breathe!"

"I've got to hold on to something!"

Behind Sandoval, Harald was uncharacteristically silent. Sandoval could feel his small hands gripping the sides of his robe. They had ridden only a short while when Harald's wavering voice called out, "Shut up that racket, men! You want to draw anything within hearing to us?"

After that, welcome silence settled upon the group; the only sound was the clip-clop of the horses.

Just as dusk settled around them, Sandoval spotted the tunnel through the trees that defined the front entrance to Quelean. Sandoval marveled at the loss of his usually keen sense of direction and distance. It seemed the last time they had started out from Will Wiggins' tower, they had arrived at Quelean from a different direction. *Maybe the elves brought us in by a circuitous route to confuse us*, he thought. *Or I'm losing my touch—or something else is at work here.*

There was no sign of the temporary tents the elves had erected for the Dwarves on their last visit. Sandoval took Harald's hand and lowered him gently to the ground, then swung down himself. It took some time to unclasp the four Dwarves aboard Bully from each other. Milton Snufflebeam, sitting up front in the saddle, was seemed frozen to the saddle horn with a white-knuckled grip. Sandoval had to pry his fingers apart and lift him down. Harald glowered at the young dwarf, disgusted.

"You will all wait out here," Sandoval instructed. "I'm going in to see Nortenaine. If I'm not out by the time Khensu rises, you will seek out Tillie, Harald. You won't have to look far, I'm sure. Just call for her. Have her take you to Tronus."

"But sir, Number One will skin us if we desert you," Harald said.

"He'll appreciate being informed, I'm sure. A soldier's duty is to remain free to fight, not get captured."

Sandoval waved his staff over the five Dwarves. A blue glow spread from the eyepiece and covered the tight group of Dwarves, who had squeezed even closer to each other in fear of the spell's hitting someone instead of just being cast around them. Harald shushed them and watched Sandoval closely as the wizard mumbled a spell. Stepping back from the group as the glow faded, Sandoval nodded to Harald and entered the tunnel. When he glanced back, he saw Harald and the boys still in a tight circle.

"You can move around normally now," he called back, shaking his head with a chuckle as he moved on.

"We might as well get some shut-eye. We may have to leave quickly," Harald said. "Snufflebeam Company, fall out! Gort, you take first watch."

Sandoval walked into Quelean unchallenged and was deciding on his next move when he saw Trelaine walking resolutely toward him. Her brown eyes held his until she stood before him. Sandoval thought briefly that she seemed to have shaken off the melancholy at last.

"Inspector Carmichael," Trelaine's husky voice had a sharp edge to it. "I have been expecting you."

"I did wonder at the ease with which I walked into Quelean. I see no guards about."

"Nortenaine and all of our warriors have gone to set up camp at the eastern border near the Valley of the Mists. They will use that as their base to face the Ileana in the open at last. It will be a glorious battle!"

Sandoval almost jerked back at the force of her declaration. Was there vehemence there also? "I am here to retrieve my assistant, Hoagy, if you would take me to him."

"You may go to him. He is in the same room you shared previously. But you will not be leaving with him."

"Oh?" Sandoval caught the hard light in her dark brown eyes before she lowered them, as if in embarrassment.

"I should apologize, but the only reason you had no trouble getting into this city was the spell placed upon it by Maelthor before he left. Normally, no human would be able to get past it, but since your heart is kindly toward the elves, you have accomplished entry. Unfortunately, exiting will be impossible."

Trelaine turned without a word, and Sandoval walked beside her toward the small guard hut.

"I'm surprised you did not go with Maelthor and Nortenaine to confront the Ileana," Sandoval said quietly, his eyes on her profile. "To see the final defeat of the Ileana."

Trelaine tossed her reddish-brown hair as her brown eyes narrowed. "What do you mean by that, wizard?"

"I have been told you are a direct descendant of the original high lord of the Ileana, through your mother, Maeleana. Would that have made you a cousin to Rolf Andelar?"

Trelaine stumbled, and Sandoval reached out deftly, his hand gripping her elbow to steady her. Two bright red spots dappled each cheek.

"You insult me, Inspector Carmichael." Trelaine's voice was low, and Sandoval recognized that her reaction was tightly controlled. "I loathe the memory of Rolf Andelar and what he did to my sister, Lilliana."

"Did you not attempt to talk her out of going to him?" Sandoval's black eyes did leave her face as he continued to probe softly.

"I loved my sister, but she was a foolish female who thought she had deceived me and that I would not discover she was meeting Rolf Andelar secretly. As if that silly wood faerie could keep such knowledge from me!" Trelaine spat the words out, her normally honeyed voice cracking in anger. She shook her head and took a deep breath. "I apologize for that, Inspector. We elves do not approve of openly expressing our emotions to such a degree. It pained me more than I can say to have such knowledge and remain silent before Lilliana and the rest of our family. I knew that if I tried to pressure her to discontinue seeing Rolf, she would resist. I couldn't tell Nortenaine or Maelthor, for they would have killed Rolf immediately."

"Wouldn't that have solved all of the Florian problems?" Sandoval asked, not unkindly.

Trelaine finally turned away from the penetrating black eyes that gazed down at her. "Nortenaine has always felt that the taking of Rolf Andelar's life would have angered the gods beyond our redemption. It is one thing to fight fairly for your cause but another to coldly execute another elf."

Sandoval realized that Trelaine was just barely containing her anger and frustration at the persistent questioning, but he posed another. "But didn't Maelthor do just that by beheading Andelar?"

"Maelthor reacted immediately upon seeing Lilliana's dead body! There was little thought involved in bestowing pardon upon the person who had caused such a sacrilege. Rolf didn't even try to defend himself or answer for the limp body he pulled from the pool. There was no more reason for Maelthor to withhold his sword's swing than if he had been facing the enemy on the battlefield. If I had been there, I would have done the same, as would Nortenaine or any Florian. That is why Nortenaine determined Rolf's death to be just and has always supported our brother. Now, you will discontinue interrogating me and allow me to leave you!"

With her face flushed, Trelaine turned away from Sandoval and walked swiftly away, leaving him to stare after her. After a few moments, Sandoval continued toward the hut. When he arrived, he knocked lightly once and stepped inside. Hoagy expelled a gasp of relief at the sight of Sandoval.

"Am I glad to see you, sir!"

"You won't be, when you find out that neither of us can leave here, thanks to a spell placed by Maelthor."

Hoagy dropped his eyes. "I know. I've already tried. Felt like someone hit me on the head. I think I passed out. Next thing I knew, I woke up on the bed. I just thought maybe … you …"

"Sorry, Hoagy. My power can't dilute Maelthor's. Maybe a Gold Guild wizard could. Oh, well, let's make the best of it. Please report, Hoagy," Sandoval said, dropping his leather bag on the bed and slumping onto a chair.

"I'm afraid there's not much to report, sir. Either all of the elves, including the women, have joined Nortenaine on the battle lines, or they are staying within their homes. I've seen no one around since I arrived yesterday, other than the one called Lenlael, who brings me food. I did see Trelaine once, when I was out walking about, but she ordered me to stay in my room. She sort of hinted that if I wandered around, something might happen to me."

"Precisely what did she say?" Sandoval raised one black brow in question.

Hoagy closed his eyes and recited, his voice even becoming more melodious, very similar to Trelaine's but with an imperious lilt. "I would caution you, young man, to keep to this hut. There is much tension in

Quelean now, and a human wandering around may be misunderstood. Some young elf may decide that you are the vanguard of a warring party and put an arrow in you."

"Really?" Sandoval took a piece of cheese from the platter on the table and popped it into his mouth.

"It truly gave me the chills." Hoagy flopped down on his bed and stretched out, his head propped on one fist.

"Was that before or after you tested the boundaries of Quelean?" Sandoval asked, smiling knowingly.

Hoagy had the good sense to look slightly embarrassed. "Oh … before, sir. But I was beginning to get concerned. If she had turned on us, they could just as well have decided to pull me out of this bed and string me up. Or do something even worse! You can bet I was relieved to find myself back here when I woke up. Lenlael told me that it was he that found me. He said"—here, Hoagy's voice took on a different lilt, sounding quite like Lenlael's—"'You are lucky, young man, that it was I who discovered you back in the woods, or you probably wouldn't have awakened in your bed.' All I could do after that was pace back and forth and hope you made it away from that horrible creature at the pool!"

The memory of the Glaistig flooded back, and Sandoval shuddered, despite his effort to treat it lightly. "It was a close one, my boy, and not an experience I ever want to repeat, though the ghost was pretty interesting."

"Oh, tell me, sir." Hoagy swung his legs over the bed and sat up eagerly.

"On our way, Hoagy. We have one more stop to make before settling for the night."

"Not a wise thing to go out, sir," Hoagy cautioned.

"I have the benefit of being able to see—or at least, sense—a spell to avoid breaching our confines. And Noona's cottage should be within that boundary anyway. Come; it is dark enough now for us to slip out."

Even though the silence of the forest was not broken by any sounds other than their footsteps, Sandoval had the uneasy, prickling feeling of being followed. Reaching out with his acute senses, he scanned the area around them as they walked, but nothing stirred his heightened awareness. Shrugging it off, he relaxed enough to bring Hoagy current on all that had happened since they had parted at the green pool. Even allowing for the young man's constant interruptions with questions, Sandoval finished telling Hoagy everything by the time they arrived at Noona's cottage. Sandoval was slightly surprised at the promptness with which Noona answered his light knock on her door. She opened it just enough to hurry them inside and close it after them.

"I knew I would see you again, Inspector." Noona's body bent over a sturdy wooden cane.

She's wasting away before our eyes. Sandoval marveled at how much more withered and pale she looked since he had seen her last. Her skin appeared almost translucent. Her voice, though still strong, was kept almost at a whisper as she looked out of her window before waving her hands over it, as if to draw some imaginary curtains. Sandoval decided that was just what she was doing—creating a spell to hide them from any prying eyes. His sight could discern a slight wavering in the air around the window now.

Noona acknowledged Hoagy by offering him a chair but said nothing to the young man. She sat on the small couch opposite the chair where Sandoval sat down and gazed earnestly into Sandoval's black eyes.

"I have the far sight," she said quietly. "But that does not tell me why you would risk coming to see me. I know there is much anger and resentment against you humans right now."

"I know, and that distresses me," Sandoval responded, "but I need your help again, Noona. Maybe to complete a riddle I've been wrestling with. I came to tell you what I learned at the green pool." At the name of the place, Noona visibly winced. Sandoval reached out and took her weathered hand. "I'm not here to bring you more pain, but to bring you solace. I do not believe Rolf Andelar killed Lilliana."

Noona lurched backward and pulled her hand away from him. "You champion her murderer!"

"No, I seek the truth, and so far, I have gotten conflicting stories of the event on that day—even the *official* one." He watched for any reaction from Noona, but she merely stared down at her hands, now clenched in her lap. "From these accounts, a picture is forming for me, and I believe it is the truth of the matter."

"Then he …" Noona began, and then she fell silent, her hands twisting together convulsively.

Sandoval waited, but she didn't finish the sentence. Instead, she rose and went from the room, returning shortly with a garment. She held it out almost reverently to Sandoval. The entire front of the gown was covered with old blood stains on the delicate mauve fabric, from the top neckline to the lower portion, encrusting the entire hemline. He knew immediately what it was—the dress Lilliana had been wearing the day she died. He took the garment and held it up, his eyes scanning the blood stain on the front of the gown. Hoagy leaned forward and gazed at the gown, his handsome young face squinting in distaste. Sandoval looked back at Noona, who had resumed her seat on the couch, her head bowed.

"Your mind is still as sharp as it always was, Noona. You loved Lilliana, did you not?"

Noona nodded silently.

"Then you must know that the evidence of this garment does not support the story of Rolf's tossing her from the ledge under the falls. Do you protect Lilliana's memory or your own skin by being silent?"

Noona raised her eyes to Sandoval's and the rheumy blue eyes cleared suddenly and became hard with anger. "I care little for my own skin. The rest is for you to discover, Inspector Carmichael of the Royal Bureau of Investigation. My Lilliana is dead; others of my kin still live."

And with those words, she clamped her mouth shut and stared off into the distance, her chin jutting defiantly. Sandoval stood and held out the gown for her, but she shook her head roughly, her eyes still avoiding his. He rolled up the gown and stuffed it into his leather bag.

Sandoval then pulled the silver ring from his pocket and handed it to a startled Noona. The old elf woman's hand shook as she took the delicately inscribed ring and stared at it with love and longing.

"It is Lilliana's ring, given to her by the dark elf, Rolf Andelar. She showed it to me just before the end." Noona's voice took on a wistful tone, and her eyes softened as she touched the ring with reverence.

"And the inscription? Can you tell me what it says?" Sandoval watched her brow wrinkle in consternation and her head shake back and forth slowly.

"It says 'To my wife-spirit, Lilliana. Our bond of love will breach the ages.'"

Hoagy's blue eyes rounded, but he said nothing. Sandoval nodded and took the ring back, slipping it in his pocket.

"They were bonded—married—to each other?"

"Yes. This is an inviolate agreement between a male and female elf and requires no approval or formal ceremony, though most do request recognition from their spiritual representative. In this case, they would have known none would come."

"Noona, do you believe Lilliana's life was taken from her purposefully?"

The old woman's eyes hardened, and the pain expressed on her face hit Sandoval with an almost physical impact.

"The hand that killed her did so out of blind faith and bitterness. That hand will also touch me."

Chapter 11

Maelthor's Magic

Sandoval watched dawn lighten the window of their hut as he threw his leather bag over his shoulder, secured the strap across his chest, and took up his staff that was sadly useless in Quelean—its ability to channel his magic was numbed by stronger elven spells. He nudged Hoagy and put a finger to his lips as the young man sat up with a start, wide awake.

"I'm going to find Harald. You must distract Trelaine if she comes. It probably won't work, but I only need a short time."

"But, sir—the barrier ..."

"Will not bar speech, Hoagy."

With that, Sandoval opened the door and slipped out. It was still too early for their morning meal to be brought, and if he was quick, he shouldn't be missed—he hoped. He knew now that there was a murderer in Quelean, one who wouldn't hesitate to dispatch him and Hoagy as well. Now there was an even more urgent need to flee

Quelean, given Noona's pronouncement the night before. It had taken some urging, but the old woman had agreed to let Sandoval and Hoagy take her with them if they were able to escape the confines of the city.

How we're going to do that is anyone's guess, Sandoval thought, as his wizard sight picked out the wavering barrier that Maelthor's spell had put in place. He was close to the spot where Harald and the Snufflebeam Company would be bivouacked. Standing just mere inches from the wavering barrier, Sandoval took a deep breath and concentrated on Harald's round, open young face. He reached out mentally and easily encountered that young dwarf's mind, still peaceful within a veil of sleep. So as not to alarm him, Sandoval nudged gently with his mind. Yet even with that slight prod, he recognized alarm as Harald woke abruptly. Urging soothing waves of assurance, Sandoval beckoned Harald to come to him. Within a minute, Harald's wide-eyed face was before him on the other side of the spell barrier.

"That's far enough, Harald." Sandoval held up his hand in caution.

"That was frightful scary, Mr. Inspector," Harald piped.

"Sorry; I tried to be gentle. We have a situation here, Harald. I need you to contact the wood faerie, Tillie, immediately."

"How am I to do that, sir?" Harald cried and then lowered his voice when Sandoval made a shushing motion. "I don't know where to find her," Harald continued in a whisper.

"Just do as I told you before, and take the boys and the horses into the forest. You won't have to go far. Call up a mental picture of her and call her name. It doesn't have to be loud. She will hear you. Tell her she must get you and the boys to Tronus on the eastern border, so you can tell him that Hoagy and I are captive here in Quelean."

"But the horses! That big black one of yours could stomp us just as well as look at us. And how will Number One get you out of here?"

"Menopet will go with you; don't worry. Tronus should not attempt to get us out of here—he couldn't anyway. He must keep an eye out for the troops from Sanctuary and notify King Filemon that we have been taken. I've no doubt he will see them coming. Now I must get back."

Without another word, Sandoval hurried back toward the hut, as the morning sun was already casting an eerie, misty glow through the trees. Harald stared after him, his brow knotted in worry, before turning away with a sigh to carry out his orders.

Sandoval slipped silently through the door of the hut and almost ran into Hoagy, who was pacing back and forth, staring at the floor. Hoagy's head snapped up, and he let out a surprised gasp.

"Steady there, son," Sandoval cautioned as he slipped off his leather bag.

"I was working myself up to a pretty good panic, sir. Lenlael should be coming with our breakfast any time now," Hoagy said in hushed tones.

The words had barely left his mouth when there was a soft knock on the door. Sandoval brushed a lock of hair from his face and composed himself before he opened the door.

"Ah, breakfast! Come in, Lenlael."

The elf stepped inside, deposited the tray on the table, and left without a word. Sandoval and Hoagy exchanged looks at the cool atmosphere Lenlael left in his wake, but they dove into the pasties stuffed with tubers and assorted vegetables. Sandoval glanced longingly into the cups the elf had brought but was disappointed when he saw it was only water to wash down the food. Finishing in brisk time, they gathered up their meager belongings and started to leave, only to find the door had been latched from the outside. Sandoval frowned at it and motioned Hoagy to follow as he went to the window, lifted the sash, and slid his large body through the small opening, feet first. Hoagy followed—it was a little easier for him, being much smaller than his tall boss. Sandoval smiled grimly and pointed to the latch that had previously barred the window, which was now on the ground.

"Took the opportunity to undo that before returning, just in case."

Hoagy grinned broadly at Sandoval, who was already retreating through the brush.

"Where to now, sir? Do we get Noona?" He spoke in hushed tones as he caught up to Sandoval.

"That is the plan so far."

"And then?"

"That's the part I haven't worked out yet," Sandoval said, weaving in and out of the trees. Hoagy skipped double-time to keep up with Sandoval's long strides.

It seemed to Hoagy that it didn't take as much time to reach Noona's cottage as it had the night before. *Maybe it's the thought of angry elves on our tail that gives us that extra speedy spring in our step,* he thought as he danced impatiently from one foot to the other, waiting for the door to open at Sandoval's light knock. When that didn't happen, Sandoval peered in the front window but could see nothing in the main area of the house. Stamping his staff lightly on the stoop, Sandoval saw the shimmer of a light spell dissipate around the door. Entering with a nervous Hoagy close behind him, Sandoval walked into the back bedroom area and halted abruptly, causing Hoagy to run into his back.

"What is it?" Hoagy spurted, but he saw immediately what had stunned Sandoval.

Someone had evidently been searching desperately for something, as clothing and other articles were strewn about the room, including some delicate jewelry. The amount of the devastation indicated an almost wrathful anger. Sandoval hoped that Noona had not been here at the time, though he guessed she hadn't been. From that leap of logic, it took only a moment to decide where Noona had gone. Before Hoagy could wonder aloud what to do now, Sandoval was off again, calling back over his shoulder, "Hurry, Hoagy. We have to get to her in time!"

By now, Sandoval was running, and Hoagy was fast on his heels. Before they burst into the clearing where Lilliana's sepulcher stood, Hoagy was sure what their destination would be. Curious to finally see the legendary elf maiden under the glass top, Hoagy's eyes didn't immediately register the slumped figure next to the bier, old arms spread against the base of the stand as if attempting to embrace it. Sandoval crouched down to touch the old elf woman's neck, hoping for a pulse.

"Is she …?" Hoagy whispered.

Sandoval nodded his head, his face set in a grim mask. Brushing the gray hair from her face, Sandoval peered closely at her. Even Hoagy, standing over him, could see the harsh red welt around her neck.

Sandoval stood, his hand still resting gently on the old woman's head. It was that tableau that Maelthor found as he and a party of elves burst through the trees.

"As I thought!" he boomed. "He has hounded an old woman to her death! Take him to the fountain in the common. We will charge this miscreant at last!"

"But … we found her this way!" Hoagy protested as two strong elves each grabbed one of his arms and practically lifted him off his feet.

Hoagy turned to Sandoval, who gave a brief shake of his head before allowing two other elves to grip him on either side and shove him forward. As they were being maneuvered out of the clearing, Sandoval turned back to see Maelthor watching as one of the elves lifted Noona's body. As he raised her up, Noona's head dropped back, her long hair cascading down to expose the angry looking welt on her neck. Maelthor's face contorted in anger, and he hurriedly draped a corner of her cloak over her face.

By the time they reached the center of Quelean, many elves had already gathered; Sandoval wondered if some mental communication had drawn them there. There was no wailing or crying for the departed elder, but a soft musical chant grew as more voices joined in the lament for their recently departed. In another time and place and under other conditions, Sandoval may have enjoyed the flawless voices and pure notes of the song. But there was no time now to wonder at the origin of the music or its purpose as he and Hoagy were made to stand within a circle of elves, back to back.

"Well, sir," Hoagy said softly, "here we are in the soup pot again, about to be eaten, so to speak."

"Have faith, Hoagy. The Florian aren't so barbarous as to stew us."

"You think not, wizard?" Maelthor's voice rose as he pushed two elves aside to gain entrance to the inner circle and face Sandoval. "We Florian are not the pleasant, compliant elves you have experienced in the past. Faith!" He spat out the word. "What do you know of faith?"

Sandoval remained silent, watching the elves outside of the circle draw closer and pause, uncertain. Consternation was written on their clear features, male and female alike.

"Well, I can't lay claim to following any structured belief system; most of us humans do have our little ceremonies presided over by wizards of the Blue Guild. Mostly, we put our faith in the natural order of things. But there are always those situations in life that require faith—"

"Enough!" Maelthor cut him off roughly. "You need not try to talk your way out of this one, wizard. You will be restrained until we can hold a proper deliberation on your fate. I hope you like your young assistant, here, as you and he will be living in a faerie hill for some time."

"Will that be with or without a trial?" Sandoval asked drily.

Maelthor glared at him with hard brown eyes, but he did have the foresight to glance around and notice the attentiveness of the community. Some of the elf faces were wrinkled with troubled frowns, and they glanced furtively at each other, though no one spoke.

"You looked at Noona's body," Sandoval interjected while he still had the chance. "Could you determine how she died?"

"I am not a healer," Maelthor responded curtly.

"I should think it was obvious, with but a glance, what the probable cause was."

"You would know better than I." Maelthor sounded triumphant.

"You know as well as I do that I did not do this thing. I was attempting to take Noona with us, to protect her."

Maelthor's laugh was harsh. No sound came from the elves surrounding them. "Protect her from her own people? You are truly foolish, wizard, if you think we will believe that. We all loved Noona."

"One of you obviously didn't."

The gathered community of elves voiced shock at that pronouncement. Murmurs of discontent traveled through them like ripples in a pool, disturbed as they were by such an accusation flung into their midst. Maelthor smiled tightly at their reaction.

"You accuse one of our people? You know little of the family of elves and our bound spirits. None could or would do such a thing! You have sealed your own fate by such a claim. Now you will pay!"

Maelthor raised his arms and began to chant in elfish. The sound was almost like a dirge, oddly discordant and unlike any Sandoval had heard from any elf. A deep red swirl of mist seemed to appear from

Maelthor's open hands, drifting and coalescing into vague shapes that surrounded Maelthor and the elf warriors who made up the inner circle around Sandoval and Hoagy. Hoagy started, jerking against Sandoval's back.

"They … they look like elves!" Hoagy choked out the words. "Are they spirits, sir?"

Sandoval thought he heard words of protest from the outer circle of elves, who began to move away. Even the elf warriors tightly surrounding Maelthor and his two prisoners took a few steps back, their eyes wide.

Maelthor called, "The spirits of our warriors killed in battle will contain these humans for transport to the faerie hill, where they will be entombed. Their souls will taste revenge and be mended."

With that Maelthor turned and strode away. The elves guarding them stood respectfully back from the tight circle of specters that had closed around Sandoval and Hoagy.

"Sir …" Hoagy's faint voice shook. "Will this be painful?"

"I don't believe so, Hoagy. But it may be wise not to look them in the eye."

"I'll just keep mine closed, if you don't mind," came Hoagy's faint reply. "I can't imagine spending the rest of my life imprisoned."

"We are not going to remain prisoners here while great changes are occurring in our world around us."

Hoagy's silence was reply enough for Sandoval. But at the sound of a soft step, Hoagy couldn't help twisting his head around. He peered through narrowed eye slits at the feet of a woman standing next to Sandoval, and Trelaine's voice was immediately recognizable.

"This is fitting for one who has taken our dear Noona from us, Inspector Carmichael." Trelaine's voice was a harsh whisper.

"Are you sure of that, Trelaine?" Sandoval responded quietly, still wary of looking directly at the elf maiden, as he'd have to peer at her through the misty barrier of the elf spirits.

"Who else would have taken her from us—and why?"

"Maelthor was also at the green pool the day that Lilliana died, supposedly at the hands of Rolf Andelar. Did he speak to you about the events of that day?" Sandoval asked.

"Maelthor was deeply disturbed and has continued to refuse to discuss what happened that day with me. But your accusations chill me to the bone, wizard. True, he is bitter and hates the Ileana, but to sacrifice one of ours—it's too unbearable. Still, he had chastised Noona on occasion, accusing her of making a shrine to Lilliana. He felt the gods would forsake us by doing so."

Sandoval didn't respond; he waited for the inevitable.

"You will be interred for a long time," Trelaine said, her mellow voice purring softly. "I have already told you that you will not be able to leave this place, and you cannot now try to force me to assist you."

Trelaine stood facing Sandoval, her chin raised defiantly, her brown eyes fierce. The tight grin that creased her face was lost on the wizard, who continued to keep his eyes downcast.

"I don't need to force you, Trelaine, daughter of Maeleana. You will help us of your own free will."

"And why would I do that, wizard?"

"Because you didn't tell Maelthor that I arrived here with a troop of Dwarves. That tells me you have an agenda of your own. If so, keeping yourself here to guard a wizard and his assistant and serve them meals in their faerie hill is taking you out of the game. The structure and way of life you have here in Quelean may be decided by the clash of Florian and Ileana clans that is inevitable now. You will miss that while you remain behind with the rest of those unable to fight."

"What do you propose, Inspector Carmichael?"

Sandoval smiled to himself—she had used his professional designation. It was a start. "I propose that you release Hoagy and me and accompany us to the Valley of the Mists, where three armies are to converge."

"Three?"

"Don't you think that I would have reported to my superior on the deterioration of the stalemate between the Florian and Ileana before I arrived here again? King Filemon and his troops should be on their way and, in fact, may even have arrived at the designated meeting place already. Are you really going to trust Maelthor to advance any changes that may affect your future?"

Trelaine regarded Sandoval's bowed head with a steady gaze for what seemed a very long time before she smiled again. "I don't trust either of my brothers much, Inspector. I believe Maelthor, in particular, may be bent on destroying the Ileana, regardless how much damage is done to the Florian. Do you really think he was that shocked to see the condition of Noona's body when he found her? Possibly he was covering … something." She shook her head suddenly, mindful of the watchful eyes of the warriors standing off from them, too far to hear her soft words but not too far to see her reaction, as the hardness in her beautiful face softened and a finger touched the corner of one eye to wipe away a tear. "I apologize, Inspector. I believe I still haven't recovered from the loss of a dear friend. At any rate, I must warn Nortenaine of what you have told me. If you will promise to take me with you and not use your magic to harm me or my people, I will release you, once Maelthor has placed you in the faerie hill."

Trelaine didn't see the twist of Sandoval's lips. She stared patiently at the bowed head that concealed his face.

"Extracting us from our current condition may be beyond your power," Sandoval said.

"Do not underestimate me, Inspector Carmichael," Trelaine said, raising her voice as she spun about and walked away.

"Are you sure you haven't just given us away, sir?" Hoagy whispered urgently.

"We will see, Hoagy. True, I've given her a chance to seal our fate."

"I just don't—"

The sound of Maelthor's voice raised in chant cut off Hoagy's remark. His strong voice was joined by other voices, and the sound grew. Hoagy was sure he could feel the air about them vibrating—he was convinced it actually was vibrating—as he and Sandoval were suddenly elevated within the circle of elven spirits. As Maelthor continued to chant, followed by many other elves, Hoagy realized they were being transported out of Quelean. Hoagy decided the best thing was to keep his eyes on the ground that was moving under their suspended feet and try not to imagine the ghosts who cradled them in phantom arms.

It wasn't long before they appeared to slow and then stop. Below them, Sandoval could see green grass on a low rise of hill. He could feel a change in the air around them as the chanting ceased, and they were lowered to the soft grass.

Sandoval heard Hoagy's frightened yipe: "Sir, where are we?"

"At our new digs, I assume," Sandoval calmly replied.

Maelthor now stepped up in front of Sandoval and roughly yanked the wizard's face up to force him to meet his own blazing eyes. "You may take your last look at the open spaces, wizard, and the outside of your new home."

Maelthor's arm swung back and around, followed by Sandoval's and Hoagy's eyes. There was no evidence of the spirit elves, but before them was the rise of a small grass-covered hill. It didn't really look that high, and no door was visible to them. Hoagy began to shake uncontrollably. Sandoval reached behind to grasp Hoagy's hand and squeeze—they were still fastened, back to back, by some invisible means—in an attempt to calm the young man. He was rewarded by the lessening of Hoagy's shaking.

"I believe it could use some windows with curtains and maybe a nice fireplace," Sandoval said, smiling calmly at Maelthor.

CHAPTER 12

HARALD AND TILLIE

"How will we breathe in there, sir? It's not much larger than a grave. I just don't see—oh, I can't do this!" Hoagy cried desperately. The young man spun toward Maelthor, his wide blue eyes blazing. "You'll hear from Baron Toogood, my good man! This will not stand!"

Maelthor ignored the young man and began to chant even louder now, hesitantly joined by the other elves that had accompanied him. Their voices, Sandoval decided, sounded slightly more shaky and uncertain than before. Sandoval also noted the absence of Trelaine within the circle of elves surrounding them.

But no ghostly shapes came at the call this time. Maelthor raised his voice, encouraging the other elves to join him in the chant that spanned the bridge between life and death.

"Revenge will neither soothe the dead nor heal the scars of battle from them," Sandoval observed. "Look closely, Maelthor, they have deserted you."

From the surrounding forest came odd, chilling wails, and smoky shapes appeared to drift from out of the trees that stood a short way from the grassy clearing around the faerie hill. One of the eerie shapes rose high above their heads, then swooped toward Maelthor. As it passed above them, Sandoval could feel the slight chill of the air around them. Maelthor raised his arms to continue his chant, but the ghostly specters that were elf warriors of old now became cruelly twisted shapes of things only barely resembling those warriors, their shadowy mouths gaping open and high shrieks emitting from them.

Now the voices of the elves that had accompanied Maelthor were loudly vocal in protest, calling for Maelthor to cease his spell. All could see the tormented shapes of these spirits writhing in agony, ghostly arms raised in protest and mouths open. The tortured souls continued their horrid howling, increasing to a pitch that would have burst Sandoval's eardrums, had the sounds not ceased abruptly with the sudden appearance of one huge specter that almost covered the entire grassy clearing where they stood. It swirled down from above, aiming directly at Maelthor.

Maelthor stood with arms still raised, but a look of disbelief and shock was on his face. The elf warriors closest to him backed away this time, some pulling their bows and nocking arrows in confusion. But there was no enemy to battle—and no time to come to Maelthor's aid, as the apparition began to slowly encompass the elf and drag him toward the faerie hill. Wresting himself away, Maelthor twisted around and ran toward the borderline of trees, followed by the other elves.

Sandoval and Hoagy stood alone in the clearing and stared at each other in confusion. That confusion faded as sounds of tinkling laughter came from the trees. At those sounds, Sandoval threw his head back and laughed loudly. Hoagy gaped at his boss, unable to take in all that had just transpired. Maybe the inspector had gone crazy from the shock of it all, Hoagy decided. Or maybe the next wave of ghosts would swoop down on them and finally draw them into the hill.

"Sir, we must leave. Quickly!" Hoagy grabbed Sandoval and began to drag him in the direction of the disappearing elves.

Sandoval patted Hoagy on the hand and shook his head, still chuckling. "I don't think you have to worry about the elven spirits anymore, young man."

At that moment, numerous bright spots of light shot out from the trees and circled wildly about their heads, finally lowering toward the ground near them and shimmering into the shapes of several faerie sprites, one of them being none other than Tillie. Also now emerging from the forest was Harald and the Snufflebeam Company. Even Hoagy burst out with laughter and ran to hug Harald heartily, embarrassing the young dwarf, who struggled for release from Hoagy's eager embrace.

"Boy, are we glad to see you, Harald!" Hoagy tried to hug Harald again, but the young dwarf swerved to avoid his arms.

"I assume the elven spirits that almost took Maelthor into the faerie hill were provided by you and your fellow faeries, Tillie," said Sandoval.

"We are always glad to come to the assistance of the great Inspector Carmichael," Tillie piped in her high voice, grinning not at Sandoval but at Harald. "If the Florian elf had not been so assured of his power to control the elf spirits, he could have banished us with a wave of his hand. But we clouded his mind enough so that he had only his eyes to rely upon. Actually, we took the shapes of images drawn from his mind of the evil spirits in their legends."

"And turned those beliefs against him, I see," Sandoval said, beaming at the feisty little sprite. "Very clever of you, Tillie, and your brave group of friends. And I shouldn't impose upon you further, but I must." His tone turned somber. "I know that Lilliana was pushed from the falls, and a child was born to her at the green pool before she died. I need you to confirm that, and tell me what happened to that child."

Tillie hung her head and gave a heavy sigh that appeared to draw in and expel more breath than could be contained in that tiny body. Her eyes were big, sparkling in the late-afternoon light. She looked at Harald, who nodded, encouraging her to speak.

"No one will hurt you, Tillie," Harald said. "I'll protect you."

It was a ludicrous statement but given from the heart and poignant to Sandoval. It also must have struck a true chord with the little sprite, for she smiled warmly at Harald and stood to face Sandoval.

"The Glaistig assisted in the birth of the child, but I do not know what became of it. When I arrived at the green pool, I saw the maiden on the ledge above the falls. I saw a hand reach out and push her over. Rolf was there to drag her from the pool, but she had already had the child. The Glaistig must have drawn it beneath the waters. That is truly all I know of the facts of the matter."

Sandoval nodded, smiling at her serious rendition of the events of that day. She seemed so intent on pleasing him—or was it just Harald? —that he was reluctant to press her further … almost.

"Both the Glaistig and Noona told me that the child died."

"I was sworn to secrecy. But I told you true that I never saw the baby," Tillie said flatly. She eyed the tall wizard but remained silent. That was all he was going to get. "Now, if you wish, great inspector, we can transport all of you to your friends. Harald tells me they are waiting in the Valley of the Mists."

"I would appreciate your transporting Harald and the Snufflebeam Company to join our friends at that place, if you are able. But Hoagy and I must go back to Quelean and get Trelaine. I promised her I would take her there."

"Oh, I surely can do that!" Tillie cried out, laughing. "I have special faerie powers, you know."

"But, sir! Won't Maelthor just snatch us up again?"

Sandoval shook his head. "I believe Maelthor and his warriors have gone to join Nortenaine at the Valley of the Mists. We will not meet them in Quelean."

"And if we go in, can we get out? What if she won't help us then?"

"Life is full of little mysteries, Hoagy. We're only concerned with big ones here. We will still arrive at the appointed place in time for any action. You won't miss much."

Hoagy frowned at his boss but remained silent. Sandoval turned his black-eyed gaze on Tillie and nodded encouragement. Tillie spun around, and putting heads together with her faerie friends, chattered excitedly. After the huddle was over, they all became whirling dots of light before the eyes of the humans and Dwarves. The Snufflebeams looked decidedly worried, but Harald merely stood stoically at attention, so the boys remained silent, though they did crowd closer to him. Then the air about them began to shimmer, as if being whipped up by the spinning faerie lights. In another moment, Harald and the boys, as well as the shimmering dots of light, disappeared, leaving Sandoval and Hoagy alone in the now silent, brooding forest.

"Well, sir, which way do we go? I was only looking at the ground when I did manage to open my eyes, so I can't tell you," Hoagy said as he scanned the clearing around the faerie hill.

"I believe we can leave the direction up to a better judge."

Hoagy stared at Sandoval, uncomprehending. *Maybe the boss means to try his own hand at conjuring up a spirit. No, even if he was capable, he doesn't have his staff.* It didn't take long for the answer to come.

Sandoval put his fingers to his lips and whistled loudly. A robust neigh came from within the trees, just before Menopet burst from hiding, with Bully in tow, and trotted up to Sandoval. Hoagy yelped happily and hugged Bully around the neck; the horse reciprocated by head butts and nudges.

"Now that's what I call traveling in style!" Hoagy cried, grabbing his bag and tying it behind Bully's saddle.

Sandoval mounted easily, looking pleased with himself, and patted the big black stallion on the neck, leaning down to speak softly in the horse's ear.

"Back to Quelean, old boy. We have a passenger to retrieve."

Without further word, Menopet swung around and trotted out of the clearing. Hoagy, atop Bully, bounced along behind with a huge grin upon his face, back in a familiar element at last. *At least until the boss gets us into another pickle barrel,* he thought apprehensively.

Back in Quelean, Sandoval left the horses outside, and they walked through the tunnel of trees. Unlike their last glimpse of the center of Quelean, this time it appeared deserted. The fountain still bubbled a colorful water sprout and everything looked normal, but Sandoval knew that it was anything but. They had barely reached the spot where they had been confined and transported when Trelaine walked up to them. Hoagy started in surprise and scanned the area around them, wondering how she could just appear as if out of thin air. *Or maybe that's just what she does.*

Sandoval, nonplussed, merely bowed solemnly. "Lady Trelaine."

"I was hoping you would make it back to Quelean, Inspector Carmichael," Trelaine said, a slight smile creasing her lips at his expression of respect, though that smile didn't change the stiff, angular lines of her face, nor soften the hard brown eyes. "Maelthor sent a messenger to tell me of the desertion of the warrior spirits at the faerie hill and the attack of other evil spirits."

"Are they going to pursue us, then?" Hoagy blurted.

"They have gone ahead to the Valley of the Mists," Trelaine answered, without looking at Hoagy; she kept her eyes upon Sandoval. "Evidently, they decided you were a lesser prize than would be the leader of the Ileana."

"Hmmm." Sandoval pursed his lips and considered her, his black eyes sparkling. "He may change his mind about that at a future date, I think."

Trelaine's eyes widened. "You think he may have killed Lilliana or Noona—or both?" Her voice rose to a high pitch of excitement. "Why would he do that? I believe you may be attempting to cause some terrible rift between Maelthor and Nortenaine. Well, it will not be—I won't let it!"

Trelaine raised her fist as if to strike him, but Sandoval didn't attempt to soothe her or stop her harangue. He merely stood silently in the face of it, with unblinking calm composure. Hoagy had retreated behind the tall wizard as he recalled a saying of his boss: "Discretion is the better part of valor." Inspector Carmichael had read that to him from one of the ancient books he had borrowed from the king's private library. Hoagy wasn't sure of the true meaning of it, but thought that it probably included not facing up to an angry elf. All elves could command magic, regardless of their gender, and though their magic was of the constructive sort, Hoagy didn't feel it would be prudent to test it.

Trelaine appeared to struggle to retain composure to match Inspector Carmichael's, though her brown eyes remained hard, almost black. She took a deep breath and said in a more normal, steady tone, "I don't understand why you think Noona's death should be connected to that of Lilliana's, so many years ago. Lilliana was murdered by Rolf Andelar, and Noona was an old woman whose time had come. We elves don't linger and waste away, as humans do. When our time to leave this physical life is here, we take that journey and leave our physical selves behind. Noona left this world alongside the one she loved above all others. That would ensure that they would walk together in spirit."

"Before we set out, I would appreciate having my staff restored to me," Sandoval said steadily.

Trelaine's brows knit together, creasing her beautiful brow. Her face slowly reddened, as if she realized that she may have been goaded into expressing too much. *What is this crafty wizard trying to do?* she wondered. Even Hoagy stepped aside and looked up questioningly at his boss.

"You must promise me that you will not use your magic to harm me or my own."

"And you will accept my word of honor?" Sandoval asked, smiling crookedly.

"I will hold you to it," she said emphatically, spinning about and gesturing for them to follow her.

They had only a short way to walk before reaching a small cottage near the center of the common. Trelaine stepped inside without asking them to join her. While they waited for her, Sandoval again noted the conspicuous lack of any other elves. Before he could voice his curiosity to Hoagy, Trelaine came out with his staff, Hoagy's sword, and a small bag of her own slung over her shoulder. She handed the staff to Sandoval. Hoagy took his sword eagerly from her hand.

"I have your promise not to use that to harm me," she stated simply.

Sandoval nodded. "By the way, where are all of the others? Are they hiding out of fear of us, or have they gone to join the battle?"

"They are not afraid of you, Inspector. They choose not to show themselves out of deference for Maelthor's wishes. It is also a tradition in our culture that all elves, even those not on the battle lines, gather in the common to pool our spirits for support in the coming battle."

"But you prefer to be at the front."

It was a statement, not a question, and Trelaine reacted to it by stiffening. Her mouth opened, as if to retort, but she evidently thought better of it and spun about to head for the tunnel of trees that would take them out of Quelean. Sandoval nodded to Hoagy, and they followed her without comment.

Menopet and Bully raised their heads, still munching sweet grass, as Sandoval, Hoagy, and Trelaine emerged from the tunnel. By now, the last rays of the setting sun were barely casting enough light through the trees to see the trail before them.

"You may join me on Menopet, Trelaine. He will accommodate both of us nicely," Sandoval said. "We will be able to make time before setting up camp for tonight."

He mounted and put his hand out to assist Trelaine up behind him. Hoagy was already seated and gazing eagerly at the trail ahead of them.

"We're on the road again, sir," Hoagy said happily.

"That we are, my boy." Sandoval smiled at the obvious statement and nudged Menopet gently with his heel.

CHAPTER 13

A CHANCE ENCOUNTER

With the red orb of Khensu gleaming like an baleful eye in the night sky, now visible below the yellow moon, Horus, Sandoval called a halt and instructed Hoagy to rustle up a meager meal for them as he unsaddled and brushed down the horses. Trelaine, who had been unusually subdued for the last hour or so, went to the nearby stream and filled the water sacks. By the time they all settled around the fire, the forest had become an indistinguishable black barrier beyond the small circle of light cast by the fire. Hoagy had managed to brew some cherok in a small pail, which was a welcome addition to the pieces of bread and cheese he had hoarded from their last couple of meals in Quelean. Hoagy ate eagerly of his allotment and sighed contentedly over his cup of cherok. Sandoval finished his allotment in silence and snapped his flint to light a cheroot as he sipped the hot cherok. Trelaine merely stared off toward the forest, barely touching her portion of the meal.

"You should take some sustenance, Trelaine," Sandoval said softly, his black eyes reflecting the fire's glow. "It will be at least another day before we reach the Valley of the Mists. Elven food is remarkably filling."

"I ate something before we left. You may share my portion," she replied listlessly.

Hoagy looked at Sandoval with eager anticipation. "We still have enough for a meal tomorrow."

"Go ahead, Hoagy—a growing boy and all that." Sandoval waved his hand toward the food.

Hoagy took the small pieces of bread and cheese and munched happily, pausing only to take sips from his cup of cherok. The silence settled about them once again, broken only by the sound of Hoagy chewing and the puffs of smoke expelled by Sandoval. After finishing the last bits of bread and cheese, Hoagy gathered the cups and plates and headed for the stream to wash them. Sandoval snuffed out the remainder of his cheroot and turned his steady gaze upon Trelaine.

"I'm curious about the differences between the Ileana and the Florian pertaining to the status of their females."

"In what way?" Trelaine didn't raise her eyes; she continued to stare down at her hands clasped in her lap.

"From what I understand, the Ileana females may become warriors and accompany the males into battle. By your admission, with rare exceptions, the Florian females remain behind and use their combined energy to support the males in battle. Was it always so for the Florian?"

"From the beginning, when Klevian established the Florian home in the Grimwood, he cast aside many of the customs of the past. I suppose he feared that allowing females to risk harm or death in battle would diminish their numbers, and it was important for them to grow as a community."

"Or lose those females to capture. Did your mother agree with the new customs?" Sandoval watched for a reaction, but thought he may have seen only the slight tightening of her hands together on her lap.

"Maeleana, my mother, embraced her new life and Klevian as her lord." Trelaine lifted her chin and her brown eyes locked on Sandoval's.

No flicker of uncertainty, anger, or bitterness was evident in that controlled regard.

"Still, that was early in the establishment of your separate clans. Did your mother ever yearn for the exciting forays as a warrior? You all probably knew what was going on in the Ileana camp during those early times."

The reaction was obvious now: the tightening at the corner of her eyes; her lips almost disappearing, they were pressed so tightly; a bitter, hard line across her face; and the brown eyes, cold.

"She missed nothing," Trelaine said, pulling her eyes away.

"You were very young but still put in charge of Rolf's imprisonment. Did you admire him?"

"I do admit to being taken with him at first. But Klevian depended on me to be able to control the faeries and report anything Rolf may have told me. And he would have told me more, but he became distracted and it was not until it was too late that I discovered the reason for that. The fool was too weak-willed to withstand the battering eyelashes of Lilliana. He seemed to think me but a child, a weakness that was to my advantage—as if I knew nothing of our history and could not feel the pull of destiny upon myself!" Trelaine rose suddenly and, spinning, walked off into the woods.

As Sandoval tossed his spent cheroot into the fire, a small, bright, spinning light landed on the ground next to him. He rose and scooped it up as Hoagy returned with a clanking bag full of pots, plates, and cups. The young man's blond brows rose as he noticed the absence of Trelaine and the message ball in Sandoval's hand. But before he could voice his question, Sandoval turned away and opened the ball with a faint pop to reveal the scowling face of Director Tantilus. Hoagy dropped his bag down next to Bully's saddle and rolled out his blanket. As he settled himself to stretch out for what sleep remained to him before dawn broke, Sandoval walked out of earshot to the edge of the clearing. Holding the ball before him, Sandoval smiled as the image of Director Tantilus berated him, the old wizard's white hair sticking out from his round head as if electrified.

"So, you've managed to make matters worse than they were before I sent you, as usual, Sandoval! I will have to—"

The rest of Tantilus' tirade was lost on Hoagy as he snuggled deeper into his bedroll.

The morning sun rose over a Grimwood shrouded in gray mist that clung to the traveling cloaks they had donned shortly after rousing from a chilly sleep. Hoagy didn't have to be encouraged to start a fire and heat water for the remaining cherok he had hoarded. Trelaine maintained a silence as cool as the damp air while they ate their meager meal, most of which she barely touched. When Hoagy offered her a drink, she merely shook her head. Sandoval appeared distracted and unaware of anything, other than the tendrils of smoke that rose from the cheroot he occasionally drew upon. Hoagy had already saddled the horses and packed the saddlebags by the time Sandoval crushed out his cheroot and rose, gathered his leather bag and staff, and slapped his leather hat upon his head.

"We'd better be on the road. Each day that passes brings the players closer together. I wouldn't want to miss being there," he said, mounting Menopet.

"You act as if this were some kind of game we are all playing." Trelaine's husky voice had an edge to it as she swung up behind him.

Sandoval glanced at Hoagy with a slight twist to the side of his mouth. Behind him, he could almost feel Trelaine's dark eyes boring into the back of his head.

"Games are serious business, as any child knows, and can have disastrous results if not monitored properly, though I still haven't put together the entire cast of characters in this one. Actually, I'm still trying to work out the rule-maker."

"The murderer of Lilliana and Noona?" Hoagy said expectantly.

"Not necessarily," Sandoval said cryptically as he gave a dancing Menopet his head.

The black stallion moved out at once, picking up the pace to an easy trot. Bully was close behind, carrying Hoagy. As the sun rose toward its noonday peak, no conversation imposed upon the soft wind that had blown off the early morning mist. The path they had been following was already beginning to widen as it bent to meet a respectable, well-worn roadway. Sandoval recognized the road that cut through the eastern half of the Grimwood, from southern traffic that ran the length of the forest to the foothills of the Thunderstorm Mountains in the north. Lesser trails branched off the main trail that the Florian elves had allowed humans and Dwarves alike to travel without molestation for years untold. As long as travelers remained on the road and did not drift westward into the depths of the Grimwood, there would be no repercussions from the generally accommodating Florian—at least, not until the present time. With tensions having grown between the Florian and Ileana clans, any traveler could now be accosted with demands for his or her identity and reason for being on the road.

As the news of the troubles between the elven clans spread to the nearest human and dwarf settlements, traffic on the roadway had all but ceased. Yet it was still the quickest route to the Valley of the Mists, unless travelers set out east from Sanctuary and skirted the southern edge of the mountains to move up through the plains. Either route was going to bring any traveler into territory populated by one or the other of the warring elven clans. At least the forest route was cooler in the summer months. As for Sandoval and his company, their choice had already been made by the fact that they had started their trek from deep within the Grimwood. With Trelaine riding along, even the most eager Florian would have let them pass without pause. The lack of any challenge only meant that all of the Florian warriors were already preparing for confrontation with the Ileana. Sandoval knew the possibility of being halted was slim.

It was thus disconcerting to hear the snap of a branch and a shout directed at them from within the thickness of the trees that bordered the road. Sandoval pulled Menopet to a halt, and Hoagy brought Bully up next to him as they all peered into the trees. Hoagy braced himself, his hand upon the hilt of his sword. But Sandoval could either see through trees or was quicker to react than Hoagy was, for the wizard chuckled suddenly, even before his young assistant saw the wizened features of Will Wiggins, his bowl-shaped white hair and bangs emerging from behind a tree He was followed by a brightly smiling Flora, the sun glinting off the reddish highlights in her curly brown hair. Flora led a plump pony by a lead line attached to the animal's bit.

"Well met, Will Wiggins!" Sandoval smiled broadly.

"The crafty wizard!" Will growled back as he strode into the road.

"At your service," Sandoval said with a nod. "I was just looking for a good spot to stop for the noon meal. I think there's a clearing off the road around the next bend. Would you join us?"

Will nodded and beckoned Sandoval and Hoagy to precede them. Sandoval nudged Menopet gently to a walk. Hoagy slipped from Bully's saddle and moved next to Flora. Will eyed the young man for a moment and then pranced ahead, following Sandoval with long strides, his walking stick tapping on the hard-packed dirt in time with his brisk steps.

"He sure doesn't walk like an old man," Hoagy said, smiling warmly at Flora.

The young woman's gold-flecked brown eyes twinkled above a mischievous grin. "He is a wonder to me also. Sometimes I look at him, and he appears ancient, and other times, he's straight with broad shoulders, like a young man. I once asked him his age, and he only blustered back at me and said something about the *impertinence* of the young. So I never asked him again."

Hoagy laughed, which caused Will to pause briefly and glare at him. Hoagy quickly wiped the smile from his face and tried to look serious. Will picked up his pace, his walking stick jamming even harder into the roadway, causing the smile to pop back on Hoagy's face, though he did manage to keep from snickering. Behind Sandoval, Trelaine briefly gazed at the two young people, her dark eyes a study in intensity. But Hoagy only had his blue eyes on the young woman who walked next to him.

By the time Hoagy and Flora rounded the bend in the road, they were deep in conversation, heads together, almost touching. Off the road to their right, a clearing opened up in the forest where Trelaine and Will Wiggins stood waiting for the two young people to arrive. Looking up, they saw the disapproving frown pinching Will Wiggins' face and the narrow gaze given them by Trelaine. Off to one side, Sandoval had dropped the saddle he'd removed from Menopet and was stretched out, his head resting on the saddle seat, drawing on his cheroot. After formal introductions, Hoagy and Flora unpacked their respective food items, tins, dishes, and utensils and, working together, they had a small fire going in no time.

Sandoval soon joined them, and they all sipped their hot cherok—or water, in Trelaine's case—and munched on day-old bread and cheese. Hoagy had produced, from some secret compartment, an apple that he sliced in quarters and passed to each of them. Flora sat cross-legged next to Trelaine, and Hoagy noticed her casting an occasional glance at the female elf out of the corner of her eye. It was only a matter of time before curiosity got the better of the young woman.

"I don't mean to pry, Trelaine—may I call you Trelaine?" Flora started hesitantly.

"You already have, young woman. What is it you are curious about?"

"I have met many of the Ileana who have stopped at Will's tower, both male and female, and you remind me of one in particular. She said her name was Haestel, but for sure she could be your twin. Have the Florian close relatives with the Ileana?"

Trelaine stiffened visibly at the name, and her lips drew tightly together. It was several seconds before her face relaxed in a half-smile. "She is the daughter of the late Iledan, high lord of the Ileana, who died in battle. I didn't know her, but we Florian aren't totally ignorant of the Ileana."

"Oh, I am sorry. I shouldn't have pried!" Flora reddened and cast her eyes downward.

"No matter." Trelaine's voice softened graciously. "My mother spoke of Iledan's family and of course, our historians recorded all who left us in the sundering. I think they take pleasure in toting up how many deaths in each battle and who has died, if they know. Maybe it has something to do with their love of order."

"This war, it is tragic." Flora put her hand lightly on Trelaine's knee, but the older woman merely ignored it. Self-consciously, Flora removed her hand. Trelaine brushed at the spot on her dress, as if to smooth it.

"We should all hope that King Filemon can bring some diplomacy to bear and save both elf clans from any more bloodshed," Hoagy said in a rush, eager to deflect the attention centered on Flora.

Instead, Trelaine rounded on him, her dark eyes hard. "Neither my brother nor our nephew, Nortenaine, would consider advice from the human leader! It would be against all of our teachings and spiritual history!" Trelaine flared.

Hoagy cast a pleading look at Sandoval and Will Wiggins, but both men merely watched the exchange, dispassionately and quietly.

"Oh, then you are of Florian nobility!" Flora blurted, her face reddening even more than before. "I do apologize. I should not have been so impertinent. Your brother must be Maelthor. I have heard he is a powerful elf and spiritual leader of the Florian. And Lilliana, the tragic maiden who fell to her death at the green pool, was your niece. I'm afraid I am a bumbling fool for having offended you. Please forgive me!"

"I'm sure I shall survive. But please, spare me more of this conversation," Trelaine responded coldly.

"I think Will and I need to stretch out and relax somewhat before getting back on the trail," Sandoval said. "Maybe you ladies could gather the berries I spotted through a break in the trees there, down by the creek. It could be a nice treat before setting out again." Sandoval even managed a twinkle in his eyes and a nod of his head in encouragement.

Hoagy just stared at him, but Flora took the opportunity to smooth over the tension that had developed around them. She rose and grabbed a tin, waiting expectantly for Trelaine's reaction. Trelaine rose more slowly and, without acknowledging the younger woman, headed in the direction Sandoval had indicated. When they had both disappeared within the trees, Hoagy turned to Sandoval.

"Sir, I don't know if that's going to win over Trelaine, putting them together like that."

"That woman needs some loosening up," Will gruffly remarked, pulling a pipe from within his robe and accepting Sandoval's flint to strike it alight. Hoagy wondered how he could keep it primed and ready for smoking without going through the scrapping, tapping, and packing that Tronus always did before lighting up. But the thought drifted from his mind as Sandoval lit his own cheroot. Moving slightly out of the circle of blue smoke that drifted over the two men, Hoagy started gathering the lunch gear and repacking his saddle bags.

"So, Will Wiggins," Sandoval said, cocking his head toward the older man, "what brings you on the road this day?"

"I've been hearing entirely too much folderol about the elf clans and their facing off for the final grand battle. Figured I've got a stake in it, being as I live around them. Besides, it might be good show. And I've never met a king before. So it should be an eventful time."

Sandoval studied Will's open face and clear, bright eyes, as innocent as a child's—they looked green today. *Thought they were blue the last time I looked*, Sandoval mused.

"That it will be," Sandoval agreed. "But do you think that as it could end up being a bloody battle, it is the proper setting for your young ward?"

"Your young man—Hoagy, is it? Is he battle-hardened then?" Will asked smoothly.

"Hoagy may look innocent, but that lad has been through a good share of battles with me. That's not quite the same thing as a young girl caught between two armies."

"And the young man is protected by your magic?" Will said quietly.

Sandoval turned black eyes on the bent white head as the old man tapped out his remaining pipe ashes. "What I have the ability to supply is minimal, I'm afraid. There are wizards more powerful than I."

"It should be pretty easy to gauge the power of an individual wizard in his area of operation then?"

"I suppose it could be estimated. Is that a subject that interests you?" Sandoval was beginning to feel itchy suddenly, as if small crawling things were scurrying all over his tall frame. He sat up, crushed out his cheroot, and stared suspiciously at the grass on which they sat.

"Oh, everything interests me," Will allowed. "You are investigating the murder of an elf maiden long ago."

It was said as a statement of fact, not a question. Sandoval felt slightly annoyed that he couldn't find his hat. Where had the damn thing gone?

"It wasn't my original purpose for going to Quelean and speaking to the Florian elves, but it seems to have grown out of that. Where is that boy?"

Sandoval rose as Hoagy emerged from the trees, carrying full water bags for the horses. He suddenly felt extremely irritated with the young man and was about to round on him and give him a good piece of his mind for having kept them waiting, when a terrified shriek came from the direction of the river.

Sandoval took off in the direction of the sound. Hoagy dropped the water bags and followed Sandoval, with Will Wiggins right behind him. Sandoval tore through the thick brush, weaving in and out of trees, his unerring sense of the direction of that chill scream guiding him until he rounded a tree and almost fell over Trelaine, who was kneeling beside the inert form of Flora. The young woman's body was contorted, as if in pain, lying on one side, her face turned upward, eyes open.

Hoagy, who'd run up behind Sandoval, gasped, "Flora! What happened to her?"

Hoagy dropped down beside the young woman and frantically searched for a pulse or some other sign of life. Sandoval stood over them, his eyes searching Trelaine's pale face. Will Wiggins walked up, unceremoniously pushed Hoagy aside, and took Flora in his arms as if she was as light as a newborn baby. He turned back to the pathway without a word. Hoagy started to protest, his face a study in agony, but his eye caught the rough shake of Sandoval's head, and he followed the wizard's burning black gaze to Trelaine's bowed head. Trelaine's hands covered her face, and her body shook in silent sobs. Finally, with one huge shuddering sigh, Trelaine looked up at Sandoval, her face bleak.

"I don't know how it happened! We were picking berries, and she bent down to reach for a large bunch. That creature struck at her!" Trelaine's finger pointed to the carcass of an oddly bloated lizard with varicolored stripes banding its body. Sandoval nudged the creature with the toe of his shoe to assure himself it was dead before reaching down, intending to pick it up. But Trelaine screamed and grabbed his hand before he could grasp the critter.

"No! You mustn't touch it! The poison exudes from all of its pores, and it is still deadly, even in death." Trelaine shoved the creature beneath the bush with the toe of her boot and then crumbled against Sandoval, sobbing again.

"It is a rastor lizard. I have seen them bring down an elf warrior in his prime. But why here, in this part of the forest? I've never seen them except in the very depths of the Grimwood and only during extremely wet seasons. Do you think it could have been intentional? Could someone be watching us?"

"It is rather odd ..." Sandoval began softly.

"You think they were after me? If it was the Ileana, they could want me dead. What better way to gain revenge for Rolf Andelar!" Trelaine's dark brown eyes hardened and the blood finally began to suffuse her previously pale face.

"I think we had better return," Sandoval suggested. "Will may need our assistance."

Sandoval put his arm around Trelaine and pointed her back toward the clearing. Trelaine let her head drop to his shoulder, and she leaned against the tall wizard. Sandoval looked at Hoagy over Trelaine's head, and Hoagy nodded silently. Bracing Trelaine between the two of them, they walked back to the clearing. Hoagy's face fell at the sight of Will Wiggins sitting on the grass in almost the exact spot he had occupied before, cradling Flora in his lap. He released his support on Trelaine and rushed to the old man.

"Sir! I'm so sorry. I—" Hoagy choked back a sob and was about to reach down to pat old Will's shoulder when Flora's head came up, and she looked into the young man's eyes.

Hoagy staggered back, and even Sandoval stopped dead in his tracks, his arm dropping from around Trelaine's shoulders. Trelaine stumbled and almost fell to the ground, her eyes wide in disbelief.

"I'm all right, Hoagy," Flora said in her musical voice, pulling herself up. "Please, don't fuss."

"Just a fainting spell is all," Will said, rising to assist her. "She saw that critter and just keeled over. She still feels a little wobbly, though. I think we'll just settle in for the night right here and regain our strength for a new start tomorrow."

Hoagy's face twisted into an uncertain smile as he looked from Flora back to Sandoval. The white wizard merely nodded again and turned to Trelaine.

"Are you all right?" he asked her.

Trelaine's face had paled again, her brown eyes like deep holes in her skull. She continued to stare at Flora. Then the blood rushed back into her face, and she lifted a shaky hand to her cheek. "I'll be all right. Such a shock."

"I think Will is right," Sandoval agreed. "We should all settle in here for the night. It will be dark soon, after all. Let's bring up the fire a little more, Hoagy. Maybe some more wood for it?"

Hoagy nodded and turned without a word, grabbing a sack and stepping back into the forest the way they had just come. Trelaine looked after him, then her head swiveled and she stared at Flora. Sandoval was certain the look in her brooding brown eyes was more of wariness than concern for the girl. He pulled a cheroot and his flint from his large pocket and struck it alight. He would need at least one smoke to contemplate these events.

CHAPTER 14

ON THE BATTLE LINE

Sandoval and the others arrived at a crossroad late the next morning. Sandoval, who had taken to walking beside Will Wiggins with Hoagy, while Trelaine and Flora rode upon Menopet and Bully, raised his hand to halt the group. Both women dismounted and joined the men. Hoagy still stayed close to Flora and even now reached up to brace her by the elbow.

She smiled at him. "I'm okay, really, Hoagy."

He frowned at her. "Well, you still look a little pale—sort of wavery."

Sandoval and Will both looked intently at Hoagy. Will moved to take Flora's hand, pulling her away from Hoagy. The young man's blue eyes narrowed, and he would have protested, had not Sandoval tapped Hoagy on the shoulder and motioned for him to follow.

Sandoval and Hoagy slipped off the road and through the trees. The remaining members of the party stood uncomfortably silent as the moments ticked by before Sandoval and Hoagy re-emerged and strode up to the anxious group.

"The Florian battle camp is not far from here. I will be taking leave of you now, Will Wiggins. Trelaine and I must meet my friends at my old dig, just up in the hills to the north of us."

Will Wiggins nodded solemnly. "I have enjoyed your company, Inspector Carmichael. I believe it is best that Flora and I go back to the tower. I think the girl needs more rest after that scare yesterday eve."

"Oh, but no!" Flora protested, grasping Will's arm in her delicate hands. "I wouldn't want you to miss seeing the king. I'm sure I'll be all right. It's just that the creature scared me so—it was like all the breath was sucked out of me. I—"

"No need to protest, my young charge. There will be other battles, I'm sure. Besides, the Florian might think it an imposition for spectators to just pop in on them," Will said.

Sandoval chuckled softly and placed his palms together, touching his fingertips to his forehead in the common salute that wizards reserved for their own kind. "Hoagy has his own orders but will be traveling with you until you reach your tower. Then he will go on to bring the rest of our company together, if that's acceptable."

Will held a steady gaze on Hoagy until the young man cast a worried look at Sandoval.

"I suppose we could stand the company, Inspector Carmichael. And Flora will have a chance to ride and keep off her feet for a while more."

"It has been an honor to spend time with you, Will Wiggins. Perhaps when this business is concluded, we may sit and talk again."

Will Wiggins repeated Sandoval's gesture with a short bow, touching his own forehead with his hands together. "An acknowledgement generally reserved only for fellow wizards honors me also. We just may meet again."

With that, Will picked up the reins of his pony and walked back down the trail. Hoagy took Flora gently by the elbow and assisted her in mounting Bully again. Trelaine stared off toward the direction of the battle camp.

"We must go now, Trelaine," Sandoval said quietly, breaking her reverie.

Trelaine turned to him, her beautiful face a vision set in stone. "I would like to continue to the camp and join Nortenaine and Maelthor."

"I promise you shall, but not just yet. I need you with me for a while longer. I hope you'll be patient."

Trelaine started to speak, then pressed her lips tightly together and nodded reluctantly. Sandoval swung up on Menopet's back and reached a hand down to assist Trelaine up behind him. The moment she was settled, Menopet leaped away to a smooth gallop. They traveled a faint path for a short while before breaking off and heading up through the scrub brush on the side of the mountain. Menopet's sure footing eventually found a rough dirt trail that wound up the side of the mountain northward. Before long, they were above the forest treetops. Neither Sandoval nor Trelaine spoke until they reached the flat shelf on the eastern side of the mountain, which had held Sandoval's previous dig.

Standing on the edge of the rock shelf were Ferrel, Jade, and Tronus. Harald and the Snufflebeam Company were finishing their meager noon meal of cold biscuits. They sat at one of the tables set up near the mouth of the tunnel where they had been working days before. As Sandoval lowered Trelaine to the ground, she turned her head and looked up at the wizard questioningly.

"You told the old man that Hoagy was to meet your friends, but here they are. A lie, wizard? And what for?"

"I felt Hoagy should accompany them back to their tower, just in case anyone might attempt to ambush them on the way. Will's walking stick wouldn't be much help in protecting himself and the girl." Sandoval dismounted, his black eyes steady on Trelaine's probing gaze.

"Implying Florians would do such a thing?" Trelaine questioned, her voice rising. Heads turned away from the action below them to stare at the wizard and the elf maiden.

"Their tower is still close enough to the border and the battle lines. Your Florian may control the road coming through the Valley of the Mists, but there are other ways of entering the Grimwood."

With that, Sandoval turned and joined his friends at the edge of the shelf. Still looking angry, Trelaine stepped over to the edge of the shelf and looked down. Below them, the Florian were camped just on the edge of the Grimwood, with the Ileana camped upon a small rise across a flat stretch of grassy plain that faced them. Trelaine's brows drew together, and her eyes narrowed as she found her kin in the Florian camp below. Nortenaine's large tent in the center of the camp was easy to spot, but the figures were too small for normal eyes to make out any distinctive identification. Sandoval's wizard sight, as keen as any elf's, spotted Nortenaine and Maelthor almost immediately, off to one side of the main battle line in a close circle with other warriors.

Sandoval turned away and walked into the cave, returning with an object in his hand. He handed the long cylinder to Trelaine. She took it and turned it in her hand before placing it to her eye, as he directed, and aiming it below on the camp. With a gasp, he knew she could see the various players up close.

"This is a marvelous object. Where did you get it?"

"One of the little toys I found in another dig similar to this but broken. Yet there was enough of the glass and other pieces left for Tronus' mechanics to create one for me. Pretty handy, don't you think? Tronus calls it a distance viewer."

Trelaine didn't respond but continued to swing the viewer to the Ileana camp. The silence was almost palpable and Sandoval, watching her closely, wasn't sure she was even breathing.

Ferrel, Jade, and Tronus joined them, and Sandoval, who had taken the viewer from Trelaine with apologies, handed it to Tronus, who put it to his eye, jumped back, and gasped in wonder.

"Ho and be damned! Looked like they were right on top of me—or the other way around. This is a marvel."

"And your men created it. Pretty good, huh?" Sandoval slapped the stout dwarf on the back.

"What'd I tell you? A dwarf mechanic can figure out anything!"

"Hoagy should be arriving soon, and since we didn't really have a chance at breakfast, I think food is in order." Sandoval motioned Trelaine toward the tables.

As she stepped away from him, Jade moved to his side and spoke in a low voice. "I had a chance to get down close to the Florian camp near the tree line. I overhead several elves speaking of the battle to come. They are ready and pretty confident. I also managed to move down to the edge of the plains in the south and met up with some Lestrami. They are all watching the meeting of these two armies with interest. They also tell of King Filemon's army moving toward them from the south."

"Good, it is progressing as I thought it would."

"A confident wizard is a dangerous one." Jade's beautiful mouth twisted in a smile.

Nodding, Sandoval walked back to the cave and disappeared inside. He returned with a basket of wrapped bundles in his arms, which he unwrapped and spread on the tables. Seeing the bounty of food, including a loaf of bread, cheese, and fruit that Sandoval added to their simple fare, the Snufflebeam Company whooped for joy. Even Trelaine sat down at a small table. Sandoval was surprised to see her actually eating some fruit and taking a cup of water with more eagerness than he had noticed in days.

"It is good to see you eating again, Trelaine. I was beginning to worry about you," he said, sitting down and pushing his unruly hair from his face.

"I must gain my strength. I will need to join my people and see them through this great battle."

"And which *people* would that be?" Sandoval asked quietly.

Trelaine jerked her head in his direction, slowly wiping a small drop of fruit juice from her lips. *Her dusky, flawless skin is truly stunning,* Sandoval thought. But there was still that something behind her eyes— something like melancholy; a deep pain that Sandoval was sure would be her undoing.

"I don't think Nortenaine or Maelthor would doubt my loyalty, however much they might question my methods," Trelaine said haughtily.

She emptied her water cup, set it down, and rose to walk back to the edge of the shelf, where she could gaze down at the melee below. Sandoval finished his slice of bread and cheese, washing it down with the remainder of the water in his cup, just as Hoagy arrived. The young man yelped happily at the sight of the food on the table.

"You've been holding out on us, sir," Hoagy exclaimed happily, as he set into the food.

"Just a little stash I left behind—in case." Sandoval smiled and moved out of the way as his hungry company gathered around the small table, threatening to tip it over in their haste for food and drink.

Sandoval rejoined Trelaine at the edge of the shelf and watched intently the milling about of the Florian below. They appeared to be gathering at the tree line, groups of elves dashing within the trees, then back out again. Hoagy walked up to Sandoval and Trelaine, one hand full of bread packed with cheese slices, and a piece of red fruit in the other. The round, succulent fruit was already dripping through his fingers, which he sucked between bites of his sandwich.

"Wow, suh, id sumpin!"

"Swallow before speaking, please, Hoagy," Jade admonished as she too was drawn back to the cliff edge and the action below.

Hoagy did so with a gulp. "I mean, this is something! Like looking at a game board with your soldiers lined up ready to battle. Ferrel!" he called. "Come look at this!"

"Already seen it, laddie," Ferrel laughed.

At that moment, Harald and the Snufflebeam Company also joined them, calling out excitedly upon viewing the scene below. With his charges distracted, Harald came up to Sandoval and saluted stiffly. Sandoval smiled at the young dwarf.

"Inspector sir, I have been mulling over this conflict between the elf clans, and I think I've come up with a magnificent plan for stopping the war. Uh, it would also not hurt in earning me credits toward my captain's rank if *certain* parties"—he dropped his voice and glanced quickly toward Tronus, then back at Sandoval—"knew of my contribution, you know."

Sandoval nodded silently, as Harald stood still at attention, arms straight and chin held high. "Let me think that one over, Harald. I'll get back to you."

Harald nodded solemnly, and Sandoval turned his attention back to the scene below. They were all riveted on the action among the trees just outside of their view. The treetops were rustling and shaking furiously, as if some huge creature was moving through them. At a shout from the throng below that was heard from their perch, a platform burst from the treetops, swooping low over the Florian camp before rising and gaining height. Almost level with the eyeline of the group on the ledge, the platform—rectangular, flat, and open but railed along the edges and containing a company of elves—swooped in the direction of the Ileana camp. Below them in the Florian camp, Sandoval could see Maelthor, Nortenaine, and a group of warriors linked in a circle and doing what appeared to be chanting. A soft, rhythmic sound came to his ears.

"Have you ever seen this effect before, Trelaine?" Sandoval asked, the distance viewer still to his eye.

"No …" came the slow, soft response. "But Maelthor has been pouring over the ancient records of our people lately. He must have found some charms that he has used to create this flying thing."

"And with the power of the entire clan directed at aiming it toward the enemy, it seems," Sandoval said.

The platform was nearing the flat-topped hill upon which the Ileana tents were erected, with their army arrayed before them. All of the Ileana raised their bows and aimed at the platform. Behind them stood the tall form of Vaester Shee, with other male and female elves, arms linked, forming a line. At a cry from the supporting line, the front line of Ileana elves let fly their arrows. At the same time that the platform swooped down upon them, the elves braced upon it with their bows ready. But at the shout from the Ileana line, the platform had begun to waver and suddenly swerved away amid flying arrows, spinning erratically to the south, as another platform shot from the tree tops.

The second platform met the same fate, joining the first at some distance to the south. The group on the ledge could make out the small figures of elves running back toward the Florian lines. Trelaine had broken from the other watchers and was pacing frantically, her hands balled into tight fists. Even as the furor below seemed to lessen and the respective armies appeared to gather together in standard attack formation, she continued to move from one point of view to the other with nervous jerks, slapping her hands against her thighs in frustration.

"I *must* go to them!" she announced finally, stopping to stand defiantly before Sandoval.

The wizard considered her calmly. "You will join them soon enough, I think."

Tronus, watching the two, narrowed his eyes suspiciously, then turned his head away from Sandoval and Trelaine to peer at the distant skyline to the south. Behind a curve of trees that jutted out, he spotted dust rising into the sky. "I think we've got more company," Tronus said.

All eyes were directed toward the outcrop of trees around which now rode a large company of mounted men. Jade reached for the distance viewer, which Sandoval passed to her. She put it to her eye and let out a loud yip.

"My Lestrami got to them in time!" she crowed.

As if the Florian below could hear her, they turned and spotted the oncoming riders, even though the new army was some way off. Sandoval could see the lead rider and his companion to his right. He didn't even need to have a wizard's long sight to recognize King Filemon, outfitted in his battle armor, and his Gold Guild wizard, Norena, riding in the lead.

"Now this is getting better," Ferrel said, clapping his large hands together. "Our great leader has brought what looks like most of the barons and their soldiers—at least, those whose baronies surround the Grimwood."

"Can I borrow that viewer?" Hoagy asked, his hand already reaching toward Jade for the piece. When he placed it to his eye, he let out a gasp. "Oh, no! My da's there, too, with his personal guard. Now why would he go and do that? He knows he can't hold a sword any better than my sister! He'll get himself killed for sure, sir!"

"Don't worry, Hoagy. I'm sure Baron Toogood will be fine. I don't think we're going to be seeing a battle today. Filemon knows better. This is probably just his version of diplomacy, although with teeth, to be sure." Sandoval narrowed his eyes, straining to pick out Director Tantilus with a unit of white wizards surrounding him.

"What a bunch of diddy-poop!" Tronus humphed. "What does that fool think he can do to stop two warring elf clans with magic? Wave his golden scepter at 'em?"

"Settle down, Hoagy." Jade sent a hard-eyed glare at Tronus, who only shrugged and turned back to the scene below, fists on his hips. "I'm sure the king has a good share of Gold Guild wizards in that bunch. Inspector Carmichael has it all worked out, right?"

Jade raised her brows at Sandoval and nodded her head in encouragement to the wizard. Sandoval merely grinned and clapped Hoagy on the back.

"Keep an eye on the direction the king is taking, Ferrel. Looks like he's circling to bring his little army up behind the Ileana. Hoagy, come with me."

With that pronouncement, Sandoval walked over to the table and, pulling out a cheroot, struck his flint to light it, expelling a large puff of smoke. Hoagy settled opposite him, his round blue eyes on his boss. Turning to catch Harald's eye, Sandoval beckoned to him. Harald, with exaggerated nonchalance, headed in a slow, circuitous route to the table. Sandoval shook his head with a chuckle before he turned back to Hoagy.

"Report, Hoagy."

"It was as you guessed, sir ..." Hoagy began.

"Guessed?" Sandoval's black brows rose. "I don't *guess*, Hoagy. I make learned deductions."

"Right. Anyway, we got to the tower, and Flora went to make us a nice pot of hag tea. It gave me the chance to show Will what I had found. He studied that lizard for a while, then smiled his strange, knowing smile and told me to turn my head away and look at the creature from the side of my eye. I figured he was going to do something to the carcass, so I squeezed my eyes shut. But he slapped me on the shoulder and said, 'Look at it sideways, you nit. I'm not going to blast you or it.'

"And lo! When I did, it suddenly didn't look like that lizard but just a piece of tree root. I asked Will Wiggins if he thought Trelaine had done it. She does seem tightly strung under all that elf coolness. But the old man only shook his head—he looked kind of sad and tired—and never said a word. So I don't know if he was agreeing with me or not. Then Flora came with the tea and when she saw the dead 'lizard' on the table, she almost dropped the pot and cups. She looked terrified—slammed them down on the table and ran from the room.

"I didn't know whether to go to her or not, but Will just sat there turning this stiff critter carcass around with his finger. So I got up and followed Flora. Figured the old man would say something if he didn't want me to. She was back in the kitchen, holding on to the edge of the sink, sobbing. I told her I was sorry to scare her like that, but wanted Will to look at the *critter*. I asked her if Trelaine was near the bush before she started picking the berries, but she didn't think so. She and Trelaine reached the clearing at the same time, and she thought Trelaine was on the other side, while she went to pick from that group of bushes. She was shocked at my suggestion and just kept repeating it was an accident.

"When we went back to the main room, Will Wiggins was gone. I just gulped down a cup of tea, grabbed the carcass, and left them. That's it, sir. Sorry I couldn't have done better."

"Don't be, Hoagy. You've given me more than you know," Sandoval said, as he took a last drag from his cheroot before crushing it in the dirt beneath his boot.

At that moment, Harald, arms behind his back, his eyes turned toward the sky, as if studying clouds, continued his stroll in their direction, halting only as he walked into their table. He looked down at it in surprise, and then shot a furtive glance toward the group at the cliff who was still watching the action below.

"I think you could have done better just walking over, Harald," Sandoval said with a twisted smile on his lips. "Anyone looking at you would have figured you were drunk or someone had hit you on the head."

"Sorry, your eminence." Harald bowed.

Hoagy chuckled, shaking his head.

"'Inspector' is fine, Harald. Now, tell us your plan."

"Well, Inspector, sir, I've been talking a lot to Tillie—the wood sprite, you know."

Sandoval nodded, waiting.

"Anyway, she told me there was going to be a meeting of the court of the faerie king and queen today at the heart of the Grimwood. It is an annual thing, you see, and usually others are banned from seeing this. But Tillie says since we are friends of Will Wiggins and the king and queen, like the old man, we could be allowed to enter. One of the great things about this annual get-together is that the king and queen preside over disputes between the magical folk of the forest and maybe can resolve the disagreements between the Ileana and Florian. We just have to swear fealty to the faeries."

Sandoval's black brows twisted together in concern, and he opened his mouth to speak but Harald cut in.

"It's not what you think, sir! It's not like we have to give up our own citizenship as humans and Dwarves and all. It's just … like a courtesy, you know." Harald trailed off at the stern look on Sandoval's face.

The inspector's black eyes seemed to bore into him but glancing quickly at Hoagy, he was reassured by the young man's smile and twinkling blue eyes. "You're speaking of a *reckoning*, I believe."

Both Harald and Hoagy looked uncertain for a moment.

Then Hoagy snapped his fingers. "It's the method of determining the truth of an argument for elves. I remember hearing about it, sir! They speak their piece, and then the king and queen look into their souls with the *seeing stones* and can see who's lying. Of course, as I remember, the liar could be banished forever, if the crime is bad enough."

"And this would stop the impending war between the elves. A nice idea, Harald. Now all we have to do is figure out how to get the two clans to agree to such a resolution."

Hoagy sat quietly, picked up another piece of cheese, and chewed while studying his boss. Harald thought for a moment before his face fell in disappointment.

"Sorry, Inspector. I guess I didn't think it out too well."

"Not at all, Harald. At least you're thinking." Sandoval slapped the table for emphasis and grinned broadly. "Unfortunately, our King Filemon doesn't have the seeing stones, but maybe he can use a familiar."

"A what?" Harald's head swiveled from one to the other.

"Oh, it's just someone or something that wizards use to enhance their magic or act as a conduit."

"How is this going to help us find out who killed Lilliana and Noona?" Hoagy asked quietly.

Sandoval studied Hoagy with a narrow black gaze. The young man, used to his master's intense concentration, didn't flinch from the scrutiny.

"I believe I already know that, Hoagy. But to expose the truth, you first have to clear the sight of the person you mean to convince. Let's make a plan."

Back at the cliff, Trelaine had discontinued twitching and pacing and spun around to see Sandoval, Hoagy, and Harald in deep conversation at the table. Clenching her fists, she advanced toward them, her face clouded with anger. Turning as Harald slipped away from the table, Tronus followed Trelaine's advance upon the wizard. As he stepped away from the group to follow her, the four young Dwarves of the Snufflebeam Company jumped up and snapped to attention. Their stance didn't last long, as they soon discovered Harald was nowhere to be seen, and Tronus was oblivious to their actions. Still, having military protocol instilled in them from babes, they rushed to march behind Tronus. Jade motioned to Ferrel, and she and the big man joined the group that surrounded Sandoval.

"I insist you take me to join my people, or I shall take myself," Trelaine announced angrily. "I am not your prisoner, Inspector!"

"I think it's about time you did just that, Trelaine," Sandoval said.

"Good! Let's get going!" Ferrel thundered. "I'm itching to get down there and hear what's happening."

"I have to agree with Ferrel, Sandoval," Jade said.

Beside her, Tronus nodded emphatically, frowning down at one of the Snufflebeams as the young dwarf tried to squeeze in closer. *Must be Milton,* Tronus thought. *He always was pushy.* Tronus shoved the boy out of his way and turned his attention back to Sandoval.

"We may be too far away to do any good now," Tronus groused. "Even for you, wizard, this is cutting it too close."

Sandoval rose and bowed before Trelaine, sweeping one arm wide to indicate she should precede him to where Menopet stood sipping from the bucket of water. Trelaine's chin jutted out in defiance, though she did give Jade and the others a nod of acknowledgement as she strode toward the horses. The others scampered to resaddle their mounts or pack up their belongings.

Tronus looked up at Sandoval with a twinkle in his eye. "You know, if I didn't know better, I'd say you keep stickin' burrs under her saddle, just to see her get riled."

"Some of the sweetest treats are often made by burning the sugar," Sandoval responded cryptically.

CHAPTER 15

SPIRITS OF ONE HOUSE

King Filemon, tall even in the saddle, with his orange-red hair fluttering in the light breeze that blew across the plains, sat his huge roan stallion with the same stately grace he showed at ceremonies in Sanctuary. Gazing ahead at the Ileana camp, he leaned toward his right and directed a quiet order at Norena, the Gold Guild wizard who had been at his side since his coronation more than thirty years previous. Norena turned and nodded solemnly at Director Angelon Tantilus, riding three tiers back in the midst of the surrounding barons and their soldiers. Angelon's round head, covered with white hair that stuck out wildly in all directions, nodded back and whispered to the White Guild wizard riding next to him. Nudging his horse out of the main group, Tantilus, followed by a contingent of fifteen White Guild wizards, broke off from the main body of the army and headed almost directly east of their position at a leisurely trot. Atop a brown-and-white spotted mare, the director's round body bounced awkwardly, like a magician's ball precariously balanced on a wobbly spinning plate. Behind the white wizards, four other wizards of the Gold Guild, each attached to separate barons, also broke off and followed the director and his group.

Behind King Filemon were arrayed full contingents of soldiers from the baronies that surrounded or were closest to the Grimwood and Mt. Thorn. These included the Toogood, Carthwait, Nestor, and Wentland baronies. Above each group flew the flag of its respective baronies, carried by the lead of that baron's personal guard and followed by as many soldiers as they could hurriedly free from their duties. These were not battle-hardened warriors, such as the elves they were moving to meet, but were mostly parade and show soldiers, whose major contributions to their masters rarely resulted in more than local conflicts with angry farmers or merchants. On occasion, the soldiers may have had to draw lines across from an irate citizenry, but they were not eager to spill anyone's blood, let alone their own—that is, with the exception of Baron Carthwait's contingent who, along with their leader, were always eager to jump into any foray.

Baron Carthwait rode on the eastern flank of the army, his chin up and a defiant, a twisted smile on his pasty, arrogant face. His Black Guard and the soldiers of his barony were ruthless fighters and even fought each other in annual games, as well as competitions with others on a regular basis. If they were lucky enough to gather together some men from the local villages who would face them in riding, sword play, or hand-to-hand combat, that was even better. Then they could satisfy their most vicious appetites for mayhem. Fortunately, only the most callow youths from the surrounding villages were eager to join those games in hopes of taking the generous purses they awarded. Some actually won a bout or two, which generally put them in line for service with the baron. The more brutal they were, the more eager was Carthwait to have them serve him. Though he rarely discussed his service with Baron Carthwait's Black Guard, Ferrel Lovelace was just one of those youths who had served the baron for years before meeting Jade Sholeen and learning the error of his ways.

King Filemon, instead of continuing to circle around the rear of the Ileana camp, guided his horse directly toward the left flank of the battle line of elves arrayed on the flat top of the hill before them. He was close enough now to see the nearest of that line of elves point to the contingent of wizards, which had broken off and were now circling behind their lines. Yet even as they pointed and appeared to shout instructions to the remaining elves in front of the closely set tents behind them, none of them moved to change his position. Filemon nodded to himself in satisfaction. Maybe it would all work out as planned in the end. He certainly didn't want to face the magic and might of trained elf warriors. Retaining the slow steady pace of his army, he moved closer to the elf line.

Director Tantilus, backed by his white wizards, swung around the rear of the Ileana camp in a brisk trot and rounded up on the right rear of that camp. Behind them followed the tight grouping of the four Gold Guild wizards, ready to direct their considerable power through the white wizards, thus amplifying that magic considerably. Elf warriors, with bows in hand and arrows nocked, surrounded the camp in a loose circle, facing outward and watching the maneuver of the humans with stoic elven calm. Tantilus slowed his mount to a brisk walk and the tight contingent finally came to a halt, facing the leading right flank of elf warriors, almost directly opposite King Filemon's army on the left flank. If one didn't know any better, they'd think the humans were supporting the Ileana clan. To dispel any misunderstanding, King Filemon and Norena, with each of the four barons, two on either side of them, trotted away from the main body of the army to halt halfway between the leading Florian and the Ileana lines, facing the Ileana.

Back in the Florian camp, those closest to Nortenaine's tent could hear the raised voice of Maelthor, as Bruel brought the news of the duplicity of the humans to his lord's attention. Nortenaine's calm response could probably have been heard, but any elves within close enough distance were distracted by the sound of horses' hooves as Sandoval and Trelaine on Menopet burst from the forest behind them. Before Menopet had come to a complete halt, Trelaine leaped from his back and ran into Nortenaine's tent. Sandoval patted the big black horse on the neck and, dismounting, bowed to the gathering Florian elves. If they were shocked to see the white wizard in their midst again, the only evidence of it was an occasional peaked eyebrow or pursed lips. *The elves redefine the word stoicism, that's for sure*, Sandoval thought.

Standing in the rear of the Florian camp, next to Nortenaine's large tent, Sandoval had a good view of the battlefield laid out across the plains that separated the Florian camp from the hill on which the Ileana had settled. He saw Filemon, Norena, and the barons approach the center of the stretch of land between both elf clan camps and turn to face the Ileana. Sandoval didn't need his distance viewer to easily see a tall but stoop-shouldered older elf emerge from the large tent in the middle of his camp and walk slowly to stand with the elves marking their battle line. Sandoval studied the man closely, noting his fine robe with gold-thread markings, and decided that he met the description of Vaester Shee given to him by Ferrel, Jade, and Tronus. The old elf appeared nervous, running his hands up and down the sides of his robe. Sandoval began to wonder whether this vessel of the Ileana was having second thoughts about helping to escalate the enmity between the clans to this standoff, when the swift movement of several warrior elves near the side of the large tent drew his eyes, including those of the Florian elves who stood watching. With a brisk step, a huge black stallion who could have been Menopet's twin, though even heavier in girth, trotted from behind the tent, carrying a large figure completely encased in red armor. The helmet on his head, with a tall red plume on top, gleamed in the afternoon sunlight. Mounting a horse brought up for him, Vaester Shee joined the strange knight.

"I doubt any of the elves have seen his like," Sandoval said quietly.

He had seen one of the elves rush into Nortenaine's tent. Now that warrior exited, followed by Nortenaine, Maelthor, and Bruel. Trelaine was not with them. The elves were clothed in long green tunics, interwoven with gold elven lettering circling a golden fountain that reminded Sandoval of the fountain in the Quelean common. Below the tunics, they sported green buckskin leggings. On his head, Nortenaine wore a thin gold crown.

Nortenaine turned to meet Sandoval's eyes, his own blue eyes clouded with suspicion and distrust. Maelthor also saw Sandoval and his company and jerked a motion toward one of the warriors coming up to them for orders. The warrior nodded toward several of his companions, and they started in Sandoval's direction, but a vocal admonishment and a swift shake of Nortenaine's head brought them to a halt. Maelthor threw Nortenaine a dark look, and Bruel whispered hurriedly in his ear, but instead of responding, he only took his sword from the warrior who held it out to him and strapped it to his side. Another elf brought up a horse-drawn vehicle and halted before the small group in front of the tent. It was an odd contraption with a seat for the driver, behind which was a platform, open in the rear, that allowed the elves to stand, bracing themselves with bars on either side. Sandoval started humming a tune.

"Do not forsake me, oh, my darlin' ..." Sandoval sang in a deep bass voice.

"It is an odd time to be singing, wizard. Is that a warding tune, to protect you in battle?" Maelthor called out sarcastically.

"No, just a little tune I picked up, about a duel." At that, Sandoval leaped up on Menopet's back.

"We do not wish your assistance in this, Sandoval Carmichael." Maelthor's voice rose angrily.

"I'm not assisting either party in this dispute," Sandoval said for the benefit of Nortenaine, who kept his eyes trained on the Ileana camp and didn't turn his head or respond to Sandoval's remark.

"Suit yourself, wizard."

With that clipped response, Maelthor and Bruel climbed onto their vehicle. Nortenaine followed, still without acknowledging Sandoval's presence. With a company of warriors on foot trotting behind, the elf who was driving snapped the reins, and the contraption rolled out toward the group of humans who were, even now, facing toward the red warrior. Trelaine came back out of the tent at that moment, clad in the same green tunic and pants as the male elves. She slipped up next to Sandoval. As Menopet danced, eager to follow, Sandoval reached out and scooped up Trelaine to settle behind him.

Across the Valley of the Mists, King Filemon and his party sat their horses in nervous anticipation, as Vaester Shee and the red warrior on their respective mounts moved forward at a slow walk to halt before them. Vaester Shee nodded at King Filemon, his sharp blue eyes scanning the four barons quickly and finally resting upon Norena. The Gold Guild wizard had not held her position for the thirty-plus years of the king's reign without having learned diplomacy in the ever-changing political arena. Never take your opponent for granted or at face value was the first lesson she had ever learned, and even though she faced what appeared to be an elderly elf, she noted the bright, intelligent gleam in his eyes and knew that neither she nor the king could afford to underestimate this person who, by his office, had great power to hold together an elven clan such as the Ileana, without benefit of a high lord to back him. King Filemon was obviously mirroring his wizard's thoughts, for his first words were delivered in an even tone to Vaester Shee.

"I am Filemon Landelaine and from the gold markings on your robe, I am assuming that I am addressing Vaester Shee, vessel to the Ileana."

"You are correct, King Filemon. And I will assume that the woman next to you is Norena, your Gold Guild wizard and chief diplomat. I do not know the barons who accompany you, with the exception of Baron Wentland. We have communicated in the past, as his barony is the closest to Mt. Thorn."

Baron Wentland nodded acknowledgement when his name was spoken. Beside him, Baron Carthwait grunted, but Vaester Shee ignored him. Next to him, the huge black stallion carrying the red knight snorted and stamped the grass. Vaester Shee glanced sideways toward the rider but did not turn to look at him directly. Filemon and Norena, being directly across from the vessel and the warrior, would later acknowledge that they felt a chill air drifting over them that appeared to come from the knight in red. Their horses were already showing signs of nervousness. Behind him, Filemon heard one of the barons trying to calm his mount; another whinnied softly.

"I would like to invite you and a delegation of your choosing," Filemon said, glancing quickly at the red knight, then back to Vaester Shee, "to meet with the lord and vessel of the Florians for diplomatic talks. I intend to make the same offer to Nortenaine in hopes that we humans may assist the Ileana and Florian in airing their difficulties and arriving at an agreement to cease any further actions against each other."

"And you humans believe this would be beneficial to your people?"

"By all means. Peace between the elven clans will stabilize the entire region of Pacifica, just as continued war could have drastic effects upon our economy, as well as endanger the lives of those humans who live within close confines of the Grimwood and the plains. Of course, this diplomatic delegation would require agreement from both the Ileana and Florian to head the talks between you."

"Enough!" came a strong but hollow voice from behind the red helmet of the knight. The eerie, echoing voice caused all of the horses to dance about and a few to whinny frantically in protest.

"You humans presume much. You will remove yourself from this place. Remaining where you are not wanted will only put you and your army in jeopardy."

Filemon shot a questioning look at Norena, just as the contingent from the Florian arrived. Maelthor directed the driver of their conveyance to align themselves next to King Filemon, who didn't take his eyes from the red knight. On the other side, next to Norena, Sandoval halted Menopet. The red knight did not turn toward the Florians but did swing his helmeted head toward Sandoval. The red helmet dipped slightly in acknowledgement of the white wizard. Filemon shot a suspicious look at Sandoval but still directed his question to Vaester Shee.

"I'm afraid you have me at a disadvantage, vessel of the Ileana. Please present your knight to our party."

Vaester Shee's rigid countenance faltered slightly as he glanced from the humans to Nortenaine and Maelthor. His voice quavered discernibly as he responded. "May I present to elves and humans alike, the wrath of the Ileana: Rolf Andelar!"

Gabbling voices rose in protest, highest of them all was that of Maelthor. King Filemon, keeping his horse steady with an iron grip on the reins, raised a cautioning hand. Behind him, Sandoval heard Trelaine's quick, rasping intake of breath at Vaester Shee's pronouncement. Unlike the other horses that were prancing nervously as they picked up on their rider's emotional turmoil, Menopet stood steadily, only tossing his great head and snorting at the larger black stallion. Nortenaine was the first to speak, his hand on the sword strapped to his waist.

"It is unexpected that a vessel alone would have the power to conjure a wraith from the dead. Am I to expect that you received some assistance from the wizards of the humans?"

The words were sneered in defiance at Vaester Shee but any response was cut off by the echoing response of the red knight.

"This vessel had no hand in my appearance, Lord Nortenaine. I have returned for one purpose: to avenge my death and that of my bride, Lilliana, at the hands of the Florian!"

"This travesty will go on no further!" yelled Maelthor, his sword as well as Nortenaine's aimed at the red knight. "I challenge this imposter to prove he is Rolf Andelar. Having been the one to remove his head from his body, I would like to see how he managed to reset it!"

Norena was the one to gasp now, swinging around to glare at Maelthor. She raised her staff, bringing it in front of King Filemon, as if it alone would protect her liege from harm. Filemon reached up and pushed the staff away from him, shaking his head in admonishment at Norena. Everyone seemed to hold their breath. A hollow laugh emitted from the red helmet, and the red knight raised his mailed fists. With one swift gesture, the helmet was lifted from his shoulders, revealing a bony ghostly stump of spine protruding from the metal collar of his armor. Norena closed her eyes momentarily, shaking her head in disbelief. Above the bony stump of spine appeared the ghostly shape of a male elf's head, with flowing dark hair wavering about it, as if truly caught in the light breeze that swept over them. The spectral eyes seemed the only animate thing about it, as they glowed feverishly toward one, then another, of the humans and elves. Sandoval recognized it as the same ghost he had seen at the green pool and nodded acknowledgement at King Filemon and Norena, who had turned toward him.

"No! It is a lie!" came the choked response from Maelthor.

Nortenaine, recognizing Rolf Andelar at once, lowered his sword and slipped it back in its scabbard. "It is Rolf Andelar," he said to King Filemon in a tight voice.

Nortenaine reached out to grip Maelthor's arm, as if trying to force him to lower his sword, but the vessel of the Florian was frozen, his eyes blazing his hatred toward the figure of Rolf Andelar.

"She could have been saved!" intoned the ghostly head.

"This spirit is unclean, my lord!" Maelthor turned to Nortenaine. "It must be banished to the realm of the unblessed!"

His handsome face sagging in sorrow and grief, Nortenaine shook his head at Maelthor. But the dark elf vessel shrugged off Nortenaine's hand and leaped from the back of the chariot, his wild eyes turned toward Norena.

"You have the power in you. We must destroy this evil spirit, or it will destroy us, as well as you humans."

Sandoval slid from his saddle and stepped between the two groups. He faced King Filemon and Norena.

"What the spirit of Rolf Andelar speaks is true. I saw him before at the scene of the murder, and I am sure I know what happened there so many long years ago."

"You are a traitor to your people and a spy. The humans are in league with the Ileana! My lord, we must silence this wizard!" Maelthor came toward Sandoval, his sword raised threateningly.

"I'm not sure how I can be a traitor to my people, and a spy for them and the Ileana at the same time, but that is neither here nor there," Sandoval said dryly, ignoring the sword being brandished just inches from his nose. "I would request that Nortenaine call for a *reckoning* to resolve the dispute between the clans."

It was as if a blast from a gold wizard's staff had struck the ground in front of him. Maelthor's reaction was violent, and the sword he swung down on Sandoval might have split him in two, were it not for the intersection of both Sandoval's and Norena's staffs that crossed in front of Sandoval and produced the result of changing Maelthor's sword to a bouquet of flowers that struck the staffs, breaking them into colorful petals, leaves, and small pieces of stalk that drifted gently to the grass at their feet. Maelthor stared dumbly at the remaining stalks gripped in his hand before recovering himself and releasing them. Turning to Nortenaine with eyes that still blazed, he raised his hands imploringly.

"My lord, you must not listen to the white wizard. He is false, and I am sure he had a hand in the death of Noona, the handmaiden. They are all in this together and bent on destroying the Florian. The gods have already left the Grimwood's sacred heart, but I am sure we can bring them back to us as soon as we rid the Grimwood of the Ileana, who would defile it. But if you allow this ... this blasphemy, the gods will surely desert us, and we will be lost to them forever!"

Nortenaine colored slightly at this unaccustomed outburst from his vessel. He glanced furtively at King Filemon and then across at the passive red knight, who still held his helmet under one arm. Finally, he sighed and turned to Maelthor. The vessel of the Florian read the answer in Nortenaine's set face, as well as the slight slump of his broad shoulders.

Nortenaine then directed his gaze to Sandoval, his blue eyes filled with weariness and pain. "The reckoning isn't meant to place blame or choose sides." He murmured so softly that he could barely be heard beyond the first row of humans and by the enhanced hearing of the elves and wizards. "In ages past, it was meant to reunite the spirits of one house, as the legend tells us. There will be no more Florian blood spilled this day. I agree to the reckoning."

Before Maelthor could do more than gasp in despair and anger, the air around them began to glow with an ethereal light.

"It is done," a tired voice intoned, seeming to emit from the air around them.

Those watching from the Ileana and Florian camps saw that odd glow around the party on the battlefield for a brief moment, before Rolf Andelar, Vaester Shee, Nortenaine, Maelthor, Bruel, Sandoval, and Trelaine disappeared, along with their mounts.

"What is this?" shouted Filemon, as Norena spun around in her saddle and searched the area around them. The barons also swung their horses around, drawing swords. Their combined voices rose in discordant indignation, finally cut off by the raised hand of Filemon.

"Who was that? Who could have made them all disappear? Did you hear someone speak?" Norena was clutching her staff and glaring angrily at the Ileana and Florian camps.

"I don't think that voice belonged to any of the elves. It had a strange, echoing sound to it. All too human, it sounded," King Filemon said.

"What do we do now? We can't just sit out here like a bunch of fools!" growled Baron Carthwait.

"Damn Sandoval Carmichael!" Norena howled, raising her staff to the heavens. "This will mean his head on a platter if you listen to me, my king!"

"We make camp and wait," Filemon said as he turned his horse and headed back toward his gathered army. "Whatever Sandoval is planning will either work, or he'll be too dead to care if his head is missing."

CHAPTER 16

THE COURT OF LAST RESORT

With Hoagy in the lead, packing Harald in front of him on Bully, and Tronus behind, his strong arms clutched around Hoagy's waist, the rest of Sandoval's company wound their way through a narrow path in a direction that was taking them deep into the Grimwood. Hoagy was followed by Jade and Ferrel, each carrying two of the Snufflebeam Company on their mounts. All of them cast anxious glances into the dense foliage that closed in on either side of the path. Hoagy had given Bully his head to keep pace with the darting, yellow light that floated above the trail in front of them. The stalwart gelding kept up a brisk pace, dodging low-hanging branches and weaving through clinging vines that hung from odd, twisted trees. Hoagy could hear Tronus behind him, cursing roughly each time a branch slapped at his face. Hoagy had placed Harald in front of him on the saddle so his keen eyes could also follow the small, bright, yellow point of light ahead of them on the barely visible trail. The deeper the small group plunged into the forest, the closer the trees enveloped them, until the noonday sun high above could not penetrate the cover. Hoagy leaned low and hugged Harald, alert for each warning of a twist or turn in the trail. When the spot of light, which even Hoagy was able to follow in the dim light, blinked out, he pulled Bully to a trot. He was not about to put his beloved horse in jeopardy—or himself and the rest of them, for that matter—by allowing the mad dash in almost total darkness to continue.

At the tail end of the group, Ferrel called out, "I think it's time to take a rest, Hoagy."

"I second that!" came the response from Jade and Tronus together.

Hoagy pulled Bully to a halt, as Harald leaped brazenly from the saddle.

"Tillie! Where did she go? I know she wouldn't desert us, sir."

"I'm sure she wouldn't, Harald. But it's time to rest the horses and ourselves."

Before Harald could protest, Jade's voice called from within the trees to the right of the path.

"There's enough space here. We can probably build a small fire."

"We could use that daffy wizard's staff light about now," Tronus grumbled.

Hoagy dismounted, took Bully's reins, and turned back toward the sound of Jade and Ferrel's voices off to the side of the trail. Tronus, without Hoagy to hold onto, grabbed the reins also.

"If you let go, Tronus, I'll lead the horses."

Tronus expelled a humph of disgust and released his grip. Hoagy picked his way carefully through a dim opening in the trees and found himself in a gap just barely big enough to fit them all, with little room to maneuver. There was enough of a break in the tree foliage overhead to allow some afternoon sunlight to filter through, so he could see that Jade was already opening her bag and laying out provisions. Ferrel came out of the forest on the other side with an armful of dead wood, enough to build a fire to heat their cherok. He used a sharp stick to dig out a small indentation in the grass that would serve as a fire pit.

"Let's just hope the faeries don't take a dislike to our lighting a fire," Tronus said, sliding down the side of Bully and stretching his short legs.

Ferrel snapped his flint and the dry wood took light. Within a few moments there was a bright blaze going under the little grill, upon which Jade sat a pot to heat the cherok. In silence, they all took the bread and cheese she offered and set about chewing and sipping. It was so quiet in that little clearing that everyone could hear Tronus' stomach growling before he washed down the first mouthful from his steaming cup—which made it more surprising that none of them heard the approach of Tillie, in her full form, until her tinkling laughter broke the silence.

"My what a noise!" She looked at Tronus. "You will wake the spirits of the forest with such a grumble!"

They all jerked upright at the sound of her laughter, and Harald popped to his feet, a broad smile on his face.

"Tillie! I told them you wouldn't desert us. But we had to stop and take some sup before going on again."

"How much farther will it be before we arrive at the Grimwood's heart?" Hoagy asked her.

"Not much farther from here. Actually, the sacred center of the Grimwood isn't truly at its center, for it moves, depending on where we want it to be."

Tillie smiled pertly at the confused looks that answered her. Jade and Ferrel exchanged worried frowns. Harald saw his friend's consternation and hurriedly filled the tense silence.

"Oh, sirs and madam—and Number One," he added for Tronus' benefit, "I'm sure Tillie means that sort of figuratively."

"No," the little wood sprite said, nonplused. "It really doesn't have a particular spot. It is the spiritual center of the Grimwood. We just know where everyone is going to be and at what time. We won't miss anything, I promise."

Tronus glared at Harald until the Snufflebeam Company giggled at their lieutenant's discomfort. To recall order among the troops, Tronus knocked one of them on the noggin with his knuckles. "All right, you boys, get this camp packed up. We're heading out. And be sure to douse that fire proper."

Harald assisted in the packing, turning every few moments to check that Tillie was still there waiting for them. He would smile wistfully at her and receive a wink in reply before continuing his packing. Waldo

Snufflebeam, who had been working next to him, had to stop each time, as Harald usually had something suspended in his hand. He finally grabbed the last item from Harald and hefted the pack, giving a disgruntled huff at his lieutenant as he stomped toward the horses.

At last they were mounted, and without another word, Tillie raised her arms swiftly, spinning into a small light that swooped about Harald's head as he sat in front of Hoagy and bounced away toward the trail. This time, she managed to keep a more reasonable pace, the little dot of light darting to and fro on the path before them, so the company had little trouble following her progress. Still, it seemed a long time before the light shot off to their right through the trees, reappearing once only to swoop back through a break in the foliage. When they followed her, they found themselves entering a large clearing that was covered by a canopy of trees and lit by an indiscernible golden glow. At the far end, seated on two small thrones, were a male and female faerie, each in long robes and wearing small silver crowns upon their heads. Flanking them were numerous faeries, dancing about and bursting out with tinkling laughter. Tillie resumed her full form before the king and queen and curtsied deeply. Then, gesturing to Harald and the others to follow her, she led them off to the side near the tree line, where they could dismount and tether their horses.

"Well, if this ain't something," Tronus mumbled beneath his breath.

"Surely we have been given a great honor to be here," Jade said in awe.

"Well, I suppose we should go and present ourselves," Hoagy said, then aside to Tillie, who was obviously flirting with a flustered Harald, he said, "Tillie, how should we address the king and queen of the faeries? I don't even know their names."

"King Hileantis and Queen Traeponae. You can just call them 'Your Majesties.' That's what we do."

Hoagy nodded to his company, and they all moved forward as one, stopping before the king and queen, who they could now see were smaller than an average elf and not much bigger than Tillie, all faeries being of approximately the same height. It made Hoagy feel a little odd to be looking down on such a dignified pair.

The king had long, curly blond hair. His dark green eyes sparkled merrily as he grinned up at them. Queen Traeponae appeared more regal in bearing, with long dark hair beneath her small silver crown. Her steady gray eyes studied each of them in turn, stopping at Jade and considering the warrior woman for a long moment.

Jade was taller than most women and even some men, including Hoagy, and had her own particular proud bearing. Next to her, towering even higher from their highnesses' point of view, was Ferrel. Yet even as they had to crane their necks upward to take the humans in, neither the king nor the queen appeared even the least bit uncomfortable. Queen Traeponae smiled up at them.

Hoagy took advantage of the momentary lull to make a low bow. Even the romping faeries had by now ceased singing and dancing and were regarding them solemnly.

"Your Majesties, please accept our sincere regards and appreciation for allowing we who are not of your kin to attend the proceedings here today."

"There are some events even we cannot control," intoned the king in a high, piping voice, his face creased in a frown.

"I would like to know your names," said the queen in a soft voice.

"I am Jade Sholeen, of the Lestrami and this is my companion, Ferrel Lovelace."

Jade bowed at the waist, pulling Ferrel down with her. Straightening, Jade and Ferrel moved aside. Tronus stepped forward.

"Tronus Longbottom, Your Majesties, of the Thunderstorm Mountain Dwarves.

And this is my lieutenant, Harald Brassbucket, and his company of young recruits: Waldo, Gort, Tumpe, and Milton Snufflebeam."

The Snufflebeam Company scurried forward to bow before the royal couple, until Tronus patted the nearest on the shoulder and motioned them backward.

The little queen eyed Harald and smiled. "You must be Tillie's friend. She has spoken highly of you."

Harald reddened suddenly and opened his mouth, but no sound came out. Behind them, they could hear some snickering laughter from the young faeries. Tronus patted Harald on the back and gave him a wink of encouragement.

"I think it is about time for the proceedings to begin," the king piped in his high voice.

Hoagy motioned for them to move back, away from the center of the forest amphitheater, as the air about them began to crackle ominously. Tronus scooted the Snufflebeam Company before him as they all lined up with Hoagy, with Jade and Ferrell flanking them, facing toward the center of the large area.

"What's going to happen, sir?" Harald said in a tight whisper to Hoagy.

"I'm not sure, but I'll bet it'll be a sight none of us has ever seen and maybe never will again." Hoagy tried to look confident, but his insides were squeamish at that moment.

"Here we go, guys," said Jade, her words dying away as lights spun around in a whirlwind of sparkling color, widening until they almost covered the entire area, the border stopping just before the startled spectators. With an audible pop, the lights were extinguished, revealing an equally shocked group that consisted of Sandoval, Trelaine, Nortenaine, Maelthor, Vaester Shee, and a tall, headless knight armored in red. Tillie and several of the other faeries clapped their hands and exclaimed happily at this event, which caused the king and queen to frown and shake their heads angrily. Effectively silenced, all watched in stunned fascination as Maelthor spun about, his sword swooping over the observers, who backed away, then rounded on Vaester Shee and the red knight.

"What trickery is this?" he bellowed.

"Not of our making," Vaester Shee answered wearily.

Sandoval, who had calmly taken in the area and spectators, smiled broadly. "Well, I suppose we should present ourselves to our hosts, don't you think?"

CHAPTER 17

TRUE BELIEVERS

With a ring of steel, Bruel pulled his sword from its scabbard and moved from Maelthor's side so that each of them flanked Nortenaine and faced the Ileana. Nortenaine's normally pale face had turned a pasty gray. The high lord of the Florian appeared to be stunned to silence, for he neither spoke nor acknowledged them. With a lunge, Maelthor thrust his sword into the red knight, but the blade merely slipped through the spirit warrior as if he weren't there.

Sandoval took Trelaine's elbow and spoke in her ear, modulating his voice so low that none of those around them could hear. "You must come with me now."

Woodenly, the elf maiden allowed Sandoval to push past the stunned warriors and step up to the seated king and queen of the faeries. King Hileantis and Queen Traeponae both sat in haughty silence as Sandoval bowed before them. He tugged ever so slightly on Trelaine's arm until she curtsied stiffly. A gasp behind him and a light gust of cold air told Sandoval that the red knight had moved next to him. Out of the side of his eye, Sandoval saw the spirit warrior bow low, his helmet still clutched under one arm. Close behind him came Vaester Shee on unsteady feet. Neither of the royals moved to acknowledge them; instead, their cold eyes turned toward the remaining elves. As if drawn toward them by an invisible hand, Nortenaine, Bruel, and Maelthor reluctantly joined them.

"The human has at last brought to us those who have defiled the sacred home of the elves by the murder of kin," their voices chimed in unison.

"What do you mean?" Nortenaine gasped, a faint flush finally suffusing his pale face.

King Hileantis stood then, his small stature not diminishing the look in his hard green eyes, nor the strength of his high voice. "We would know why you have forsaken this place of your birth." In his hand he held a crystal ball, which swirled with varied colors.

This must be a seeing stone, thought Hoagy, wishing to get closer to it but not daring to do so.

"This *creature* murdered Lilliana, a maiden of the Florian." Nortenaine pointed at Rolf Andelar, his voice hoarse with emotion. "It was his act that forced the gods to desert us and go into hiding. His act has stained our ancestral home with blood."

Queen Traeponae stood suddenly, her arm sweeping toward Nortenaine as if to brush away his emotional response.

"You have been misled by those close to you. This reckoning will open eyes that have been shut against truth."

Maelthor pushed Nortenaine aside and glowered down at the diminutive faerie queen. "I demand to know by what authority you presume to bring us here. And how you propose to hold us against our will. Your little show of transportation doesn't impress me."

The little faerie queen cocked her head up at him and a tight smile spread over her lips. "You are welcome to leave—if you can."

Maelthor nodded curtly toward Nortenaine, then spun around and stalked toward what appeared to be a path out of the clearing. As he neared the tree line, he ran headfirst into an invisible barrier with a loud smack and fell backward on the grass. Pushing himself up, his face reddened with anger and bewilderment, he stalked back toward the group. Before he could vent his bitterness, King Hileantis cut him off with a wave of his hand.

"I would ask you, Maelthor, as well as the vessel of the Ileana represented here, why you have transformed the faith of your forefathers into twisted versions of bitterness and bigotry." The king's gaze turned toward Vaester Shee.

"But we Ileana have only upheld the one faith of our revered ancestors, the original elven warriors of the old days," Vaester Shee sputtered.

"We Florian have been the vanguard of the faith as our fathers carried the strain of purity when they severed themselves from the Ileana, who had been tainted." Maelthor's voice rose and he turned a hate-filled gaze toward Vaester Shee.

Queen Traeponae laughed a tinkling laugh, like the chime of a silver bell. "Ah, yes, purity and piety—those are always good excuses. Your revered ancestors, you say?" She looked from one to the other. "Those ancestors you so honor stand before you!"

Maelthor and Vaester Shee both gasped in shock. Sandoval heard Trelaine's sharp intake of breath and saw the reaction of Nortenaine and Bruel in the stupefied looks they directed at each other. Sandoval could also hear muttered exclamations from his group of friends. He turned his head to look at Trelaine, but her head was bowed, and her dark hair, falling forward, covered her face. Sandoval did note that her hands were clasped together in front of her, and she twisted them convulsively. When he turned back to the little faerie queen, he noticed an odd tingling in his head and a soft ringing in his ears. His hand automatically gripped his staff tightly, for security as much as for support, as the air around them wavered, and an image appeared all around them, as if they were insubstantial motes drifting on the air, encompassed within, but not a part of the actions being played out before them.

Horrified, but unable to move, they viewed the cataclysm that resulted in the reformation of the planet: a massive red planet—the legendary Angel of Death—that covered the sky from one end of the horizon to the other; land masses sank beneath roiling seas, while others burst open, spewing fire and smoke into the air; people were crushed and burned beneath structures thrown about by massive explosions;

hot blasting wind seared all animals and growing things and above it all, the terrifying vision of the planet was bearing down on them. But instead of impacting them, it swept by, pulling behind it a trail of noxious vapor, steam, and debris that rained down on them and covered the earth and drew darkness about them.

Then, from within that darkness, came shimmering sparks of light that cut through and touched the torn and scarred landscape to bring forth small sprouts of green. And from small beginnings, that magic spread its light and life onto the planet. Sandoval knew that time was passing in what they viewed as a remarkable pace, but it all was clear to him. Odd forms of animals and plants grew up around them, and tiny sparks of life burst from gloriously colorful flowers and spun about, streaking into the air, which shimmered and quivered about them like a living thing. Myriad flying creatures, from sparkling butterflies and dragonflies to tiny, winged faeries, filled the air. And men appeared, and Dwarves crawled from caves to blink in the new sunlight and gather together. The new creatures of this world found their own places, drawn by their nature to open spaces or to the close, dim green comfort of the forests and glens. Within the forests, faeries found their forms and gloried in their aliveness, bringing from it new shapes, from chortling goblins to trolls, which grew to frightful giant sizes. In the air above them, birds swooped and sang, and higher above, sweeping in, out, and among the clouds, soared dragons of all colors and sizes.

Sandoval was sure that if he turned his head and concentrated on one area, such as the formation of the human settlements, he would see the growth of the villages and cities and the sprouting of sculptured fields filled with crops of all sorts. He would see mankind lift itself up—men building ships to sail seas that gleamed brilliantly blue, and structures to house themselves, and tools to work with, as well as fight with.

But all eyes were glued upon the twirling figures of faeries that danced and sang and spun webs of magic to bring forth the animals of the forest, and with them sprung the huge form of an elf warrior. He was clad in short tunic and leather vest, and his flowing, reddish-gold hair framed a beautiful, angular face. He brandished a gleaming sword, which he aimed at the sky, as if in salute. This image hovered over them, now changing to that of a beautiful, stately elf maiden, with flowing golden hair encircled by a thin band of silver and a sparkling gown of myriad colors. Then it changed back to the elf warrior. The image flip-flopped in a dizzying array and soon appeared to become one. As they continued to stare upward, the figure brought its sword down and touched the earth. A clear ringing tone vibrated about them, and those watching gasped in amazement as the ground opened up, and from it were lifted the tall, lithe forms of female and male elves of varied skin and hair colors, and they brought with them stately horses upon which to ride, and about them were risen towering trees and a lush and teaming forest. Beyond that, the observers could see a span of grassy plains, upon which rode the elves on fleet steeds, their cries of joy reaching to the heavens. The figure turned to the silent, awed observers, bowed its head solemnly, then winked out.

The spell lifted, Nortenaine, Bruel, and a silently weeping Vaester Shee bowed before the king and queen of the faeries and were about to prostrate themselves, when King Hileantis waved them back.

"There is no need for that. We do not wish to be worshiped. Too much pain has been caused by such slavery to ideals. Know only that we are all part of this world and created of the same elements."

"No, my lord! This is a trick that these faeries have created with the help of the Ileana. You must not accept this!" Maelthor cried.

Maelthor pulled Nortenaine around to face him, his hands gripping the elf lord's arms and shaking him as if to wake him. Nortenaine pushed him away, the fear in his eyes replaced by a sadness and sudden realization. He shook his head, his body appearing to slump wearily. Sandoval moved to stand next to him, his hand lightly touching Nortenaine's shoulder. Maelthor stepped away from the group and glared at them, each in turn, his blazing brown eyes resting lastly upon his twin, Trelaine.

"I do not believe this. You must not."

"On the contrary," Sandoval interjected, his black eyes moving from Maelthor to Trelaine, "you killed Rolf Andelar because you *do* believe and always have."

Maelthor glowered at him, his face twisting in a bitter smile. "I should have killed you, wizard, when I had the chance. You have caused dissention among the Florian, and you have tried to turn my sister against me, as well as Nortenaine."

Sandoval would not be cowed. "You drove away your lady mother because she wouldn't agree to disown her people, the Ileana, and also because you didn't want her to ruin the work you had done, instilling your own bitterness and self-loathing for your Ileana blood in your sister."

"It cannot all be laid at Maelthor's door, Inspector," Vaester Shee interjected. "I, too, am guilty of a similar distrust and revulsion for those who didn't fit my ideal of elfkind and our way of life. I have striven so desperately to identify the Ileana separately from all things Florian that I have clung to what we always believed was the *true* faith of the elves."

"Ours is the true faith!" Maelthor growled, moving toward the Ileana vessel.

Sandoval placed his staff firmly in the ground between the two vessels and stepped in front of Maelthor. Nortenaine and Bruel flanked him on either side. Maelthor's hard brown eyes rounded in surprise. He whirled on Trelaine, whose head lifted. Her brown eyes, like bottomless hollows in her drawn face, stared balefully at him. One hand came up, outstretched, a finger jutting forward to point at him.

"You killed them both in your pride! You are an arrogant fool!" Trelaine spun around and faced Vaester Shee and the silent red knight. "I carry the blood of Iledan within me. I am the true lady of the Ileana and should lead them. I could have been the princess you deserved." Her voice rang in a desperate plea.

"So you simply killed your rival," Sandoval said.

"No! She fell—"

"Yes, you told me the actual version of what happened that fateful day. As if you were there and saw it—because you were, Trelaine. You said Maelthor would not speak of the events of that day, and the historical record certainly was not accurate." Sandoval turned to Nortenaine. "Sorry, we had to practice a little deception to read them. Trelaine described the scene perfectly, but she left out the part where she pushed your half-sister off the ledge to the rocks below."

"He lies!" Trelaine cried, grabbing the front of Maelthor's tunic and shaking him. "Tell them that is not what you saw!"

"I did not see Lilliana fall. I came when Rolf was pulling her from the pool. I could not have guessed—oh, Trelaine, you have shamed me!"

Sandoval turned to King Hileantis, who held the seeing stone before him. It seemed to grow in size and as the colorful swirl of mist within the globe cleared, they all saw the form of Lilliana, balanced upon the slippery ledge, just at the edge of the cascade of water. She was already drenched, her long blonde hair matted about her face. Below, a dark-skinned elf burst from the forest and dashed to the edge of the green pool. It was Rolf Andelar, his arms raised in entreaty, his voice calling out to her, pleading. They heard the unspoken words and watched in dismay as Lilliana smiled and reached out her hand toward her lover. Upon that hand sparkled a silver band. Sandoval heard someone among his friends sniffing tearfully. Then they saw a hand reach out from the veil of water and shove Lilliana roughly off the ledge. As cries rose from the group of observers, the mist about the falls cleared, even as Rolf lunged into the water to pull his beloved from the rocks. Clearly through the mist of the falls, they could see the form of Trelaine, her face glowing in wild hate and triumph.

"And so the deed was done!" Sandoval intoned, like a rolling rumble of thunder as the scene in the seeing stone faded. "Perhaps you had regrets when you saw your brother dash your hopes of becoming an Ileana princess by killing Rolf. You may have buried that day deep within your mind, but that sepulcher in the forest was a constant reminder to you. And when you saw Hoagy and me meeting with Noona at her cottage, and her giving me the dress, you knew that I knew. Yes, though I didn't see you, I felt your presence. I knew immediately that much blood was not caused by the rocks she fell upon in the green pool. And you knew, because you had a clear view from your vantage point on the ledge above, just what transpired below. But you must have known that even if Noona agreed to go with Hoagy and me, she would never have betrayed her people. There was no reason to kill her. Not as compelling a reason as the one you had to commit yet another murder, but you were foiled in succeeding by a power greater than yours."

With a shriek that jolted the hearts of all in that clearing, Trelaine threw her head up, her arms reaching toward the sky, and crumbled to the ground at Sandoval's feet. Maelthor stared down at the crumpled form of his twin, then whirled on Sandoval.

"But the blood! If Rolf Andelar did not kill her, where did all the blood come from? There must be something missing. This is a false message. My lord, I cannot—"

Nortenaine cut him off with an abrupt gesture. He looked at Sandoval, the mixed emotions he felt now flashing across his smoothly sculpted face. Sandoval knew the question his friend wanted to ask—although he didn't want to hear the answer. By then, Hoagy and the others had closed ranks and joined up behind Sandoval.

"The blood was from the birth of Lilliana and Rolf's child," Sandoval continued in an unhurried fashion, even after a few more incredulous gasps and a low, quivering moan that came from the helmet of the red knight. All of those watching the drama unfold backed away from the tall elf spirit, as he seemed to loom over Sandoval now. "There were two others at the green pool that day: Tillie, the woods faerie, and the Glaistig, a faerie with a lust for blood, which lives in the green pool. The Florian carry her image in their legends and warnings of her abound. But the cautioning connected with the green pool has since gotten mixed with memories of the murder of Lilliana, followed by the swift demise of Rolf Andelar. It has become belief that the spirit of Rolf Andelar kills those who come too close to the green pool. In fact, the Glaistig happily takes care of that herself. She particularly likes young men." Sandoval glanced at Hoagy, who shivered involuntarily.

"But she protects children, and when Lilliana gave birth, the Glaistig assisted her and took the child. I could not extract the information from either the Glaistig or our Tillie as to where the child was taken. When I attempted to find out more about the fate of the child from Lilliana's handmaiden, Noona, my inquiries only sealed her fate. Trelaine quieted that voice in the only way she knew—by strangling her as she knelt to bid her farewell at Lilliana's bier."

"Trelaine …" Nortenaine groaned, his face twisted in agony as he looked down upon Trelaine's curled form.

Maelthor grabbed the front of Sandoval's robe, but Bruel hastily pulled the vessel's hands away and restrained him with a look. Maelthor shook free from Bruel and dropped to the ground to take his sister in his lap. Trelaine moaned, opened her eyes, and stared up at him. He pulled her up and held her tightly against him before the accusing faces of Nortenaine and Bruel. Trelaine slowly raised her head and glared in hatred at the specter in red armor, who stood silently.

"You could have given me my true birthright. I curse your memory!" she shrieked at him, her hands raised and claws extended toward him. "I gloried in your death!"

The red knight stood stoic and unresponsive. Nortenaine's face flushed in anger as he stepped toward her, only to be restrained by Bruel.

"She had a child," Nortenaine wailed, "You've killed more than two people! You have destroyed a part of the future of the Florian."

"I demand the death of both Maelthor and Trelaine," Bruel pronounced, directing his appeal to King Hileantis and Queen Traeponae.

"I didn't know …" Maelthor muttered, still holding Trelaine's inert body in his arms.

"Your hatred directed her hand!" Nortenaine's voice rose. "That same hatred has kept both clans killing each other for too many years and could have destroyed us completely!"

"We will not have death upon our hands and will not consent to elves or humans exacting such a sentence here. We do request that you allow us to take Maelthor and Trelaine with us. Neither the Ileana nor the Florian will see or hear more of them." Said King Hileantis.

"You will carry them to—" Nortenaine began, but King Hileantis raised his hand to silence Nortenaine.

"By the power of the first one. You need know no more. Give us your assent." Queen Traeponae cut him off gently.

Nortenaine nodded sadly without looking at Maelthor or Trelaine. Bruel gave one stiff nod but did throw a fleeting glare in their direction. Trelaine shrugged off Maelthor's embrace and stood defiantly. As they watched, the figures of Maelthor and Trelaine, along with all of the faeries, began to fade. The last image was of Trelaine, her fists raised to the skies, howling with rage, as Maelthor hung his head in despair.

Beside them, the specter of Rolf Andelar extended his hand, palm up, toward Sandoval. The wizard nodded, pulled the ring from his pocket, and dropped it into the specter's hand. Rolf closed his mailed fist over the ring with a contented sigh, stepped back, and began to glow brightly. All eyes watched as the glow widened and transformed into the figure of the Ileana elf as he was in life—tall, bronzed, and muscled. One hand held that of Lilliana in all of her youthful beauty, with her glowing silver hair. Her sparkling blue eyes were directed upward at him. He held up the silver wedding band, and Lilliana raised her other hand to receive it on her finger.

A sharp intake of breath came from Nortenaine. He reached out his hand longingly toward the twin spirits, his face a study in grief. Bruel's hand grasped his father's shoulder as another specter appeared beside Lilliana. Sandoval nodded toward the image of Noona, who nodded back at him and winked. Then all three figures faded out slowly. For a brief moment, there was a total silence within the clearing, and then the loud honk of a blowing nose brought them back to the present. Waldo Snufflebeam wiped his nose with his handkerchief and dabbed quickly at his eyes. Tronus glowered down at him until his face relaxed in a smile. Harald sighed heavily and only stared off into the forest, thinking of his lost Tillie.

"There were only three!" Nortenaine exclaimed suddenly, swinging on Sandoval. "The child still lives!"

"Oh, I think so," Sandoval responded

"The faerie king said *by the power of the first one*," Hoagy piped up. "You said Trelaine was foiled in succeeding in another murder by a greater power. That can only mean …"

Chapter 18

A Prayer Answered and a Case Closed

Sandoval smiled at Hoagy. "As you have guessed."

"The first elf warrior was the one we saw in the vision," Nortenaine said, turning to Vaester Shee, who had remained silent throughout the sentencing of Maelthor and Trelaine.

"Yes, our common ancestor, Queleastor, he was called," Vaester Shee said.

"But the child! What happened to it? I must know." Nortenaine swung around to Sandoval.

Hoagy smiled knowingly at his boss.

"I think what we all need is a strong cup of hag tea and a nice fire. The forest does get damp later in the day, don't you think?" Sandoval quipped.

Nortenaine frowned at the white wizard, but Tronus merely chuckled as they all began to feel an odd tingling sensation.

"Here we go again, I think."

The echo of Tronus' words trailed after them as they all appeared in an instant within the main room of the tower of Will Wiggins. Sitting in a large chair before the fire sat Will Wiggins, and his ward, Flora, stood near him with a tray full of tea cups and a steaming pot. Harald and the Snufflebeam Company hurried over to the long table that also contained trays of fruit, bread, and cheese and took their places with eager faces, followed by Tronus, Jade, and Ferrell. Sandoval again marveled at the size of the room that could easily accommodate all of them, as the last time he was there, it seemed to be a snug little room with just enough chairs before the fire to fit whoever needed to sit. In this case, there were sufficient chairs for him, Nortenaine, Vaester Shee, and Bruel.

"Sit, sit." Will Wiggins waved his hand at them. "No need to stand on ceremony. I know who you all are, so no need to introduce them to me, Inspector."

Nortenaine slumped into one of those chairs. Already overloaded with too much to mentally digest for one day, his wary blue eyes did not leave the face of Will Wiggins. Sandoval lowered himself into the chair next to Nortenaine, as Vaester Shee and Bruel also seated themselves. Flora passed around cups of tea, placing the pot and empty tray on the table and returning to stand next to Will.

"My explanation only covered part of the dire events of that day at the green pool. There was more that occurred before the end of Lilliana and Rolf."

"I beg you, Sandoval! I cannot bear to see more," Nortenaine groaned..

"You will need to bear with me a few moments longer," Sandoval said, taking a sip of tea, sighing, and placing the cup on a small table next to his chair.

"I will not add to your grief, though you must know that Lilliana felt she could not bring her child to you, for Maelthor would demand that it be put to death. Instead, she meant to dash herself on the rocks of the green pool, killing them both in her despair. But when she got to the pool, she went into labor. The Glaistig heard her and came to her aid. She agreed to assist Lilliana but only if she could take the child. Lilliana, in her grief and still determined to take her own life, assented. After the deaths of Lilliana and Rolf, the faeries came to the Glaistig and took the child. Even the power of the Glaistig must bow to a greater force. After all, she really couldn't take the child into the green pool with her, could she? In any case, the faeries took the child from her and placed a *glamour* upon it, to disguise its true nature and keep it safe, and they placed it with a human—not that Trelaine didn't make an attempt to finish her off anyway. But Trelaine recognized the child too late to plan carefully, and she made only a clumsy attempt of putting her own *glamour* on a piece of wood, to make it look like a deadly lizard."

"With who …?" Nortenaine gasped.

"Oh, I say a human, but really, probably more like a good imitation of one."

Slowly, all eyes turned to Will Wiggins and Flora. There were sharp intakes of breath, mixed with audible gasps, as they all gaped at the young elf maiden who now stood beside Will Wiggins. The rough clothes had been replaced with a delicate mint-green gown. Flora still had the reddish-gold hair, but now it came down over her shoulders in soft waves, and the pert face had been transformed to one with a delicately sculpted bone structure and a soft peach-toned complexion—not as pale as her mother, Lilliana, but neither the bronze-toned skin of her father, Rolf Andelar. She was a beauty to take the breath of every male in the room. Soft brown eyes sparkling with gold flecks took in those who gaped at her in disbelief—all except Hoagy, who smiled broadly.

"I knew it!" he announced.

Nortenaine and Bruel both rose and went to Flora. Nortenaine took her gently in his arms, tears rimming his eyes. He released her so Bruel could embrace her. They took her by the hand and drew her across the room to Vaester Shee, who bowed before her and kissed her hand.

"This is a great day," the old vessel said.

"One I never would have expected." Nortenaine smiled down at the elf maiden. "I can't thank you enough, old man."

All of them turned to Will Wiggins, but instead of seeing him, they beheld a young male elf, tall and bronze-skinned, like the Ileana, with long, burnished-gold hair and bright, flashing blue eyes, who smiled once at Flora, then faded away. Nortenaine, Bruel, and Vaester Shee looked at each other, their faces filled with awe and recognition.

"Wow!" yelled one of the Snufflebeam boys.

"I'll be bollixed!" Tronus crowed.

All spoke at once for a moment, while Jade took Flora's hand and led her to the table. The young elf maiden lowered herself to a bench next to Jade, seeming relieved to be in the company of another female, but her soft brown eyes were filled with sadness and still glanced over to the spot where the old man had disappeared.

"I have spoken with many elf warriors from both the Ileana and Florian clans as they came past the tower over the years," Flora said in a soft voice to Nortenaine. "I knew my true nature many years ago, when Will Wiggins revealed it to me. I so ached to go to Quelean and Mt. Thorn to see my mother and father's people. Rolf and Lilliana visit me in my dreams, and I feel them with me all the time. I tried to speak to Trelaine about them, but I saw the wild madness in her heart and the hate she felt for me."

"I think there was more than that, Flora," Sandoval said softly. "Trelaine saw you as what she could have been—a bridge between the Ileana and Florian—and she hated you for it, as she hated your father for turning to Lilliana, rather than her."

"That is behind us now." Nortenaine came to Flora and took her hand. "You will go to Quelean with me and meet your people. Then we will resolve our differences with the Ileana, and you will go to Mt. Thorn and meet your people there."

Vaester Shee nodded. "Yes. We have been fools to turn our backs upon our heritage, Ileana and Florian. With your permission, Nortenaine, I would like to go with you to present ourselves in unison before both of our clans. But first, we must pull back our armies and relieve King Filemon of his watch."

Nortenaine nodded solemnly. "I have been wrong in turning away from the evidence that was available to us all. My father's fear and hatred infected me, even as I tried to ignore it. Even Maeleana tried to change his mind and those of her children. And Maelthor used it to gain his ends with me. I feel great sorrow at having turned my back upon her when Maelthor cast her from the clan."

"We must start anew now." Vaester Shee bowed toward Nortenaine. "With your permission, I will gladly act as vessel to the Florian and Ileana until you can find one to take that place. I think it is time the Ileana chose their own lord to lead them. I am weary of that position and would return to the contemplative life, which one of my position should embrace."

"It is possible that your position could serve all of the elves. But we may speak of that at another time," Nortenaine said.

"My apologies are due to Tronus Longbottom, Jade Sholeen, and Ferrel Lovelace for the cruelty I showed to them. I will regret it all of my remaining years." Vaester Shee turned sorrowful eyes at them.

"There wasn't much permanent damage you could really do to them," Sandoval said. "I am sure Will Wiggins was keeping a wary eye on all of us *and* informing our dragon friends. No wonder they looked so unscathed when I saw them here."

Vaester Shee nodded. "There was much power here."

Sandoval only smiled and sipped his tea.

"I think our rides are here!" called Harald, at the sound of whinnies and stamping hooves from outside.

The Snufflebeam Company and Harald charged out of the front door and exclaimed at the sight of not only Bully and Menopet but Jade's and Ferrel's horses as well.

"You know, I like magic and all, just like the rest of them," Ferrel said in an aside to Jade, "but I'm about ready for some elbow-rubbing with Hogarth at the Dragon's Lair and a good bowl of his stew."

"I know what you mean, big man. I think I can already taste a mug of cold Bergen ale."

Sandoval's ears pricked up at that comment, and he smiled broadly, nodding to Nortenaine.

"I think it is time we all headed for home," Sandoval said. "I have a report to write, and it's going to take me a while to condense the events of this day sufficiently for Director Tantilus and the king. In the meantime, I'll send a quick message ball to tell them the case is closed. And all are well."

Flora looked around at the cozy room she had shared for so many years with Will Wiggins. Her brown eyes were touched with tears as Bruel took her hand, his smile encouraging.

"We can wait for you to prepare what you wish to bring from your personal items."

"Only a few clothes, which I don't need. I am ready now," Flora said resolutely, turning toward them with clear eyes and an eager smile.

Nortenaine ushered them ahead of him and bowed quickly to Sandoval before following Vaester Shee out the door. Tronus tapped out the pipe that had gone dead and stuffed it in his pocket. As Sandoval, Jade, Ferrel, and Tronus headed for the door, Sandoval paused and stared longingly up the narrow stairs.

"What are you thinking, wizard?" Tronus grumbled

"Oh, I just thought it might be beneficial to take a long look at the books and artifacts Will may have left behind, although I do suppose I can come back. I doubt he'll take up residence again."

"And just who was he?" Jade asked as they stepped outside.

Sandoval smiled and shrugged with exaggerated innocence, which caused Tronus to laugh heartily. Jade shook her head and turned to mount her horse, when a crackling sound filled the air and tingled against their skin.

"Not again!" Tronus roared.

Sandoval turned with the others to look back at the tower, which began to shimmer in the afternoon light, wavering as if it were turning to liquid before their eyes. Then it disappeared in the wink of an eye, leaving behind not the least indentation or bent blade of grass to mar the spot where it had stood.

"By Ludlow's beard!" Ferrel said.

Sandoval glanced around, but there was no sign of Nortenaine's party. They had slipped into the forest moments before. A frown creased his brow, and his mouth twisted in a half-grin.

"I guess I won't be rooting around in Will's artifacts after all. Oh, well, I do have one that I happened to borrow," he said, as he reached into his bag and pulled out a carved wooden plaque.

"Borrowed?" Hoagy laughed.

"Well, I was going to bring it back after making a sketch of it. It was stuck between some books on Will's bookshelf that told the tales of the first elf, Queleastor. Now, isn't that odd?"

They all bent over the gleaming, polished wood on which had been carved and painted a picture of a tall elf with bronze skin and striking blue eyes.

"Look familiar?" Sandoval asked.

"Well, I'll be damned," Jade said, shaking her head. "It looks just like the image of the elf figure that we saw in the tower."

"Queleastor, the first elf?" Ferrel said.

"The elf god?" Tronus queried.

"Anything's possible, I suppose," Sandoval said, stroking Menopet's smooth neck muscle. "Though I have a feeling he'd term himself more of a guardian than a god. God is a heavy burden to carry, and any who would want to be so called would probably not be welcome to the elf clans now. No, the Florian and Ileana who visited this area regularly on their forays found the old man nothing special, though some of them did wonder about his ability to seemingly appear and disappear at will, so to speak. From the reaction of Nortenaine, Vaester Shee, and Bruel, I would say that a new legend has been born here, one that will help to reunite them under their common ancestor." Sandoval chuckled to himself.

"Wonder how long it will take us to get to Darren's Choice?" Ferrel said wistfully.

"You may have to wait a couple of days for that stew and ale," Jade laughed.

"Oh, I think we may be closer to home than we think." Sandoval winked at them.

The End